The Dead M

By

James Alan Vincent

The moral right of Brian Fletcher, writing as James Alan Vincent to be identified as the author of this work has been asserted in accordance with the Copyright, Designs, and Patents Act of 1988.

All rights reserved. No part of this publication may be reproduced, stored in a retrieval, or transmitted in any form or by any means, electronic, mechanical, photocopying, recording, or otherwise, without the prior permission of both the copyright owner and the above publisher of this book.

This book is entirely a work of fiction and any names are purely the author's imagination and the author's opinions are not representative of those of the publisher.

All characters in this book are fictitious, and any resemblance to actual persons, living or dead, is purely coincidental.

ISBN: 978-0-244-12949-1

Copyright Brian Fletcher, writing as James Alan Vincent.

Acknowledgements

I would like to thank Gaynor Mapp for all her helpfulness and especially her constant encouragement in helping me to write this book. Even when my spirit was sometimes low her input was invaluable, and especially in posing for the front cover picture in the cemetery in Devizes. That was a day to remember.

Sometimes in life we are in the wrong place at the wrong time through no fault of our own. And yet the consequences can be terrible beyond anyone's imagination.

Prologue

Friday 20 March 1965

The White Lion pub in Holborn, London was a little noisy, but friendly with a good atmosphere. There was much laughter, and if you were on your own you soon got talking with someone. But that's of course if you wanted to. There were several people holding gatherings. One gathering in particular was for Alan Jacobs, a young man celebrating the end of his apprenticeship after five long years. He was sitting with five of his friends around an old long oval oak table.

The decor was in the usual style of an old pub. But clean, with those hard wooden seats and polished oak tables. There was a long bar with a brass rail along the bottom and a few stools parked along the bar. It had the old beer pumps with a varied selection of beers. Twenty old beams painted in black were on the ceiling. On the walls there were some old faded paintings of past Lord Mayors of London, which looked a little creepy from the lights but made the place just a bit different.

The pub also boasted a small snug that held up to eight people, where sometimes local so-called businessmen (who were really local villains) would book it for private gatherings, and if you did book it you could have a personal waitress service.

Big Dave Irons was the landlord, a popular and jolly man who always had his pet under his arm a dog called Sawn-off. It was a small fat black-and-tan sausage dog. Jimmy had been there now for the last twenty-three years. He'd put on some large T-bone steaks with a surprisingly good wine for Alan and his five friends.

The meal they all had was excellent, and they had finished with a large slice of Black Forest gateau each. For a pub the food was fantastic. Having enjoyed the pub from the age of eighteen, the place was a favourite of Alan's. Tonight he had been celebrating his twenty-first birthday. However, it was a low-key event. Anyway, he had to get up for work. Because he started every day at 4 a.m. as he was a baker. Sadly he had to leave his friends in the pub at 10 30 p.m. So he could get the last bus home. Looking at his watch he saw he had about four minutes to get the last bus and realised he would have to run to catch it. Now he had to get a bit of a sprint on, and even though he was full to bursting he couldn't miss the bus.

Annoyingly it was now drizzling with rain which didn't help, as the wet made the pavements a little slippery. There were more than a few people milling around or going home from various types of entertainment such as the cinema, as it was a Friday night. Unfortunately, as he ran around the corner he slipped on the wet pavement, where he crashed into four men who had also been out celebrating. They were welcoming home Benny Dolan, who was a well-known Gypsy street fighter. He was known as Benny the Fist. He'd just been released that very day from a three-year prison sentence for almost killing a man in a previous street fight three and a half years before.

Alan had accidently banged his head into Dolan's head, which had the effect of pushing the wrong button. Benny immediately went nuclear and set about Alan with a ferocious attack. The young man had no chance whatsoever because he was just a tall, thin twenty-one-year old lad, a simple baker who, after five years, had just finished his apprenticeship.

Benny was now brutally destroying Alan. While he was sitting astride his chest he stupidly pulled out a knife and stabbed him in the neck. Alan was desperately trying to defend himself. Benny was now beside himself with rage. The three other men, to their credit, tried to pull Benny off. That was a difficult task because he weighed sixteen stone and was made of solid muscle and hard bone. When he was about to stab Alan again a very loud shout fortunately took his attention away.

Henry Lambert, who was walking by with his girlfriend Dorothy, had noticed the one-sided fight and yelled at Benny to leave Alan alone. Benny was now ready for anything, due to his temper and his low tolerance of alcohol. Suddenly he got off Alan, stood up to his full height of six feet three inches, and shouted.

'You want some as well, do you?'

'Do you want to go to prison, you idiot, shouted Henry.

'Idiot, am I? So make me stop, then.'

'Look he's half-dead,' replied Henry.

'Fuck you screamed Benny, fuck all of you. Still enraged, Benny ran at Henry with the knife, but Henry managed to sidestep him and punched him hard in the jaw really hard. He'd put all his weight into that punch – it came from the hips – which broke Benny's jaw and knocked him out stone cold.

Benny's mates tried to grab Henry but they were quickly dealt with in the same manner. Henry was a very good ABA amateur heavyweight boxer with ten years' experience. Being five feet ten inches tall and weighed in at fifteen stone. His training had taught him how to handle himself.

By now, despite the foul weather, a small crowd had gathered. As the fights ended and the rain increased it soon melted away. The rain, which had started as a drizzle, was now pouring down and was soaking anything and everyone. The wind – which was sweeping dead leaves and discarded bits of paper around your feet – had now become very strong, but it was the end of October. People were walking with their heads down, and nearly everyone was hurrying home. That included a variety of ladies with their umbrellas turned inside out, who were still trying to protect their hair from getting wet. Several men, except for a couple, were getting no protection from the rain. Some people were trying to catch buses to get back to their warm homes. It had turned into a filthy night. You were much better off indoors on a night like this.

Henry very carefully picked up Alan into a sitting position, but he was in a bad way. After taking off his own raincoat he covered Alan up the best he could to keep him dry and warm. Someone thankfully had called for an ambulance. Henry managed to stop him from bleeding to death and he also managed to calm him down until the ambulance arrived.

The ambulance crew covered them both with thick red blankets and took them both to the hospital. Henry's girlfriend (*and future wife*) managed to get a taxi home.

By now the police had arrived. Benny was now fully recovered. One policeman, a sergeant, immediately recognised Benny as a persistent offender. They arrested him for GBH. It still took three of them to finally subdue him before they took him away.

When Dolan was later brought to court for the umpteenth time the judge, after looking at Benny's terrible police record, could see a long history of violence.

'Mr Dolan,' he said, 'please listen to me very carefully. Somehow you do not seem to have learned anything while serving your sentence in prison. Neither have you shown any remorse, nor indeed any regard for your victim. And so this time I have no choice but to send you to prison for eight years to reflect on your life and your role in society.

'Take him away.'

Benny started to shout and scream abuse at the judge, his counsel, and anyone else in his way. Suddenly he started to fight his police guard as he tried to run away, but he was soon covered in police officers as they dragged him away to start his well-deserved sentence. The sentence went down badly with his family, the Dolan family, very badly indeed. Twelve months later, while in prison, Benny was having a shower when the other three men in the shower quietly walked away from him. He realised they had disappeared, but now he saw they had been replaced by four big men. Suddenly they came at him with home-made knives and gang-stabbed him to death in the shower.

His family then swore to get even with anyone and everyone they held responsible, no matter how long it took. Sometimes the Dolans waited years to dish out revenge, which, according to them, was best served cold. That incident had happened some years ago now but had still not been forgotten by the Dolans. Nor, indeed, forgiven.

Anyone who belonged to Henry Lambert's family was considered an enemy of their whole family. In short – according to the Dolans – it was because of Henry Lambert that Benny had been arrested by the police, which was a ridiculous thing to say.

Hatred was born into all the Dolans. If you hurt one, then you hurt all of them, period, with no respite.

In 1976 Alan Jacobs was still happily making his living as a baker, and by then he had his own bakery. Suddenly, out of the blue, he was left a public house in Soho called the Black Swan. It was left to him by his grandfather, who had sadly suddenly died from a heart attack behind the bar while serving a customer. His grandfather had had the pub for fifty years, and his father before him for about the same period of time. Alan had no hesitation in moving in. His master baker, Jimmy Watts, bought his bakery shop. So he took up the bar towel and set to work in the Black Swan with his pretty wife Alice. The pub was also a free house. He now owned the freehold of the very valuable property. After just a few months he had turned the pub into a little goldmine. Sadly, after many years in the pub trade, Alice became ill and could no longer work. Alan decided he would rather retire to look after her. And so the Black Swan went on the market.

Chapter One

Sarah Lambert was sitting on one of the comfy chairs surrounding the large modern dance hall at the American airbase at Mildenhall in Suffolk. It was a Saturday night: rock and roll party night. The music was fantastic. It was difficult to keep still because there was a brilliant band on, whose lead guitarist was just amazing. People were standing round the stage watching the band playing. The music got inside you and made your limbs bounce along. It made you feel alive. The whole place was full to bursting and everyone was in a great mood. Americans certainly knew how to throw a party.

Sarah was watching her best friend Delia Simms dancing the jive with a very good-looking sergeant first class in the American air force. They were having a brilliant time even though the sergeant was smaller than she was, but she was very tall at five feet eleven inches. They looked so happy dancing together and so athletic. Delia could actually dance. She was no beginner, like Sarah, who danced like a bag of cement. Sarah had been asked several times to dance. But she was so bad everyone gave up on her because the Americans were fond of their jiving and the Lindy hop style. Dancing was taken very seriously by most of the USAF airmen. They didn't want to look ridiculous in front of their buddies because, after all, it wasn't really cool.

Sarah had just turned eighteen. How she wished she could dance. She felt a bit like a wallflower. She had bravely tried to dance with a couple of fellows and had managed to trample all over them. They had never asked her again. She was determined to learn how to dance. The trouble was that she was a dedicated language student and could speak Spanish, French, and German fluently. She also spoke some Russian. She had been a natural at languages since she was ten years old. Her ambition was to join the Foreign Office as an interpreter when she had gained her degrees. All she seemed to do was study.

Saturday nights and Sundays were her only release. She so wished she could dance. The trouble was that she had no time, or anyone to practise with. She was far away with her thoughts when ...

'Hello, hello ... Excuse me, can I have this dance please? Hi ... Hello ... Are you there? ... Are you in?' The voice, which was now laughing, seemed to come from nowhere.

Then she set eyes on Kenny Santana for the first time, and her heart did a somersault. He was standing right in front of her and was asking her again,

'Can I have this dance, please? I'm Kenny. What's your name, honey?'

Everyone who could dance was on the floor rocking to the song 'Johnny B. Goode'. It was very loud but very exciting, and the whole place was jumping.

Slowly Sarah stood up next to this six feet two inch fifteen-stone Adonis.

'Sorry, can you say that again?' she said, smiling as she held her hands next to her ears. Kenny Santana laughed and repeated his request again.

'Can I please have this dance with you? My name is Kenny Santana. Tell me what your name is, honey.' Now he was laughing, showing his ridiculous even line of brilliant white all-American teeth set in a bronzed and handsome square-jawed face. He had the loveliest smiling face she had ever seen. Sarah was smitten, big time.

'Oh, hi ... I'm so sorry. It's Sarah.' She couldn't believe he had asked her to dance. He had this swarthy, typically Latin American look. He had the blackest hair, and his lovely smile lit up his gorgeous face. He had the sexiest dark brown eyes, which seemed to dance when he spoke to you ... which made you want to dance with them. He also smelt divine. She couldn't believe her luck.

'Oh, look, I'm so sorry, I was miles away. If I could dance I would, but I can't. Look, I'm rubbish, so if you want to try with someone else, that's OK with me. Still, if you want to give it a go then that's also fine by me, but don't blame me if I cripple you,' she said, and laughed.

Kenny smiled and said, 'Hey, I'm a sucker for punishment. You can cripple me anytime, honey. Let's go just follow me.' Holding her hand firmly, he led her on to the dance floor, but he walked right across it to the other side and through a door marked *Lounge*.

'So, what's your poison honey? And tell me your name again. Mine is Kenny Santana and I'm from Hoboken, New Jersey. You and I, little lady are going to get married pretty soon, so we'd better hurry it up because in three months' time they are shipping me home to the States and I want you to come home with me.'

Sarah stuttered. She thought. *Did I hear this correctly?*

'What? Are you mad? I just wanted a dance, that's all. Not a husband. So tell me now. Who put you up to this, Kenny Santana? You must be mad or very drunk,' she said, and laughed again.

'Neither, honey, and I'm very serious.'

She just stared at him. Sarah was five feet eight inches tall with a willowy look about her, and she had the most amazing grace and the light blue eyes of a child. When she walked it was poetry in motion.

Kenny knew she was very young but he could see she would turn into a real beauty she had a wonderful figure and a lovely smile. Even though her smile was a little crooked, but she was a really genuine person. He could see she was a very strong girl, and also strong-willed. Her hair was beautiful: she had a full mane of thick blonde hair that framed her lovely blue eyes, and her hair bounced off her shoulders when she walked. It smelt fresh and wonderful, and it shimmered with the lights from the glitter ball hanging low from the ceiling. Kenny wanted to bury his face in her silky hair. However, all he had at that moment was hope. But he also had a hunch it would work out.

'Honey, listen, I can't dance either. That's why I brought you straight back in here. I can't hang around, and besides I really can't dance a step.' They both laughed.

'Look you don't know me. You know nothing about me. And so, Kenny Santana, I'm going. I may be only eighteen, but you're not going to make a fool out of me.' And she turned to walk away.

Kenny quickly grabbed her hand.

'Listen up, Sarah. I told you, I haven't got long to go in this country. I can't hang about and once I've gone that's it. I will lose you forever, but that's not on my agenda, honey. I want you to marry me, and believe me this is not a joke. I'm serious.'

'Yes, well, that's all well and good. As I said, Kenny, you don't know me and I don't know you, so will you please let go of my hand because this joke has gone far enough. I am not amused. If you think this is funny then go and find another sucker. Then she said it again, but this time very loudly and very seriously in perfect Spanish.

'Sarah,' he said with real emotion in his voice, 'please just sit down and listen to me. So what the hell am I supposed to do, then?' He also said that in Spanish. 'I have watched you for most of the night and also for the last seven weeks. You sit there with your friend, but your friend has all the dances. I was too damn scared to ask you to dance because I can't dance and I don't want to make a fool of myself, or indeed you.

'But I would like to dance through life with you, both of us together. Can't you see I'm serious, really serious? Just listen to me. That's all I ask of you. Look, please sit down and I'll get you a drink. Just one drink so what are you having? Can't you see you're driving me mad?'

'OK, Kenny, but just the one drink, and make it rum and Coke with plenty of ice, please.'

'Would that be white rum?'

'No, that would be dark rum. It has more flavour.' Then she smiled at him.

His legs turned to mush at her smile.

After they sat down, Kenny ordered the drinks – doubles – from the hovering waiter.

He told her all about his life and his family, who had now all gone. Sadly he was the only one left. Both his parents had both been killed. His mother was Irish American she'd been killed in a car crash, and his father was a fire officer who had died in a big warehouse fire down by the river. His mother had been from Irish stock and his father had been a Spanish immigrant. All he had was one auntie who had brought him up after his parents' deaths, but she had now returned to Ireland.
She now lived in a home for people with dementia. She didn't know who he was any more, so he was all on his own. But with her he

wouldn't be. Kenny told her 'he was a policeman in the USAF. He was twenty-six years old and he would be leaving the air force soon to take up a position as a police officer in the NYPD. They always took in ex-service police first because their training was similar. The prospects were good and he could offer her a good life. Now they had just three months to fall in love.'

Fortunately Sarah had already fallen for him. She knew he was the one for her she just knew it. Now she was beside herself with strange feelings and wonderful dreams – talk about being swept off her feet – but she was not going to admit to Kenny how she felt ...

But he already knew. It was all in the body language; it was all in her eyes. So it was pretty obvious to him although he didn't say in case he spoilt it. After all, he had been taught how to read body language in the USAF.

'Honey, I wish I could take you home to my parents but I can't. I am a good man and I will promise you faithfully I will take good care of you. No, I will take the greatest care of you forever.'

Sarah laughed.

'Hey, did you know you sound like Frank Sinatra? My dad had most of his recordings. I was brought up with the sound of Frank Sinatra, Tony Bennett, and Sarah Vaughan. He named me after her.'

'Jesus. I'm so glad you weren't called Frank, then,' said Kenny. They both laughed.

'Well, anyway, all the folks down in Hoboken sound the same. That's where Frank Sinatra was brought up. In fact when he was younger he lived just two blocks away. And did you know his dad was a fire officer too?'

'No, sorry, I didn't know that, but I bet my dad did.'

Sarah suddenly looked at her watch.

'Oh look at the time, Kenny. I have to go. My friend Delia will be wondering where I've got to. I'm staying at her Auntie Pam's place – which is just down the road, so to speak. She's so strict about what time we have to be in. OMG, we're already late, and now we're going to be in big trouble.'

'Where do you live, Sarah? Can I ring you or call on you?' he asked her.

She blurted out, 'I live in London in Notting Hill, which is a long way to go home. I live with my brother Tom and his wife Laura. Tom's a brewery rep. He's about the same age as you. He wants a pub and one day I know he will get one. I live with them at the moment. It's my home as well. I own half of the house. 'So then, Mr Kenny Santana,' she said as stood there writing something on a piece of paper, 'this is my phone number. Now you can ring me, but please make it after 7 p.m. I have to go.'

As Sarah came out of the door marked *Lounge* her friend Delia walked past, looking for her.

'Hey, young lady, where have you been?' Delia looked at Kenny and thought,

Well, that explains a lot, and grinned.

(That was in the spring of 1986. Sarah and Kenny got married in the August of the same year. They quickly moved to America to start a new life, and what a great life he gave her.)

When Sarah returned home the next morning she was all flustered and scared about what Tom and Laura would say. She needn't have worried they were happy for her. She had to tell them exactly what happened. Laura said she wasn't to keep any juicy bits out, and to tell them everything. If she really wanted to go ahead with it she ought to do it. After all, she could always come back home no matter where they lived.

Tom and Sarah were born when their parents were in their late thirties. Henry Lambert died in a terrible accident a few years later. The official version was that he fell off his bike. Some said he was pushed, but whatever the cause he was crushed under a lorry. Yet others said it was a deliberate act and that the lorry driver was paid to run him over. However, before it got to court the lorry driver was found dead in Kensington Gardens. Apparently he'd hanged himself because of the guilt. But the rumour persisted. He was murdered by a family called the Dolans, who had paid the lorry driver to run over Henry Lambert. They needed to get rid of the lorry driver in case he talked. In fact he had already begun to open his big mouth, especially after a few drinks.

Henry Lambert was killed in revenge for beating Benny Dolan years before. They blamed him totally for getting Benny arrested and then he got the blame for Benny being stabbed to death while in prison. A year later, after Henry's death, tragically Dorothy his wife died of a broken heart. Now that's what everyone said. But they were as close a couple as you could get. Both Tom and Sarah inherited the three-storey house in Chepstow Road, Notting Hill. At least it had been paid for by then. Tom had always wanted a pub, and so did his wife Laura. When he was thirty-three, and Sarah had gone to the States, he sold the house with Sarah's permission. Then he bought a pub called the Black Swan in Soho London.

Alan Jacobs who was the owner at the time, and Tom already knew him well because he had been calling round on a regular basis from the brewery where he worked for a number of years. On Tom's last visit Alan, who was also the landlord, told him he was selling up, and if he wanted a pub why not purchase his? If Tom liked the idea Alan would leave some of his own money invested in the pub. Which was really a personal loan let's say over ten years and then he could pay him back with only a very small amount of interest.

Tom jumped at the chance and he never looked back.

Sadly Mr Alan Jacobs had no children of his own and, unbeknown to Tom, he had known his parents very well. But that was many years ago now. Alan was already a wealthy man. He was very happy to make Tom's dream come true. That was because Henry, Tom's father, had saved his life some years before Tom was born. Alan had been getting a beating from a man called Benny Dolan. There was no question that he had saved Alan's life, no question at all. In fact Alan was thrilled to bits to be able to pay back the kindness to Henry's son. However, he would never tell him about it. It was a secret he would take to his grave.

The Dolans were a notorious Irish family from Gypsy stock who had settled in London back in 1843. They started off by mugging people and breaking and entering virtually any building they chose to. If they were caught they came back, or sent someone else back to dish out severe beatings, with some resulting in death. They ruled by fear and all stuck together. They obtained property by bullying and threats, they took over prostitution and gambling dens. They became legitimate by going into bookmaking. They looked respectable, but a lot of people disappeared and yet no one knew why. But the Dolans did. The police were well aware of what was going on, but to prove it was impossible because witnesses were bought off or just simply vanished.

There was one policeman called Richard Howard who was the main witness to a shooting. When he was a young probationary policeman on his first all-night patrol he had watched – scared shitless – from a doorway, while four Dolans beat a rival club owner with metal bars. The man was in such a mess his face no longer existed. His nose was in the gutter with his ear and part of his lower mouth.

One Dolan shouted,

'Finish him off. He looks disgusting.' Another of the Dolans, a young man called Harry Dolan, was trying to make his name, and he pulled out an ex-army Smith & Wesson .38 and blew the man's head off. He shot him five more times. So they asked him why the hell he had emptied the six shots into the man, because the first one had killed him. He looked at them as though they were stupid, shrugged his shoulders, and said,

'I liked it. What's not to like?' His reputation was established.

Then Harry saw a movement in a shop doorway. After spotting a young policeman trembling in the doorway he walked over to him. He was standing in a pool of his own urine, and there was also a foul smell emanating from his new police trousers. Last night his young new wife had ironed them to perfection. Harry said to him.

'Hey, PC 295, you didn't see anything, did you? Look, are you married? Have you any children?' Harry was quickly joined by the other three menacing men.

'Yes, I am, but only three months ago. No children. But hey, look, I never saw a thing.'

'If you do open your mouth, PC 295, then unfortunately some of my gang will be down to pay your pretty wife a visit. We will take some pictures and send them to all the coppers down at your nick. Remember to do yourself a favour and walk away while you can.'

They left the rival club owner's body as a warning to other people. The young policeman said nothing. Within six months he had obtained a transfer to Manchester and thirty-nine years later he retired as a top police commander. If any pictures had been taken of his wife he would have been forced to leave the police, but he said nothing and looked the other way. As it turned out he had a good long career.

Even now the Dolans were a feared family who owned a lot of Soho and its surrounding streets, which many years ago they had poached or taken from the Maltese gangsters. The Dolans liked to purchase any property that came up for sale in the Soho area, one way or another. The Dolans had always employed clever lawyers where they kept them on lucrative retainers. But if they thought a lawyer had ripped them off then the consequences were grim – not just for the lawyer but for always, including his children and anyone else connected to him. If you hurt one Dolan you inadvertently hurt the lot of them. It was as though they all belonged to the same tribe, and in essence that was true. Cut one head off and they grew two more, and so on. The trouble was that they were just evil, and the best way to punish them would be to kill them.

The family had now multiplied like rats down a sewer. To kill them was not the easiest thing to do. And yet some had tried and failed miserably.

Gone were the days of slumming it in a caravan for the Dolans with their black-and-white cob ponies. Now they lived the high life in the villages in Surrey and on various luxury mobile home sites. The top man, or godfather for want of a better saying, was now Harry Dolan, who lived in Park Street, Mayfair with his wife Joan and his eldest son Noel. But then there was Alex, and then Jason, and they both had separate homes. Harry also had a sumptuous villa in Marbella in Spain.

CHAPTER TWO

Tom Lambert and his wife Laura quietly moved into the Black Swan. He was now aged thirty-three and Laura was thirty-one. They both took to the pub trade like ducks to water because over the years of being a rep for the brewery Tom had seen it all and how some pub landlords operated, some good some bad. He had taken it all on board and had learnt a lot. Even after having three children Craig, Stephen and Helen, they managed to run a very successful pub they became a very popular couple. Over the years they had many offers to sell the Black Swan but they managed to resist them all, then over time the novelty was beginning to wear off a little. But they often talked about buying a property in Spain to use as a holiday home but to keep a main house somewhere in Surrey. They wanted to live a more simple life to enjoy a little peace and quiet. After twenty-six years in the pub trade the time had come to sell up. Now they had decided to call it a day as their three children had no interest in the pub trade at all. But sadly the trade had changed beyond belief.

There was Craig who was now 24, Stephen was 21 and then last but not least there was Helen who was now 16 and a lovely looking young girl. She was a little slow and had not grown to her full height, but although they had all worked in the pub and its restaurant, the novelty especially for the two boys, had now worn off. They were sick of having no life and working odd hours while their friends had normal jobs working normal hours, and now they wanted the same. So they decided they would look for a daytime coffee bar. But none took a remote interest in the pub any more.

The Lamberts became, like a lot of landlords, utterly fed up with all the long hours for hardly anything in return because all the extra income brought in by longer opening hours simply went on wages. What was the point in killing yourself just so you could employ someone; it also meant more hands in the till. Tom had caught many an employee stealing. It was a regular event and now he was sick of it. Also the regular amendments of the employment contracts and the meddling food and health inspectors put most people off.

Now they decided it was time to go. They offered the pub up for sale in the *Daily Pub News*, which was a newspaper to the pub trade. Within hours there were plenty of replies and for some reason there was interest from America, France, Germany, and even from Australia, so in the end they decided to have a closed auction to see what the best offer would be, that was the advice given to them by the estate agents. When Harry Dolan saw the Black Swan up for sale he wanted it. And so he decided to make a direct approach to Tom Lambert asking him for his price, in fact he could name his own price within reason. Harry owned a few properties in Soho and the Black Swan would be the crowning glory. It would make a lot of sense because it was sitting between his other properties. He must have it.

In fact he had approached Tom Lambert via a third party several times in the past only to find he didn't want to sell the pub to anyone because it simply was not for sale, but now it was. The trouble with Harry Dolan was he couldn't take rejection of any kind, to him stabbing him in the heart was the same thing. Now he was determined to get it one way or the other.

Tom Lambert turned Harry down flat which according to Dolan made him lose face. But it was to be expected. Tom didn't want dirty money or even to talk to Harry Dolan. So as far as he was concerned he would never get it as long as he was alive to tell the tale. There was a long history between the two families, a long bad history.

The pub did go to a closed auction it was handled through Higgins & Stockwell the large estate agents and auctioneers in Soho.

Harry put a bid in for the pub, but he knew the highest bidder because it was in the interest of the main auctioneer Mr David Higgins to tell him. Harry Dolan had incriminating filthy photos of David Higgins being flogged by another man while he was handcuffed to a bed. And there were also more pictures of him with various men of a homosexual nature taken at one of the brothels owned by Harry. So if they were released David could kiss his lucrative marriage goodbye, he also had a gambling habit and was in debt to Harry for £23,000.

Harry was not in a generous mood he was not inclined to give David Higgins any more time to pay. Higgins had a choice, he either gave up the information that Harry wanted or go broke overnight a simple choice really. Now if he told Harry the highest bid then he would be debt free until the next time because Harry would write off the £23,000 but still keep the films, after all they were worth a lot more than £23,000.

David Higgins was a well-respected estate agent who was married to Bethany, a very wealthy Christian woman whose father at one time used to be the Bishop of Westminster. Both of them were staunch regular church goers. They were the pillars of society, or so it seemed. There was no choice but to tell Harry the highest bidder's price. So all Harry had to do was pay another £10,000 over the bidding price. If anyone asked, then it was to be in another name and after all it was a closed auction, a secret auction no less because if Tom Lambert found out he would pull out for the spite of it.

The price was £2,500,000 lock stock and barrel. Harry offered £2,510,000 which was accepted. It quickly went through to the solicitors to sort out the paperwork. A couple of weeks later one of the Paralegals from the solicitors, a young woman called Jenny Tucker was in the Black Swan having a drink with her friends from work. After she and her friends had been drinking for an hour, the door opened and in walked Noel Dolan who was the eldest son of Harry Dolan. Noel had been drinking all day. Even when sober he could be unpleasant at the best of times. And yet he could charm the birds out of the trees when required. He liked to fight when he was drunk, but that was nothing new, all the Dolans did. However he had also been barred from setting foot in the Black Swan for life. He didn't go unnoticed by Tom the landlord who was busy serving a few drinks at the time.

Noel had started to brag to people he knew, he would soon be serving them drinks. When he was asked what he meant by that remark he touched his nose, winked and laughed. But that was seen by Tom Lambert. Tom walked over and asked him to leave he told him 'he was not welcome in his establishment, not now, and not ever.' Noel immediately kicked off but was so drunk he could hardly speak properly, let alone stand up straight. When he spoke again he looked at Tom and snarled 'you've had your time here, so now it's our turn.' Then he stumbled out of the Black Swan into the street laughing. 'You'll soon see you bastard' he shouted 'you'll soon see you fucking faggot, your time is almost up.

You have no fucking idea what's going to happen. You bastard Lamberts are finished now, all of you, finished.'

Tom shook his head in disgust but it troubled him. Now he walked back into the pub visibly shaking. Quickly walking over to the girls he asked them what Noel had said. The young girl, the Paralegal called Jenny Tucker who worked for the firm of solicitors handling the sale told Tom what Noel had said. 'He was round the solicitor's office this very morning with his father Harry Dolan to sign some papers concerning a well-known London pub. And she thought it was the Black Swan.'

Tom rang his solicitors the first thing in the morning to cancel the sale, because he knew that somehow the Dolans had made the highest bid. After talking and thinking about it, he decided they were not going to get the pub. Laura and his kids totally agreed with him. There would be someone else because the interest had been incredible high. But this time he would sort out the buyers himself. He would also vet them, and then he would sell it himself. In fact there was a wealthy family from Newcastle, the McDonalds from McDonalds Brewery who had shown an interest in his pub.

Norman McDonald and his wife Rita, their son Andrew and daughter Elizabeth were a lovely very experienced genuine family who wanted a pub in London. They already owned a chain of pubs in the north which consisted so far of sixty seven pubs and restaurants; this would now be pub sixty eight. Tom decided to contact them.

The McDonalds had been very disappointed when their bid for the Black Swan had failed. This news concerning the pub was brilliant within hours they had come down by train to view the pub again. They immediately offered Tom the £2,510,000 and shook hands on the deal. Tom found out after checking their references they had no connection whatsoever with the Dolans. In a matter of four weeks they had sold the pub to the McDonalds family from Newcastle.

After the sale of the Black Swan, the Lamberts decided to take a month's holiday to Alicante in Spain where they had been given free use of a beautiful Villa which was owned by the McDonalds. They also had a chance to take a good look around for a holiday home. Their two boys Craig and Stephen plus little Helen all worked at the pub, they would probably decide what they wanted to do after the holiday. So they had lots of options, but running a pub again wasn't one of them. Craig wanted to set up a coffee house with Stephen, there were lots of opportunities available and little Helen would always be looked after too.

Harry Dolan was more than furious with his son Noel, he was absolutely gutted. Noel had stupidly lost them the one asset he longed for, just because he couldn't keep his big mouth shut. Now he had unfinished business with Tom Lambert because Tom would not let him have the Black Swan so now Harry wanted the pub more than ever. But now he wanted Tom Lambert dead.

This was something Harry Dolan would not forget in a hurry because he had lost face now that was not acceptable. There would be consequences even beyond his thinking. The door to hell would soon be opened...but stupidly all by himself.

CHAPTER THREE

The man known as Duvall had just come out of the shower the time was now 10.10 pm. Having just arrived back from Australia he was just a little jet lagged. Even first class can do that, but his shower had helped him to relax. Now he was drying his hair with a towel with one hand and lighting up a very expensive Cuban cigar with the other. Already he'd poured himself a large Jim Beam Bourbon into a very expensive crystal whiskey glass. So then wrapping himself in a large white Egyptian cotton dressing gown, he finally settled down in his old favourite wicker chair on his large balcony. He listened to the quite evening, where the air was balmy and sweet all was so still. His apartment was on the fifth floor which overlooked the harbour with all the lovely yachts, small boats and restaurants. Now they were all presenting a lovely exquisite picture he wished he could paint the scene with the Mediterranean Sea in the background. The apartment was in a sought after part of Nice in the South of France. In the distance you could see the planes coming into land and taking off. The airport was just ten minutes away. He loved being in the South of France, having lived many times in the arse end of the world's trouble spots. Now he truly appreciated what he had.

Switching on his music system he listened to Mozart with his eyes closed, the CD was called Mozart for Meditation.

It was good to relax after the long haul flight back from Australia where he had been commissioned to dispense with someone's services. But he was after all in waste disposal. He was enjoying his cigar and then irritatingly his mobile rang. Checking the time it said 10.47 pm, he thought who the hell is phoning at this time of the night. It couldn't be a relative because he had none. Maybe it was a wrong number, maybe an inconsiderate idiot who wanted a job carrying out and wouldn't wait until the morning. As it turned out it was the latter.

Duvall was an ex legionnaire. However he now made a good living in waste disposal meaning people, his price was high but he really was the very best, he would travel anywhere if the price was right. Duvall was aged fifty three, he was five feet eleven inches tall but extremely fit, having served in the French Foreign legion for twenty-seven years, and being a weapons expert he was also an expert in explosives. On many occasions he'd been seconded to serve with French Special Forces, so highly rated were his sniper skills. There were occasions when he was covertly flown in to carry out a wet job on a subject and often more than one. Yet his wages were in his view not compatible to what he did for the French Government. He'd served his country all over the world in the worst places imaginable. Having seen and done terrible things for his country. Now he was hardened by all of what had taken place he had no feelings left for anyone or anything. Feeling like a dead man inside now all he cared about was money and high class women. But he didn't mind paying for them if they were the best.

Feeling let down by his country and his pension which was a mere morsel compared to less skilled people than him. So he now sold himself to the highest bidder. A life was £15,000 per person and there was no problem in him getting any work, he'd worked for different governments from time to time and his reputation was awesome. Once committed to the job no matter what or where, he finished it.

Automatically the recorder switched on it said. 'Yes, how can I help you?' After listening very carefully he switched to manual, he said 'Listen to me, my price is high but so are the risks and its £15,000 per item.'

Duvall was his name and that is what people who knew him called him. He only went by that name....or did he? Nobody really knew his full name. In fact his real name was Eric Bezier.

Duvall had finally agreed to meet Harry Dolan at Bristol International airport forty eight hours later.

Harry told him he would pay him for his time plus all expenses. He certainly didn't want to meet Duvall in London because Harry was a face. Thinking about it, Bristol was the best place to meet because it was neutral, also a quiet place and besides he didn't even want his family to know what he was planning. His stupid son Noel had a big mouth, so recently demonstrated to everyone within earshot.

Duvall had arrived more or less on time. His plane had touched down at 10.47am on a very dull dreary day which threatened heavy rain any minute. Being a typical looking French man with a sort of Algerian look about him he had a permanent tan. But he looked tough and very capable, the sort of man you didn't mess with. His hair was cropped short and had now turned mostly grey. Balanced on top of his head he wore a pair of Ray-Ban Aviator sunglasses, he was wearing a dark blue tailored blazer over a light blue fitted shirt with no tie, grey chinos and black city Derby shoes. Over his shoulder he wore a very expensive Gucci man's bag. There were a few complimentary looks from some of the ladies of a certain age in the airport. That was normal for him, he always totally ignored any woman over the age of thirty five, he only bought the best, and whatever and whoever it was.

Harry was patiently waiting in the arrivals when he spotted Duvall, but Duvall had spotted Harry first because he had a hat in his right hand which was a pre-arranged signal.
  Duval thought, Dear God, these English people have no idea how to dress. Now this guy looks like a pantomime baddie. His hair is too long, he looks unwashed, his jacket looks cheap and the trousers were a joke. But he also wanted to laugh at Harry's shoes. And why would you wear all those rings on your fingers? Fat fingers are a sure sign the guy was unfit for purpose. He also wore a ridiculous chain around his fat neck with a cross hanging from it, a throwback to god knows when.
  Yet he was not even looking in the slightest like a religious man. Duvall was far from impressed. Harry looked like a down an out wearing someone else's cloths taken from a skip and then getting dressed in the dark.

Harry waved at him smiling and showing a line of white teeth interspersed with gold caps. Now he walked eagerly up to Duvall, where he shook his hand. His dark blue shirt was open to reveal his revolting greasy grey and white chest hair, the worst was the many hairs sticking out of his large ears, and his nose. The jacket he was wearing you could plainly see once belonged to a suit. It was a brown striped ill-fitting one. His trousers were dark blue, while he was wearing a pair of ghastly slip on brown shoes. After pumping Duvall's hand a little too enthusiastically, Duvall grimaced. He wanted to wash his hands he could also smell cheap body deodorant and he was worried if Harry could afford his services.

They drove into Bristol to a smart hotel according to Harry, where he'd booked a table in the restaurant for an early lunch. The Frenchman looked at the hotel and winced. The place was old and in need of a refurbishment. As they entered the hotel he saw the carpets were years old and he could feel his shoes sticking to the floor. There was all brown furniture with old patterned chair seats. The curtains were old, solid heavy red material and full of dust.

As the waiter appeared he seemed to be about a hundred years old, he smelt of cigarettes and brandy. Which was probably a help yourself job from behind the old wooden bar. The waiter introduced himself as Victor.

'Good day sirs, I'm your waiter for today' he smiled as he led them to a table.

Harry asked 'could he recommend anything to eat.'

'Yes sir I certainly can. I recommend the fresh Scallop's sir.'

So Harry ordered the Scallop's for the two of them without even asking Duvall what he would like. Their lunch arrived in quick time but was totally disgusting. The Scallops were served with sauté potatoes with fresh vegetables. The wine tasted foul.

During this horrible lunch Harry gave Duvall pictures of Tom Lambert and his family who were all in Spain taking a whole month off whilst looking around for a property to purchase.

Harry asked 'aren't you hungry, the scallops are delicious, shame you left them Mr Duvall. But still I've heard that flying can do that to you.' He scooped most of Duvall's scallops onto his plate. Duvall had not touched them, well only the one.

They were well over done and certainly not fresh. Duvall ate them regularly in his local cafe bar back in Nice.

Victor knew they were the only two people who had booked into the restaurant. He had to get on the right side of them after all he could do with a good tip. But sadly it was not as busy as it once was, he thought how times change. But he blamed the take away restaurants which had sprung up everywhere. He was lurking against the old bar when he saw the distaste spreading on the Frenchman's face. Quickly he slid over to their table bending forward with his chin almost in Duvall's plate, to ask 'if the meal was to their liking.' Victor could plainly see the old English guy was scoffing all the scallops, and yet the French guy had eaten just the one.

Harry blurted out with his mouth full of half chewed scallops, 'yes lovely thank you.' Harrys eating even disgusted Victor who over the many years had seen it all.

The Frenchman still looked disgusted as though he'd found a slug on his plate. He couldn't figure out why the food a simple enough meal could taste so putrid and looked like a stray dog had thrown up on his plate.

Victor had turned to slide away to his position next to the old bar keeping a steely eye on the plates ready to pounce on them as soon as they had finished the meals he had a feeling this was not going well.

Duval thought Victor had been dug up for the day he was about six feet five inches tall with a body so thin a crow would swallow in one go. Yet he'd never seen a man that thin and he was stooped over as though he was bowing to a head of state. But his trousers were hanging from his hips and his belt had been on the last notch and yet his shoes so it seemed were the size of meat plates. His hair was long and greasy, the bowtie he was wearing was stained with soup or some sort of liquid. But the worst part was his nicotine stained fingers and he smelt like an ash tray. Victor's nose resembled one of those cartoon noses. It was large and bulbous at the end, but mostly purple in its entirety probably due to the drink. He reckoned it was a love of brandy.

Duval thought oh well the money would soon be in his bank that would make up for Harry's failings. Now he just wanted to get away as soon as he could, he really didn't like Harry's company and there was a nasty aura about him. To him he looked like bad luck and knew that could be catching, the sooner he was gone the better he would feel about things.

He'd looked at Harry or rather the way he was eating, because he ate with his mouth wide open giving you a flash of gold teeth now and again with the odd bit of food from the overspill falling from his large open mouth, where he managed to catch the fallen food with the back of his hairy hand then sucking and scooping the food back into his cavern of a mouth.

He had the look of a ravenous dog that had no teeth on one side of its mouth chewing on the one good side. Yet you could tell this was a practised movement born from years of eating this way.

Duvall doubted if Harry could even spell manners let alone show any. In short he was gross, but at the end of the day money is money.

Harry looked incapable of doing the job himself. Duvall thought he looked to be in his seventies but he could be wrong. However he did get the impression he would keep to his word, it would be a bad idea not to....for Harry that is. 'I don't care how you do it or what you do' said Harry 'but just get rid of the bastard and his wife and kids, they all have to die, and it's as simple as that. They've been in Spain now for nine days and this is the address. It's a Villa outside Alicante. I've written it down on this envelope for you, it's also got Tom Lambert's mobile number written on it, that's if you have a need for it. His wife's mobile is on there as well.'

'Did you understand the conversation we had last night Harry. Do you agree the terms I mentioned to you? So its £40,000 now to be sent by BACS right now and then the £35,000 when the job is completed, but if you want to argue then I will say goodbye. There is no room for negotiation, not ever, do we fully understand each other Harry, because I do have to know this minute.'

'Yes off course I do understand, but please just do it.' He gave Duvall a small file, inside were all the photographs taken of the Lamberts.

Then Harry used his mobile phone to tell his bank to deposit the £40,000 into Duvall's bank account by BACS (*Bankers automated clearing services.*) 'Like I said I don't care how you kill them or what you have to do, but just do it. The time was now getting on. The time was exactly 4pm. Duvall realised he had to be back at the airport to check his baggage in at 4.35pm. 'Ok' said Duvall, 'let's do it.' Shaking Harry once more by the hand he stood up and walked to Harry's Jaguar car, the next flight to Alicante was 6.35pm that evening. Duval couldn't wait to get out of this damp grubby country, and well away from Harry.

Tom and Laura Lambert and their three children Craig, Stephen and Helen had been in Alicante for nine days. Their villa had five double bedrooms all of which had balconies overlooking the huge swimming pool. It was a lovely place which had hanging baskets supplied and kept in order by the gardener. The swimming pool was kept clean by the pool cleaners, a pool table and an outside table tennis table including a full size tennis court were available whenever they wanted them. The Villa had its own bar and a small cinema room with luxury seating for twelve people. There was also a barbeque area with plenty of outside seating and plush Hollywood loungers. The garage was a good size double.

The McDonald family from Newcastle had kindly given Tom Lambert and his family the use of the Villa for as long as three months. They had it rent free as a token of their thanks for getting out of the Black Swan as quickly as possible allowing them to move in more or less straight away. There was also the use of a car rental company who were always on standby for whenever anyone arrived from the UK. Tom had already taken a good look around the area, he loved the houses and so far they all agreed it was a nice place to live. However, time will tell and maybe after three weeks it will be looking different, because it usually does. When the sun shines it's great, but rubbish when it rains, they say if you take the sun away from Spain, what have you got?' There really is nothing that great about anywhere with no sun. It's also the people who make a great country not the sunshine. There are hundreds of things to take into consideration when moving to a new country. But it was just not possible to see all the faults in one visit, and being on holiday is not living in the same way either. For the time being, their thoughts were to purchase a holiday home and not to live in Spain on a permanent basis.

By the time Harry Dolan had arrived at Bristol airport for his return flight it was raining quite heavy.

'Jesus wept Harry, does it always rain in this lousy damp country of yours' asked Duvall.

'Yeah' laughed Harry 'always but we never run out of water.'

It was now time for Duvall to check in, he stepped out of the car but straight into a puddle, he looked down and curled his lip at his wet shoes. Once again shaking hands with Harry, he said 'this is the last time we can meet, when the job is done send my money to this same account in France and please make sure it's all there Harry.'

'It will be, trust me, it will be. I may have need of you again Duvall.'

'Make sure it is, because I have no wish to come looking for you' he winked and slowly walked off through the door marked departures. Turning for one last time he smiled at Harry, and then he was gone.

At that moment in time, a very cold chill ran down Harry's neck and shoulders right into his lower spine. Was it a bad omen and being from gypsy stock it didn't bode well? For a split second he wanted to stop Duvall, but the parking attendant was giving him grief to move on. The chill was still in his back as though someone had walked over his grave. But it was too late now. Far too late for everyone involved. Duvall had gone. Harry tried to ring him on his mobile to stop him. Unfortunately his mobile was out of battery, probably due to him spending a long time arranging the money transfer. Now he just had to get on with it he would drive back to London, but the feeling he had was wrapped around him like a filthy down and outs blanket. Unable to stop it, it was just too late.

Part of him said idiot, you can live without the pub, but there was no way he could lose face, he couldn't live with that as people would lose respect for him in no time at all. Being the one they all looked up to; he was the one who gave out the orders that's the way it is.

Harry was the boss he was the one who everyone was accountable to, and if he lost face he would no longer be feared. Every business is ruled by the fear of failure.

The Dolans were well numbered, in all there were seventeen men scattered around, all of them wanting to be the top man so there was a lot of rivalry amongst all of them. Harry was the one and only boss always looking over his shoulder if he lost respect, then his sons were not going to follow him in the running of things. That's the way it was because if the respect was gone there would be no crown to hand down to any of his sons, and that was not going to happen on his watch.

Tom Lambert had become a pain in Harry's side, he desperately wanted the Black Swan and now it was gone. Again having been thwarted by another Lambert, well now he had to pay the price. He wanted to wipe out the Lamberts, but he did have some misgivings about it, not for long though. However in the end he was glad to pay the price to keep his respect, but unfortunately he forgot one important person, one more very important Lambert....The dead man's sister, Sarah (Lambert) Santana. She had moved to America thirty years ago and was all but forgotten.

CHAPTER FOUR

After living in America for the last three years Sarah Santana had finally received her American citizenship. Kenny Santana after working his butt off for five years was now a Lieutenant in the NYPD. He had moved on up the ranks and was a good well respected cop, and a future captain. Already with four commendations to his credit he was now a detective. Kenny was clean, he hated bent cops, he was a straight talking no nonsense cop. He and Sarah had tried to have children from the start but sadly she couldn't conceive. Sarah had also joined the NYPD and as you can imagine she had to take a lot of stick. She was not only a lovely looking woman, but a very tough one. She had been studying Karate-Jutsu-Kan which was a lethal form of martial art and was now a second Dan. Now she wanted to try for a third one. After Sarah had been working in the department for four years she was eventually head hunted by the FBI. She was one of the best shots in the department. Being a natural she could beat any man with ease in the martial arts. No one could disarm her. She had won her department the shooting shield for the last three years during pistol competitions, it was hers to keep but she gave it to the department. Sarah was well thought of and commanded respect which was a rarity in the NYPD for a woman. She was able to speak fluent French, Spanish, German, and some Russian.

Because of her language skills she was put in charge of the undercover documents such as issuing new and old passports in various names for the undercover teams for both men and women, issuing driving licences in different names, all with various addresses and all were genuine. Another job was to arrange bank accounts and saving accounts, again all genuine. She had been issued with several passports and driving licences, and bank accounts which she used from time to time. No one knew when you may need them. But she always had a few just in case of an emergency.

Sarah also worked in counter intelligence and was good at whatever she set out to do.

Try as they might, Kenny and Sarah couldn't have children, it was her body's fault as she had PCOS (Polycystic Ovary Syndrome) sometimes, that's just life. And sadly you have to move on with it. Life was for living and not for crying. Life was good but very busy. Both of them were still madly in love and wished they could see more of each other. However, she had now moved to the FBI while taking up training to go undercover. Kenny was not that pleased about it. That's what she wanted to do and once she made her mind up that was it. She had a steely ambition to get to where she set out to go, and always gave her all. She turned out to be the best they had. Once she started a project she finished it, no matter how difficult it had become.

Sometimes she never saw Kenny for a week or even more whist working away. But that was the nature of the job, the money was good but the hours weren't. So you just did what you had to do.

One late afternoon as she was heading to her office there was a commotion outside the main bank. There were two armed robbers who had entered the bank where they shot and killed an off duty police officer called Jack Mallory who at the time was with his wife Elizabeth withdrawing some money for their much needed holiday. A nervous bank teller had pressed the alarm button, within minutes the police had arrived. Jack had quickly pulled his hidden weapon. One of the robbers quickly shot him first. Jack Mallory died with a shot to his head; the gun was a fearsome Magnum .44.

Jack's wife Elizabeth screamed out and bent down to cradle Jack in her arms but he was dead, half his head had been blown away. She was roughly grabbed by one of the robbers who held her by her long hair. She screamed out, but now with a gun to her head she kept still. The robber shouted 'shut the fuck up bitch.' The two robbers walked out the bank screaming for the police to drop their guns, the police had no choice.

However, Sarah was in the crowd that had now gathered. Quickly ducking down behind a taxi she pulled out her Glock 19 mm. suddenly, she popped up from behind a taxi. Now she stood there holding her Glock with both hands, she shot the first robber in the head, he was dead before he hit the ground. The second robber shouted drop your gun or this bitch dies too. Holding Elizabeth by the hair with the Magnum pressed hard against her temple he screamed drop the gun. Sarah had no choice she lowered her gun. Then the robber moved as if to shoot her. Quickly raising her weapon she shot him twice in the head. It was two fantastic shots, they were certain the robber would have killed Elizabeth Mallory, but Sarah was a crack shot. After the shooting Elizabeth Mallory became a friend and would soon turn out to be her greatest friend.

Kenny never asked Sarah what she did and besides most of the time she was not allowed to talk about it, and if he did know he would have been worried, it was best not to ask. Some of the things she was involved in were mafia incidents, local corruption including politicians and even police officers who were paid kick backs. Sarah knew it was a bit of a waste of time as money always talks, it always does. That's the way of the world - it's just the way it is. She never talked about what she did, not ever but she did notice that a lot of her former colleagues treated her a little differently. They had heard about her undercover work which sometimes involved investigating other police officers. She had never been allowed to investigate her old department for obvious reasons.

One mid morning at 10.20am, and after 20 years joining the NYPD, Kenny Santana was shot dead. He'd been asked to come in that morning even though it was officially his day off. Sarah was away on a job down in LA and Kenny hadn't heard from her for a couple of days so he went into work that fateful day. Calling into the Bagel shop before he crossed the road into his office on the 4th floor of the police station, he purchased some bagels. While he was sat at his desk reading the latest news from the local paper and munching on a bagel with ham, cheese and pickle, he had the call to go and see about a domestic incident. Finishing his coffee he grabbed his jacket and the details and walked to his police car.

John West had always been a very unstable man. West was now aged thirty-eight years old and looked a little scruffy. His hair was long and greasy and he was unshaved, his jeans were worn and faded and he wore no shoes just flip flops. There was a large scar down his right cheek which had been carved out by a drug dealer for nonpayment for drugs. However, after a recent three-year prison term he seemed to become more stable and his probation officer had found him a job. His new job as a delivery driver was a god send, he did actually enjoy his work, but he enjoyed heroin a lot better. West never took lightly to people who had threatened him and were authoritarian.

But now his elderly landlord Mr Victor Goldberg was telling him he had to leave the premises because he was behind with his rent. It was only four months and he had promised to pay it back. The trouble was he had got himself hooked on heroin again, he needed money for that or he would not be able to work it was a vicious cycle. Sometimes West was sick of his wife's nagging and moaning and his kid was always demanding something or other. Jessica his wife was always on his case. When she realised the rent had not been paid for four months she had a row with him, which ended up with her and their seven-year-old son Nathan being locked in the cellar, but only after he had beat her up. Now she wasn't a pretty sight. Mr West had gone into a rage he needed money for his habit.

Mr Victor Goldberg was once again sick and tired of all West's excuses. He'd run out of patience with him, because after all he had a business to run. Now he owned two tenant blocks. After discussing things with his wife Mary, they decided this time Mr West simply had to go. After he rang the door bell he waited and then he rang six more times. John West came to the door and demanded to have some more time to pay. 'Look, give me until the end of this month. I will pay you back, I promise I will, oh and where's your wife Mary, Mr Goldberg, she is normally with you, is she okay.'

Mr Goldberg said 'yes she's in the car thank you. She'd hurt her ankle and can't walk very far.'

'Well let me say hello to her, I like your wife.' West quickly skipped down the six steps past Mr Goldberg who was left standing outside the door? West jogged along to Mr Goldberg's car, a brand new dark maroon Chevy which was parked on some wasteland at the back of the building.

'Hi Mrs Goldberg' he said in a friendly manner as he got closer to her window which had been wound down because of the heat. 'Hey that's a nice car. Do you know something funny Mary, I can't even afford a steak meal, yet you're bugging me about a small amount of rent,' he laughed. 'Hey Mary, that isn't right is it, do you feel that's right, well do you. Are my wife and my child including me supposed to go and live on the streets Mrs Goldberg?' West just stood there looking at her but now he was far too close for comfort.

Mrs Mary Goldberg was feeling very uncomfortable, she noticed there was a lump in the front of West's shirt and it looked like a hidden weapon. Mary had said to Victor before they left, 'look babe please tell him by a lawyer's letter, I don't feel this man is right in the head, please don't upset him.'

Mr Goldberg had replied 'Mary, these vulture lawyers cost a lot of money remember what it cost before with that other tenant Mr Blackman, now we could've had two weeks holiday with what that lawyer charged us. So I'll deal with it. Let's go and see him we can talk to him and explain we also need the money. After all it's not cheap renting out properties and there are always the repairs to consider nothing is cheap today. Let me talk with him.

Yet now West was at her window and now he was leaning into their car. She could also smell his sweaty armpits and his breath was not that sweet Heroin can do that to you. Now she started to wind up her window he was smelling gross.

Mr Goldberg had now also caught up with West by the car's half open window. 'Mr West, look we can't give you any more time, can we Mary.'

Mary replied 'Mr West, it's our business and we need to eat too you know. This is the fifth time you have got behind with your rent this year. So I'm sorry but we have to draw the line on this sometime. I'm sorry but that's the way it has to be, you will have to leave but you should have paid the rent. I'm sorry we're not a charity.'

John West told Mr Goldberg, 'get back in your car and go. Hey look it's a new car so you're obviously not short of money are you?' Suddenly from under the front of his shirt West produced a .45 in his hand. Mr Goldberg quickly sat in the car next to his wife.

'Look, please don't do anything stupid or silly Mr West' but Mr West just laughed

'Why you people make me sick. You're throwing me and my family out onto these mean fucking streets and for what, a handful of corn you tight mean bastards.' And then he pulled his gun from under his shirt then he just shot them six times in the heads. Afterwards, it was a mess there was blood, bone, scalp and snot everywhere it was all over the windows and the windscreen. Muttering you mean fucking bastards, he turned around then walked back to his flat. When he was half way up the six steps he stopped.

'Oh fuck this' he said. Then he was looking at the floor where he was muttering something else to himself. Suddenly he changed his mind as he walked slowly back to the car. Stopping again this time by the car's shattered windows. Now he reloaded his gun and shouted 'you mean son of a bitch' to Mr Goldberg who was already dead along with his wife. He shot them both six more times again leaving an even more terrible mess. Both were unrecognisable they looked like mincemeat and no-one could hope to recognise them now neither would their five children. Now satisfied, West walked back to his apartment where he slammed the door shut shouting 'son of a bitch.'

This senseless bloody murder was seen by a man called Sam Hardman. He didn't actually see the shooting up close but immediately afterwards. Mr West was walking away from the Goldberg's car with a smoking gun in his hands. Then he noticed he had stopped outside his door and then he returned to the car loaded his gun again he shot the Goldberg's again through the shattered car window. Sam thought the man must be deranged. Noticing the side windows of the new Chevy had been smashed and blood was all over the windscreen, he immediately called the police and told them what had happened. That was about forty five minutes ago. He'd seen plenty of gunshot deaths while in Iraq while serving with the Delta unit. There was not a lot Sam could do as the landlord and his wife were obviously very dead and beyond any help. The shooter was now armed and very, very dangerous, shooting the pair of them like a madman would do.

God it was so hot. Kenny Santana had switched on a small fan which to be honest was a waste of time because all it did was to blow hot air around. Now he was sitting in a warm draft because the weather was hot and humid. It hadn't rained for weeks, and all the windows were open. Everyone was complaining about their clothes sticking to them, it was almost too hot to move. Suddenly he was called out to a domestic violence incident. Because there was no one else available to deal with the situation so he had to go. Everyone hated these call outs, it was all or nothing and normally a pain in the butt to deal with. Still he thought maybe it would be a little cooler on the outside. No one would bet on it. Kenny had the misfortune to step in at the last moment. He'd been told the perpetrator. A man in his late thirties called John West was threatening to kill his wife and his seven-year-old son.

The information was given to them by a neighbour who had heard West shouting and his wife and son screaming. The neighbour wouldn't give her name as fear of reprisals by West. Apparently his wife and child were being held in the tenant basement below her ground floor apartment in Queens. Mr West had previous dealings with the NYPD before and had served a three-year prison term for attacking a police officer. At times he could be a violent man. West had a long record of violence going back into his troubled teens. Dangerously unpredictable with a habitual drug habit, he was normally a heroin user.

At the same time the call came in, there was a union dispute at a meat processing factory where all available police officers were attending the awaited riot which usually followed in these cases. Without the police being there it would no doubt have got out of hand, because it had done so a few times before in the not too distant past and this time the police were not taking any more chances.

John West was apparently holding his family in the basement that was the information given to Kenny from his department. Unbeknown to Kenny, West had already shot the landlord and his wife to death. Therefore, Kenny Santana unfortunately went in blind to deal with the now unknown dangerous situation. West was now sat down on an upturned beer crate behind the front door and looking out from time to time from his letter box as Kenny drove slowly up to the building where he parked as near as he could to the door. Stepping out of his car very slowly, so as not to cause undue alarm he lazily walked up the six large steps to the door. Each step seemed to be a little steeper because of the heat. As a precautionary measure he undid his waist holster which would enable him to be ready to pull out his standard issue Glock 19 hand gun. As he came to the front door he stopped to wipe his face with his handkerchief.

Ringing the bell four times there was no answer. West moved his head away from the letter box. Kenny shouted through the letter box 'POLICE' 'Please come out Mr West, we need to talk. Hey there's no reason for anyone to get hurt. I have all day Mr West so please will you open the door for me. Maybe you can make us a coffee and we can all sit down to talk, it's too damn hot for anything else, what do you say Mr West. Look no one wants any trouble, come on man open the door. Hey man it's too damn hot to argue.' Kenny wiped his neck again as he spoke. But he was dripping sweat which was soaking into his fresh clean white shirt. Even his sun glasses were slipping of his nose in the heat.

Sam Hardman hurriedly came to the bottom of the steps.

'Officer, are you mad? Don't you know he's just shot his landlord and his wife to death in their car round the back? My God haven't you seen them, there're stone dead in the car shot to pieces.'

Kenny asked him 'say again.'

Don't you know he's shot them? Sam looked at his watch. 'Jesus Christ officer, I told your department 55 minutes ago. Where's your back up. Please don't tell me they just sent you, they can't have surely.'

Kenny quickly turned around to the worried neighbour and shouted out 'WHAT are you sure.' There was a loud boom after West had poked the 12 gauge Winchester shotgun through the letter box. He'd pulled the trigger which blew out Kenny's backbone from close range. As Kenny was going down West quickly fired the repeater again into the back of Kenny's head. What was left of Kenny lay on the fourth step where it was now beginning to be blood soaked. There was no chance he could be alive as his back and his spine were blown away. Part of his head was lying on top of a long abandoned rusted parked car whose roof was covered in pigeon crap.

But now part of Kenny's head lay on the top as well. Kenny never stood a chance. No-one had given him the right information, yet it cost him his precious life.

The worried neighbour, Sam Hardman heard manic laughing from behind the locked door. Quickly picking up Kenny's Glock 19 he put all fifteen 9mm slugs through the door. They all caught West in his head, face and chest, when he ran out of rounds he reloaded the Glock 19 with Kenny's second clip from his blood stained belt holster. So again he shot all of the other fifteen slugs through the door. When the police finally kicked in the door, West resembled a vegetable strainer. Sam used to serve with the Delta force in Iraqi, also in Afghanistan. He was no amateur when it came to weapons as they were issued with the same Glock 19. Sam Hardman could not understand how lax the police had been. Tragically it cost the life of a brilliant young honest officer who had many years of policing in front of him, but now tragically, he was dead, just blown away.

Sarah Santana was simply devastated and broke down when they told her the sad news. She was given two months compassionate leave. There was also a lot of leave due to her. Some in her department doubted whether she could ever get over this tragedy, but eventually she did. Her only family Tom and Laura and the three kids all came over from England for the funeral, where it was a horrible time. Without her family which was all she had left in the world, she would have had a job to cope with Kenny's death on her own. But they were an invaluable help in such trying sad circumstances. Tom had asked her to come back to England for a break but she refused, she wanted to get back to work as soon as possible. No-one realised Tom had a sister because she left for America when she was only eighteen years of age thirty years ago. Sarah had been long forgotten.

No one knew who took the call from Sam Hardman, they never found that out and it seemed someone was clearly ducking the issue. But it was a very busy day due to the union problems and the phone had been ringing all day. They were desperately short of staff but the facts remain. A damn good officer had lost his life due to an error so it must not happen again; it was just not good enough. After an internal enquiry no one was held responsible for the balls up. This incident happened in June 2010.

Sarah was awarded a huge amount of money plus insurances. Now she had no need to work any longer, but she did carry on although now in a more sedate reduced training role. She was now a third Dan in Karate-Jutsu-Khan which she taught in her new role as a training officer. She was still a lovely looking lady now aged forty seven but only looking in her thirties and was very fit. After the killing of Kenny, Elizabeth Mallory became closer to Sarah, she was a good friend and someone to lean on, and the same as Sarah had been for her when Jack had died. Sarah was asked to be a personal body guard to Ed Warren who was her boss. After six months she was also asked if she would like to be a body guard seconded to the CIA which would mean she would have to protect the President of the United States, also the president's wife. She turned that one down because of the travelling involved. Her language skills would be a great asset but even though she was offered a considerable increase in her wages and allowances, she wanted to stay at home.

Her work outs at the gym were a daily event; she could lift three times her own body weight. Sarah was as strong as an ox, but she never looked it. She still managed to look sexy, but not in a sexy way. Many a man had tried to date her, but that was bottom of her list as she still missed Kenny so badly. There was nothing that could be as bad as Kenny being killed, but she was wrong.

Three years later one terrible Sunday morning in May she had the most dreadful news from Spain. It was the Spanish police who'd phoned her. She thought there was nothing that could compare with the death of her husband Kenny. However, this news was incredibly bad. Her brother Tom aged 55 his wife Laura who was 50 and the three children Craig 24, Stephen 21 and Helen 16 were all killed in a fire in Spain in Alicante whilst on a holiday. She knew Tom had sold the pub because she was due her money back plus some interest from her money left in the pub. She had the same solicitor as Tom who she gave the Power of Attorney to, and then he would sort her legal papers out for her. Somehow the Villa they were staying in had caught fire trapping all of them; unfortunately they had all burnt to death. Suddenly she dropped her phone and stood there in shock, but thankfully at the time her friend Liz was staying with her for a couple of days, she saw Sarah go into total shock. She knew the news was bad, and then Sarah collapsed onto the floor.

'Sarah, Sarah,' shouted Liz, she splashed some water onto her face to shock her out of her collapse; she really looked in a bad way. The water did bring her round but she had turned white and was now trembling. 'Sarah tell me what's wrong, please tell me, it's me Liz, tell me for God sake what's the matter with you.'

Liz managed to sit Sarah up against the sofa. Now she told her to stay still while she quickly poured her a brandy. Sarah was just staring into space quietly crying, she couldn't take it all in then she howled, and howled. Liz was holding onto her tightly. 'Oh darling what's happened to you, please tell me.' After ten minutes Sarah sat up and started to explain the phone call from Spain, they both went quiet. Then both started to cry while they hugged each other.

'Oh my God Sarah, it seemed they were only just here on holiday and I met them all. How can all of them be dead? How the hell can this happen, what caused it to happen, that doesn't make any sense.'

This was too much to bear for Sarah who had turned 48 a week before. If it wasn't for her friend Elizabeth Mallory, she would have had a job to even get out of her bed. Liz had stayed with her and nursed her back to some sort of normality. She said she would stay until she was able to go to Spain to sort things out, funerals and family insurances, and all the legal proceedings which had to be sorted out. Liz offered to go to Spain with her. Sarah said 'when she was ready she would talk to Liz about it, and when she felt able to cope with the business in hand.'

She thanked Liz for her help and told her without her help she would be in a right mess. But she knew when the time was right, Liz would only get in the way. Sarah had always had a very strong sixth sense on things and now it had kicked in, none of what she had been told seemed to make any sense to her. Because all the bodies were found burnt to death in their beds which meant none of them even tried to get up and out of the villa they rented. Usually people try and get out and are found in a huddled state somewhere in the bedroom or somewhere else in the buildings where the fire broke out, this just sounded so very wrong to her.

Five days later on the Monday, Sarah suddenly woke up fully alert at 5.05am. She knew exactly what to do. Looking around her bedroom she saw two large framed photographs. In one was her late husband Kenny and the other her brother's family. They seemed to be looking at her and Tom especially seemed to say please find the truth Sarah, find the truth. She got out of bed now fully awake and looked out of the window to the four floors below there were people who were heading for work. It was just another day in another year in another country, and nobody knew of her grief. But it was business as usual. And besides why should anyone else care about her. Elizabeth was still in the next bedroom she was still sound asleep, so she left her there a while, at 7.27 she rang her boss Ed Warren on his personal number and spoke to him. 'Ed, there is something not quite right about the deaths of my family unless of course they told me differently. I don't like the sound of this. Look how can all of them be in their beds and none of them tried to get out, that doesn't ring true.'

'I have to say I agree with you Sarah, maybe they just told you wrong, but if it is true then you have to go and find the truth because to me something sounds very wrong. Go and take a look, but remember I'm here for you, by the way you take your own sweet time on this and don't you rush, just do what you have to do. And try to remember what I've just said - I'm here for you. Oh and you're still on a salary, don't you hesitate to ring me if you find yourself in trouble. I have worked with the Spanish police before; they can be good or the latter. Please remember to ask for anything and I will do my best to help you. Goodbye Sarah, and have a safe journey.'

Ed thought well if she does find out something's wrong then God help anyone who gets in her way. That would be something they wouldn't forget in a hurry. Once her fuse was lit there was only one outcome. Knowing for certain she would dig out the truth because what she had been told by the Spanish police seemed to be utter bullshit. A hurricane was about to settle in Spain by the name.

Sarah Santana. Ed Warren also thought it was implausible that all five of her family were found in their beds and all burned to death. There would have been one of them who would have warned the others, it was beginning to make no sense, no sense at all. Someone knew the truth and Sarah would find it, he had no doubt about that.

She immediately took extended leave from the FBI. When Liz came into the kitchen Sarah was fully dressed after showering, where she was now cooking bacon and eggs for the both of them which had woken up Liz. Sarah explained that she was going to England the next day and then on to Spain. Her boss Ed had paid for the flights and she was to take all the time in the world to sort things out. The two friends went shopping for holiday things like sun cream and after sun, also a swimsuit and some shorts for Sarah, plus a sleeping mask and a neck pillow. Sarah tried to explain it would be first class but Liz wouldn't have it she bought Sarah the neck pillow and sleep mask regardless. At 8pm that night they said goodbye. Both hugged and kissed each other as friends do before they parted.

    Boarding a BEA first class seat the next morning on the Tuesday, Sarah flew to England and then on to Spain. Yet all the time she had a bad niggling feeling about all of this, it was a cop feeling that all was not well, because she felt that somehow she'd not been told the truth.

CHAPTER FIVE

Tom Lambert was trying to decide whether to eat out or to eat in. The Spanish weather was wonderful. After three days of wind and rain the weather broke early in the morning, it was now just blue sky and the forecast was good for the next ten days. Maybe they would all like a barbeque; they had been at the whitewashed Villa now for nine enjoyable days. It had five bedrooms with balconies and the swimming pool was huge. He asked his family 'what they would like to eat for dinner.' They replied. 'They didn't mind,' which put him back in the driving seat. 'Okay a barbeque it is then, anyway the weather is so good let's do that.' Tom asked Laura his lovely wife if she could make the salad and he would sort out the meat and make a garlic sauce later. Before he left for the butchers he had lit the barbeque so it would be just right for when he got back. He left them all to their devices which was messing about in the large swimming pool while he popped down to the butcher's shop which was about three miles away. They also needed some wine from the store next door to the butchers. He was going to do pork chops and spicy Spanish sausage with a crisp green salad and fresh bread with garlic butter and of course garlic mayonnaise.

'Craig' he shouted 'keep your eye on the barbeque will you, it's lit but make sure it doesn't go out.' His son acknowledged him with a wave and a laugh, 'don't worry dad' he said. Tom jumped into one of the hired cars, a Yaris. Tom and Laura had one each and he drove off to the small shopping mall three miles away with a shopping list. He looked at the sky, it was just all blue and the sun was giving off a warm temperature of 24 degrees at 12.15pm. Laura waved him goodbye, yes a barbeque would be just ideal in this weather she thought. But now she was thinking about a swim. It was so hot today and the sun was bringing out all her hated freckles the same as little Helen, but Tom loved every one of them.

The weather so far had been poor but warm, and anyway now the kids were all having a good time in the pool because the weather had now turned fantastic. Laura still thought of them as her small kids although they were now all adults in their own right except little Helen who had never really reached her natural height and was a small girl for her age with slight learning difficulties, but a lovely looking girl, and very angelic. So now she decided to join them. Donning her all in one yellow swimsuit she was ready to go. Putting her hair into a knot with a hair band she jumped in to join her three children. They all cheered 'It's about time you got into the water with us mum' shouted Stephen and they all agreed.

Throwing the large yellow ball at her while laughing, it landed in front of her splashing her. 'Right' she said and threw the ball back again. They were throwing the large yellow ball to one another laughing, and then throwing it back, but this time as Stephen threw the ball, he suddenly disappeared under the water but he never came back up again and now the water was turning red, very red, because he'd been shot through his heart.

Craig shouted out 'Stephen.' Quickly diving under the water he grabbed hold of Stephen as he came up with him, but he too suddenly dropped backwards with a neat bullet hole in his heart sinking in the pool with his brother. Helen screamed out 'MUM, MUM' Laura had been looking the other way fiddling with her swimsuit bottom, which was a little tight. After all she hadn't worn it for a couple of years, probably longer than that. She said it had shrunk while not accepting she had put a few pounds on.

She looked round as Helen had screamed for her. Now she wasn't sure what had happened and thought the kids were having a laugh. Looking at Helen again Helen suddenly slumped backwards and just disappeared under the water which was now turning a horrible red spilt wine colour. Laura was now hopelessly confused. She laughed out loud as she thought they were having a bit of fun, just having a laugh by winding her up as all kids do. They had always joked around with her, however, this time she was not amused she thought they had gone too far. But the colour of the water was now turning an even more horrible red colour.

Laura didn't know what to do she shouted out 'OK, OK, enough now, this has gone too far stop it.' But then reality set in, they had all been shot, or had they? What was going on, what was happening. She was dumbstruck. Picking Helen up from the bottom of the pool she really was simply dead. Because there was no mistaking the bullet hole in her heart, this can't be happening. She screamed out 'HELEN, HELEN.' Craig had now sunk to the bottom of the pool and so had Stephen. She tried to get them all out but she had no strength left. She managed to pull them all into the shallow end which was only two feet deep and managed to lay them on the pool steps. The bodies were so heavy she was now totally exhausted, and then frustratingly she saw them slip into the pool again. She could see they'd all been shot and then Helen had started to slip away into the pool again. Pulling her back again then sadly the last thing she saw was the glow of the sun shining through the water as she sank beneath the pool with a bullet smashing into her heart. All the bullets were dum dum which meant they spread on impact. Laura died within three seconds, almost immediately.

The water was now a horrible mess having four dead bodies floating about with their life blood pouring out. Dum dum bullets were devastating on impact they went in with a neat little hole but then smashed the surrounding area into mush with a much larger hole from the back of the impact. A shot to the heart and surrounding area was pretty much resulting in certain death. The scene was one of total bloody carnage. It was an easy killing zone. A practice range, it was easy. At the back of the Villa fifty seven yards away, there was a plot of land with three small derelict houses. None of the houses had any roofs left, just some rafters sticking out like skeletal fingers.

All around there were some old rusty farm implements, broken rusty buckets and rotten fence posts with rusted barbed wire still attached but all the metals were badly rusted. Also missing were the windows along with the doors. The land was on a hill which now belonged to the McDonald family. They had bought the land to stop anyone else building on it so they wouldn't be overlooked which would be the case if anyone else built on it as you could distinctly see the swimming pool and the barbeque area.

Understandably they wanted to enjoy their privacy and to be able to relax without anyone looking at them.

    Duvall had no problem bringing in his favourite sniper rifle, the M21 &.62 mm from over the border in France. The deadly weapon held a 20 round magazine and was very accurate. He had used this mostly all his military life whilst serving in the French Foreign Legion as a sniper. Knowing the weapon inside out he'd used it many times before on consignments. Duvall was also a crack shot, and also with the pistol and most hand guns. The M21 was set up on a two legged tripod on the window ledge of the ruined building while keeping it steady with the butt pressed into his shoulder making it secure whilst holding the rifle in the old window ledge. There was no way he could miss at this range. To concentrate Duvall always chewed gum it calmed him and you needed to be calm when taking your shots. To him it was standard practice. As the Americans would say it was a turkey shoot.

    Tom Lambert gave Duvall the perfect opportunity as he drove away. Duvall looked through his scope and watched all of his family frolicking in the pool. The first one to go was Stephen as he jumped into the air to catch the bright yellow ball - he was shot in the heart in midair. Craig went to his aid then he was shot straight through his own heart. Then there was little Helen who screamed for her mother but she too was shot through the heart. Now he watched the mother go into a complete frenzy, unsure of what to do next so he let her get on with it for a while. He'd toyed with her until he became bored. He'd noticed she managed to pull all of the children into the shallow end and he could see she was exhausted. And then they began to fall away from her. He decided to put her out of her misery, moment ally she turned to look in his direction. But then she too was shot through her heart.

    When Tom arrived back home sometime later he watched him pulling his family from the water. Tom's screams were loud and pathetic or so it seemed to him. He shot him in the same way. Then he waited, but after a while he could smell roast pork.

    Yet it was Tom's back which was being barbequed he'd fallen onto the lit barbeque after being shot now he lay there in the sun while roasting away.

Tom Lambert had been gone for 105 minutes. When he returned, he drove the car onto the front of the Villa as per usual. Honking the horn to let his family know he was back as he always did. This tooting of the horn was heard by Duvall telling him Tom was back. After carrying the shopping into the kitchen, the first thing he noticed was the silence. Putting his shopping down on the marble work top he listened to the silence but now he grew alarmed. Walking out onto the patio with his hands on his hips, he was thinking his family were playing a joke on him because they were always joking around. 'Okay, ok, where are you lot then,' noticing the water first, it was an odd colour, you couldn't quite see to the bottom of the pool at first, but what he saw next pole axed him. There was his family half submerged in the swimming pool which had now turned red with their blood. Craig was next to Stephen; both had been shot and poor little Helen had been shot the same way. Laura had a perfect bullet hole in her heart, the same as her kids, the impacts from the bullets were simply lethal.

Standing by the barbeque looking into the bloodied pool Tom jumped in and brought out his wife Laura, then he brought out Helen, then Stephen and Craig where he laid them near the kitchen door which was now in the shade? Going back to the pool to look again he didn't understand why or what he was looking for because Tom was in shock. Turning around he walked back to his family then once more he turned again to look at the pool but now his back was almost against the barbeque which was still alight. It was hard for him to take all this in, this can't be happening. Looking up at the sky with his hands raised up he screamed out 'WHY, WHY, someone please help me, my family are dead. SOMEBODY HELP ME – PLEASE.'

And then a shot rang out where he too was shot in the centre of his heart. Falling with the impact of the bullet he fell backwards tipping the barbeque over. Now he lay on the burning griddle amongst the red hot coals.

Tom was dead even before he hit the ground. The still burning hot coals carried on burning into his back making him smell like a side of barbecued pork.

Duvall looked at his watch. The time was now almost 2pm. There was a reason why he didn't use a head shot, because if he did then the skulls would show bullet holes his intent was to burn the villa down with all of the bodies inside in their bedrooms, leaving nothing to chance. He'd waited until it was 10.30pm. Feeling satisfied that no one else would be coming. Slowly walking over to the back of the Villa he climbed the 5ft wall. Wearing a wetsuit with surgical gloves, he picked the bodies up and dragged them into the kitchen. After working out which bedrooms they all slept in. He carried them to the bedrooms where he laid them on the beds.

Finding more petrol in the garage, even though he had brought his own, he poured it over everything that would burn, especially the bodies. With his extensive experience of such things he knew the fire would destroy any evidence of gunshot wounds. Waiting until 1amhe lit the whole place up. But not before he closed all the doors and the window shutters. He wanted to really burn the bodies to ashes. Now satisfied the Villa was ready to burn, he flicked a match between his fingers then he lit a trail of petrol from the top of the stairs to each bedroom. The trail started to burn slowly at first but he wanted to get out before the bedrooms ignited. When he reached the bottom of the stairs he flicked a match to light up the staircase where he had splashed petrol half way down the stairs. After pouring lots of petrol into all the rooms and on the furniture downstairs and upstairs and then all over the kitchen floor and inside the bottom units and also in the kitchen wall cupboards.

Taking off his wetsuit and trainers, he carefully threw them into the kitchen, after making sure there were no prints left, well not from him. Then he quickly walked to the back door where he had left a five yard fire gap. Opening a large bag he put on some new clothes and trainers. Lighting up a newspaper he threw it onto the kitchen floor which immediately lit up, he watched the trail slowly set light as it slowly at first snaked its way on it's terrible destructive journey from room to room. When he was satisfied, he locked the kitchen door. Carefully looking around but now satisfied, he quietly slipped away to his car which was parked a mile away. Now he was wearing dark blue trousers and a dark blue T shirt with a black cap and a pair of new trainers. Half way home he managed to change again, he was leaving nothing to chance these days the forensic guys could find things you would never even think of. Once he was home he would also destroy the clothes he was wearing. He still had two cans of petrol in his boot he couldn't take the chance of being seen stopping at a petrol station they all had CCTV's. The lunatic terrorists had changed everything. Arriving at his car at 2.23am there was nobody around. As he drove off up to the main road which had a steep incline near the Villa. He stopped then he looked back he could see the lights of the fire flickering inside the Villa but no flames were coming from the roof, it looked as though the lights were on. And then he casually drove back through the night to France. This time he'd deserved his Cuban cigar. Duvall was devoid of any feelings for anyone, child, old person or anyone else not even for animals, he was a completely dead person inside. Having seen too much and done so much killing can turn you into stone. However, he'd tried civilian life but it was not for him, he just couldn't handle it. Killing was just a way of life for him, it did pay for good cigars and his expensive habit of hiring escort girls, but they were only the very best. All the girls he hired had to be no more than thirty five but the best age for him was if they were in the twenties, but with lots of sexual experience.

At 6am the next day a local builder called Pepi Garcia had smelt smoke when he got up. His wife Louise was already in her kitchen making him eggs and toast and said to him 'Pepi what's that smell, something's burning but I have found nothing here, can you smell it too I've been outside there's nothing here burning.'

'Yes I can smell it too. I think it must be the English family burning some wood. I'll check it out on the way to work. Mind you it's a little early for that at this time of the morning.' After his breakfast he headed out to work down the narrow lane. When he was almost at the bottom he noticed a dark plume of smoke lazily drifting into the clear blue sky of yet another gorgeous morning. Now he was slightly annoyed and a little curious as he drove along the side road to the Villa which he drove past every day. When he came within a few yards of the building, he wound down his windows but he immediately felt the tremendous heat. Quickly he called the police and the fire brigade who all arrived within twenty long minutes.

Daring not get any closer because of the heat, he guessed the fire was still burning inside the Villa. But by then there seemed to be a dozen or more local people who had turned up to see what the smoke was all about yet all of them giving their opinions of what they should do. One of the men thought they should break down the door. Another one said 'no don't do that, look can't you can see the heat around the main door. If you go in you will be incinerated as the air could cause a catastrophic blow back blowing out flames. It was too dangerous. If there are people in there then take it from me they are all dead by now, how could anybody survive that fire, nobody could.' There were a couple of plastic blow up chairs that were used to sit in while in the pool, they were about two feet from the kitchen window but they had now melted and the plastic chairs near the window had also began to melt, so fierce was the heat inside the villa.

When the police arrived first, they told Pepi to get back and then go and make a statement with one of the police officers. The police thought it prudent to wait for the fire brigade, they told everyone to move their cars out of the way leaving a parking area for the fire brigade who turned up with three fire engines minutes later. They immediately set to work, they were afraid the rush of fresh air would turn the Villa into a raging inferno. The fire captain told everyone to get back as there must be gas containers inside. Then one of the shutters in the upstairs bedroom blew out letting out a huge flame which roared out into the morning air making everyone jump back. The next window blew out and suddenly the whole Villa just seemed to explode into flames.

They all quickly backed off the building, they had no choice now they had to wait while they did their best to try and dampen down the outside and surrounding area. But the building just turned into a horrible burnt colour. Sirens wailing the ambulance turned up but no one could get near the Villas rooms, they just had to wait until the place cooled down. A few hours later when they finally managed to get into the building they found the Lamberts all burnt to nothing with only dental records that may be able to help them if even that was now possible. The only clue to which the bodies belonged to were in a briefcase in Tom Lamberts hired Yaris car, it contained a diary of various names and phone numbers including the Villas owners the McDonalds. There was a recent picture of his sister Sarah Santana in her new Karate-Jutsu-kan martial art suit and her FBI T shirt. Sarah was holding a large card which said 'THIRD DAN Tom, I've done it.' She was smiling and on a chair next to her was a Bulldog special .38mm in its holster with the extra rounds belt and clips and her FBI identity badge. Under the picture was her phone number, and a message which read....to Tom my only brother from your sister Sarah Santana with much love, miss all of you guys, hope to see you all very soon....Little did she know the significance of the message.

Three days after the terrible fire at the Spanish villa. Sarah had just arrived home from work. She'd had a very busy but hard day be it a pleasurable one. She had been teaching some new recruits which were now her favourite part of the job. The time now was 3.30pm. Kicking off her shoes she walked to the fridge to get a beer. A new batch of recruits had started today at 5.30am so she was particularly tired and needed a pick-me-up. Elizabeth, her best friend was staying with her for a couple of days, they were planning a holiday together and Mexico was on the agenda. Liz had just made a pizza for them both with a salad. 'Hey Sarah, how did your day go.'

'It was manic as per usual Liz but a good day. We had some good recruits today.' Sitting down to enjoy her beer the phone rang; she picked it up and thought no peace for the wicked.

The news she had was just mind shattering and painful a Spanish police woman had rang to tell her that Tom, his wife and the three kids, all five of them had been burnt to death in a serious fire which had destroyed the holiday villa where they had been staying in Spain. The police woman offered her condolences.

She had wanted to know if Tom had any enemies she could think of. There may have been a family disagreement which had turned violent, that was the theory at the moment a family dispute had probably taken place, but they were still not sure. It was hard to tell as the fire had left no clues as to what had happened that terrible day.

After five days Elizabeth could see Sarah was back to her working self and once she made her mind up to do something then God help you if you got in her way, there was no stopping her.

So she told her again she would always be here for her and then she left for home but not before Sarah had thanked her.

Ed Warren had been in the FBI for 35 years and Sarah was the best he had seen. Because she was simply outstanding, he had worked alongside her on a few occasions and had grown to depend on her, he loved her as a friend. She had also saved his life in a situation more than once. Everyone without exception in her department thought the world of her, she was a one off, she was a lovely lady....but if she was riled in any way then you had better look out. If you pushed her she was one mean bitch of a woman, even so she was always in control. Knowing her well she had been his body guard. Ed knew this was the end for her, he knew she would resign, but then again he'd been wrong before. Remembering she took it really hard over her husband Kenny, no one had expected her to stay on, she was still madly in love with him. And yet his sad death was only a few years ago. Sarah had decided to take extended leave so she was not yet retiring, proving Ed wrong, again.

Sarah was very much her own woman and very attractive, she could well take care of herself. She had never had another romance or even been out on a date, well she had been whilst working undercover and had acted as bait as they say, to ensnare certain individuals, but not on a serious date. She still missed her husband Kenny so much, she felt even now she couldn't betray him, not until the time was right....if that time ever came. She was simply not bothered about meeting anyone right now. Her love was her work and she put all her energies into it, maybe it was possible she would meet someone someday, but she couldn't put Kenny's death behind her yet. Now she had her family to bury, but she also had to find out what the hell had happened because no one seemed to know. She now intended to get to the bottom of it.

The next morning Sarah boarded an early flight to London. She was also booked on a connecting flight to Alicante in Spain, where she would be met by an Inspector from the Department of Justice, a sort of Spanish equivalent of the FBI. The visit was organised by her boss Ed Warren FBI. Ed had worked with the Spanish before and had found them to be really helpful, also extremely efficient, contrary to what some people thought about them. Some people thought they were a Mickey Mouse organisation, but that was far from the truth, they worked in closely with the Spanish Legion, a sort of SAS police department who took no prisoners.

They were actually trained by the SAS and SBS, all of them were very fit and able, the entire Legion was from Spanish origin, it was and is a tight unit of very professional men and women.

Their first love was to protect Spain, anything less and they were out of a job. There is a great pride in being in the Legion; it was a prestige job which came with a lot of respect which is more than can be said for a lot of police units from around the world. The entry level was harsh and tough; it had no time for cry babies, the training was brutal and all of them were trained in all kinds of different weapons and explosives.

CHAPTER SIX

Harry Dolan had a text from Duvall; it read 'please pay the remainder immediately.'

Dolan replied 'on the way, thank you for your time. I may have need of you once more.'

Harry Dolan was not a happy man. There was a look of unhappiness about him. Now he was feeling down and very miserable. Surprisingly, he also felt a little guilty but it was a lot more than that, yet he couldn't put his finger on what the problem was. He would never admit it to himself, but the guilt thing was something he was not accustomed to, somehow he knew he would pay for it. Now there was something bugging him, something was making him feel very uneasy. He'd had a bad feeling that things were going to go wrong which would be very soon. This feeling he couldn't shake off. It was as though a curse was now upon him it felt heavy and seemed to be dragging behind him like a ton weight, and now he had a job to sleep. Harry decided to seek the advice from an old friend called Cynthia Smith; she was a gypsy medium and Clairvoyant. Not having seen her for a few years now he wondered if she still had the gift. A few years ago he used to live with her, but things didn't work out, they both wanted different things. Cynthia wanted the simple life, but he wanted the world and even then it wouldn't be enough for him. They eventually parted as friends. She lived a quiet life in one of his luxury mobile homes in Epsom. Harry decided he would take an unexpected trip to see her, if of course she was in, if not then that's the way it was she used to be very good at what she did and always had been.

Joan, his long-suffering wife of forty years, asked him what was wrong he seemed upset and miserable. Now she never interfered with his work or even asked any questions, because she knew better after forty years of being married to him, and the experience that brought her. She ought to know by now not to ask nosey questions.

That's because she hated to wear black eyes as he was not slow in issuing a smack in the face or two when riled about something, he was best left alone. Harry said nothing to her. He just gave her a hard look that said 'mind your business woman.'

And then he left by the back door telling her he was going into town. However, he never went into town, she knew that...because you don't use your car to go to town when you actually live in the town.

Instead Harry drove his midnight blue Jaguar to one of his three luxury mobile home sites on the outskirts of Epsom near the race track. It was one of his three sites his younger son Jason ran. Harry had put him in charge of the mobile home businesses and he may bump into him. On this occasion he would sooner not because he had some private business. Now he needed to talk to an independent friend, that friend was Cynthia. After several knocks on her the door, it slowly opened to reveal a very nice looking lady, a little overweight but still very attractive, even in her sixties.

'OMG Harry, do please come on in, how are you. It's been such a long time.'

Harry walked in, kissed her on the cheek then he sat in a comfortable armchair.

'Harry, how is Joan.' But she was looking through him in a strange way, 'oh dear Harry what have you done. OMG you have done something really silly haven't you.'

'Cynthia, look can you just listen please. I need your advice so keep this down will you, and don't let on to anyone, especially Joan that I have been to see you for a reading because this is private. I don't want anyone else to know I came here to see you, can you do this for me.'

'Of course Harry, I never divulge anything to anyone and you of all people shouldn't have to ask me that. Anyway, I can see you're upset over something. We go back a long way my love, so come on in and sit at my table. Would you like a drink, maybe a tea or coffee, as you know I don't keep alcohol in the house as it dulls your head speaking of which, your son Noel should stop drinking so much? I can see lots of trouble, listen to me you have to stop him drinking Harry, or it will end in disaster.'

'Ok Cynthia, I'll have a coffee. I've already had a word with Noel, I know he's an idiot at times, he's a good kid really he's just trying to be me.'

'Harry my darling, you have to relax so let's catch up, and then I will give you a reading. Would you like a reading for the future or do you want to contact anyone who has passed over.'

'Oh it's just a quick future reading please Cynthia. That's if you don't mind.'

'I can see something is very wrong, so what is it Harry, you can tell me.'

'Nothing Cynthia, look can I just have a quick reading. I just seem to be a bit lost and I need to take the right path if there is one. I feel I need some guidance.'

Sadly she already knew he had no future, but according to the spirits neither did his family. And this was one reading she would have to lie about. It hurt her to do this but what choice did she have. She had known Harry since he was a small boy. At one time he used to be a sweet shy child, but his father Alvin was a bare knuckle boxer, a gypsy champion. Alvin brought up Harry the hard way, his father was never wrong and it was a brave man who argued with him, power went to his head. Later it also went to Harry's head that's just the way it was. It was no wonder he behaved the way he does he used to have a soft heart but now it's as cold as steel, but a lot harder.

They had their coffee and then afterwards Cynthia gave Harry a reading. It was a good reading he was well pleased, but the real reading she had was one of death and destruction. She did warn him of someone called the dead man's sister who would be coming to greet him, but not in a good way. That's all she dare say to him, she could offer no more information other than that. She knew they were all going to pass on very soon but sadly not in a nice way. It was because off what Harry had done so he must have to pay the price in this world or the next. Cynthia really believed that, what goes around will eventually come around and it was not that far away. How could she tell him what she knew, because it would make no difference to the outcome as it couldn't be stopped?

Harry was covered in the signs of death and all those who were close to him, which was totally beyond her control. Harry asked her who the dead man's sister is, but she had no answer to that, she just said 'Harry I don't know, I wish I did, but I simply don't know.'

'Well Cynthia, you must have a clue because I haven't, the dead man's sister. What dead man are you talking about and what does she look like this woman. Tell me if you can see her, is she alive or is she dead, has she passed over, because I just don't understand. So can you try and explain some more.

'No Harry,' she cried out loud. 'She is coming to greet you, she wears two colours, light and dark but never announces herself until it's over, that's all I can say about her. She is also very hurt because you have hurt her in some terrible horrible way.'

'Jesus and Mary mother of God. I haven't hurt anyone of that description, not at all Cynthia. Look this makes no sense, and you call her the dead man's sister, but why.'

'I just don't know Harry, that's the message coming through to me, the dead man's sister. And that's all I can see. I know it's strange but that's all they gave to me. You have to be very wary now and trust nobody. Be very wary of strangers especially women, in particular tall attractive women.'

'I have no idea what this woman is about, the dead man's sister. Cynthia, it makes no sense to me, can you at least explain what she looks like, how old she is, and have I met her before. Hey you're scaring me now. As it is I'm getting bad dreams so tell me what you see. You say I've hurt her badly somehow. Well that's news to me. I think you know more than you're saying.'

'Harry my darling, that's all I know. Someone, a woman aged about forty or a little older will be visiting you very soon. Yet definitely not in your dreams but in real life, she's real. I can't say what she is going to do, but she is coming to visit your sons as well, also Joan your wife.'

'What all of them, but why, what is she going to do Cynthia, you have to tell me.'

'I can't say what, *but of course she knew,* just that she is almost here and she has to seek retribution for something you have done. Only you can figure that out Harry, only you. So look into your past, and not too far into your past, and then maybe it will make more sense. It's up to you, because only you know what has happened. However, it can't be undone because people have recently passed over and now you have to face the consequences whatever they may be. And that's what I'm getting Harry. Look, I'm sorry about this.'

'But Cynthia don't you have a name for this dead man's sister, a clue or something, anything.'

'Harry, the only thing I have been given is a warning, that she is on her way and has travelled many miles across water to get here. She's almost here now. She is a very strong woman with a lot of skills which she will use but you can't run Harry, she will find you in fact she will find all of you. I'm sorry about this Harry but you did ask me, and the spirits have told me the truth as they never lie. I'm afraid that's all I have to say. Look this has exhausted me to the bone. I'm sorry but I need to clear my head and this has come as a shock to me.'

'Well thanks Cynthia at least you're always honest about what you see, but sometimes you're wrong and I hope this time you are, because it wouldn't be the first time would it.'

'Yes there is that, you're absolutely right Harry. I'm not always one hundred percent. Anyway I have no more to give today darling. I'm so drained, I really am, I have to rest now and I have a client to see in one hour.'

'Ok Cynthia I can see you're tired. Hey look I'd better be going as there's work to be done.' He left a £50 note on the table. As he walked to the door he gave her a kiss on her cheek.

But she managed to stop herself from reeling back in shock, because he felt like a slab of ice. When he drove away she broke down knowing she would not see Harry or his family again. Yet this intense feeling she had was always right. OMG what had he done. Then she clearly saw the figure of Tom Lambert and his family, they were all in spirit, all dead and they all looked so very sad.

Harry Dolan used to be a fair minded man. He had four sons at the time but one son called Jake was shot dead one night by some drug dealers in Soho. Jake had nothing to do with them. Apparently they just shot him for fun. They shot him up badly in an alleyway by the dustbins at the back of the Happy Pizza parlour. When the police finally caught them they had disposed of the weapon so there was no proof it was them who had carried out the murder. However, they were drugged out of their heads but a girlfriend of the shooter had hidden the gun, a .38 snub nose police special revolver.

She had walked away in the opposite direction, and then she caught a late night bus and rode into town she got off at the Embankment. When no one else was looking she threw the weapon into the middle as far as she could throw it where it sank without trace. That effort got her boyfriend off a murder charge so the resulting case was dropped for lack of evidence. The shooter had gone into the Pizza parlour and washed his hands leaving them clean from any residue from the gun. When Harry eventually found out who had killed his son it changed him into an animal. So acting from a tip off he found out where this man lived and had him taken to a farm building where he was tied to an old tractor wheel and beaten, until he got the truth out of him.

The next day they took his girlfriend and did the same to her. They both pleaded with Harry to stop, he did, only to show them where they were going. It was in the large hole that a digger had dug for them. They asked him what he was going to do them he told them he was going to shoot them in the head which he did. And then he buried the pair of them and covered them with lime with the help of his men.

After Jakes death, Harry was never the same again. Jake was the favourite son, he was the eldest and the brightest one, and now he was no more. His life seemed to be filled with hate and then he became more demanding but also more unpopular. People thought he would get over it, but he never did.

Joan was Jake's mother. But she too never got over the death of her son. She still had three sons left but after the death she just ate and ate and became a large mess. Yet she used to be a very attractive woman but she started to drink and her favourite tipple was gin & tonic with lemon. She drank like a fish every night after that and Harry had given up on her and found his love life amongst the many women he employed at his businesses.

There were also the prostitutes in his house in town, it was really a brothel run by Noel, his second youngest son. Alex was now the eldest son who ran the betting shops he was a fierce enforcer. But the youngest son was Jason who managed the three mobile home sites in Epsom and was the quietest of the remaining three boys.

Jason was a sensitive man who never liked violence of any kind but he always supported his family and sometimes things just had to be done. He was also gay, he thought he had kept that a secret but Harry and Joan knew, his brothers didn't, they never rubbed along that well.

CHAPTER SEVEN

Sarah Santana landed in Alicante. She was not a hard woman to miss as she stood at 5ft 8inches tall with short cropped blonde hair. She was slim with steely blue eyes and looked like she had come straight from a Hollywood movie set. She also had a very sexy walk which was not put on either. Looking good she was wearing a black polo neck jumper and a pencil slim skirt to just under her knees with four inch heels. There were no airs and graces, she was straight talking and to the point. Sarah was a head turner but that never impressed her, she knew where she was going and had tunnel vision when she wanted something.

After she landed she was met by a policeman and was ushered through to a security office where she was told of the latest results. The police still seemed to think it was a family dispute as there was no evidence of anyone else who may have been there or indeed involved. She could tell the police wanted to wrap this up as a family dispute. After all they didn't need the bad publicity the tourist season was almost on them so they wanted to bury it quickly. They wanted to demolish the villa it was not a good advert for Spain. She asked 'if they could take her to the villa as she wanted to see the place for herself, she wanted to feel the atmosphere wanting to take it all in. But most of all she wanted to know exactly what had happened.'

'Of course' said a well spoken Spanish police officer called Juan, 'I will take you first thing tomorrow,' he said in perfect English, he thought to himself well this is my lucky day if I can work with her.

'No, if you don't mind I want to go now please.

The Spanish cop replied. 'My orders are to take you with me Sarah, that's my job.'

Sarah looked at him and said in perfect Spanish 'Really, well Juan, now you listen to me. I want to go by myself and I don't need a chaperone. I'm a big girl and can take care of myself, so if you don't mind please give me the address.'

There was something pretty scary about the look in her eyes which worried Juan and he didn't want to get on the wrong side of her, because she looked a very capable person, a very capable woman indeed. She held his gaze and it was obvious she meant business. Her look told him, she was on a mission.

They had booked her into the Airport Hotel where she had arranged a car from the police pound, it was a red BMW but she asked for a darker one, so they gave her a dark blue one. Red was a giveaway colour. The car had a sat/nav but by the time she had organised things it was getting dark so she decided to have an early night. She would go on her own in the morning, at first light.

Juan spoke to his boss and told him what Sarah had said, he was told to go to the Hotel for eight am and not to let her out of his sight at all costs. Or there would be trouble.

Sarah was in the shower by 4.05 am, she left for the villa at five am, slipping out of the Hotel by the back door. She set the sat/nav and drove away. The receptionist had been told to ring the police if and when she went out, but Sarah had figured that out, that's why she decided to take the back way out, and so far unseen.

When Juan arrived three hours later at eight am he thought she was still in bed, so he waited until nine am before finding out she had gone. He knew his boss would nail his balls to the floor, and he certainly wasn't wrong on that point.

Sarah had no problem finding the area. It was a nice affluent area with very expensive detached villas. A lot of them were surrounded by high hedges and tall pine trees to give shade. However, you couldn't fail to notice the burnt out villa. In the early morning light you could plainly see some of the roof rafters sticking out like burnt ribs. It was set on the end of the long road with about a hundred yard gap between the last and one villa. At the end of the road it narrowed next to the burnt out villa to a tight single lane, the hundred yard gap was building land which was also owned by the McDonalds family.

The villa in some part was now almost flattened. But looking like a bomb had blown it up, yet the chimney breast was still intact with the fire grate in full view. It almost resembled something like a picture from the Spanish civil war. You could still smell the burnt out building, it had a curious smell about it. As she slowly drove down the road leading to the villa she had a bad feeling about this. Looking at the time it was now 6.17am when she parked in what used to be the driveway. She sat there for a few minutes reflecting on her life and all the memories she had of Tom and his family. She held on to the steering wheel where she gripped it rigid. She was quietly shaking and then cried for a while. Really she wanted to scream for them. There was the picture in her head of little Helen and her two lovely looking brothers Stephen and Craig who were so protective of Helen, and then Tom and Laura who were always so very happy together. Now Sarah was a very tough lady but she couldn't help herself. Eventually she stopped crying and composed herself, she looked around the area and then stepped out of the car. She had a pair of Adrian Phelps handmade sunglasses perched on top of her head as she looked at the burnt out villa, she was wearing tight blue jeans with a white T shirt and a yellow scarf, her sneakers were light blue bought from Bloomingdales in New York. She looked amazing and had a large man bag as she felt it had more room than a woman's.

    Sarah was here to do a job and not to look pretty. But however that was still a look she gave, she couldn't help it. In the bag she had her Apple laptop, her Apple mobile phones and her Apple tablet, cameras and tape measures. She had sample bags for small objects she might find, also finger print dust and the new tape especially made for taking finger prints which lifted off any prints she may want to check out. In other words she had a mini forensic kit, which was given to her from her boss Ed Warren at the FBI. This could prove if her family were indeed murdered. The first thing she smelt was the villa, the smell was still lingering, a smell of burnt wood and plastic and all smells churned together with a damp after affect. There was also a faint smell of petrol. There was broken glass and melted glass all over the floor.

    She could see the broken bits of the gas bottles after they had exploded. They didn't have gas installed, just bottled gas which a lot of houses in Spain still do, and all the pieces were blackened. You could still see the fridge and the washing machine all twisted and blackened you could plainly see the kitchen utensils, saucepans and frying pans lying twisted and bent. Curiously the plastic washing up bowl which had been in the sink was for some reason still in a perfect shape. There were dishes and plates all over the kitchen floor with knives and forks all in a heap and various odd shoes burnt blackened, and melted. And yet strangely there was a local picture in a frame completely unmarked. On the back door which was still standing there was a dark blue police cap with the words NYPD which she had sent to Tom a couple of years ago, that too was strangely unmarked. Taking it off the back door she put it in her bag, and then she started to cry again. But this was so painful. Then she felt sick and threw up. In the far corner there were two small teddy bears completely unmarked. One was wearing a little vest saying 'NYPD will protect you' which she had sent to little Helen, the other one was laying in the other bear's lap, both of them had belonged to little Helen. Sarah scooped them up and cried into the bears holding each one to her swollen eyes, and then she gently put them into her bag. She stood a while thinking about what to do next?

Suddenly she heard a vehicle coming which was hooting its horn. It was then she saw a small scruffy builder's truck coming from the opposite direction. Pepi Garcia was driving the small truck. He stopped outside the villa and said 'good morning.'

'Yes it is, now composed again she asked him, 'I wonder if you can help me please,' in perfect Spanish, 'did you see what happened here, it was my brother and his family who died in the fire. I am trying to understand what happened. Can you tell me anything because I have come from America to try and get some answers? I don't understand what happened and how it happened, but most of all how it had started.'

'Mother of God, I am so sorry for your loss senorita. I was here first. I called the fire service and the police.'

'Would you please tell me what you saw? Oh I'm so sorry my name is Sarah and you are.'

'Pepi, and as you can see I am a builder. I live just over the hill look you can just see my red roof.'

'Did you see the fire Pepi.'

'Yes I did.

At first when I got out of bed I could smell burning. I thought the English family were burning some wood. On my way to work, I came across the villa I saw a small plume of smoke, but when I arrived to see what was causing it I tried to inspect it, but the villa was ablaze inside, not on the outside at that time, but on the inside, you could clearly see the heat from the fire but you could also feel it too. It was all around the building, some other people came along and one man wanted to go in, but I saw the heat around the door and told him not to go in as once the air got in it would explode. I told him there would also be gas cylinders, so we all stood back in case they did explode. I have gas cylinders we have no mains gas here. There was a strange thing though. Now the entire window shutters were closed which was very odd.'

'Why did you think that was odd Pepi?'

'Because I come this way every day and since the people came which had been about nine or ten days before I think, oh sorry I mean your family. The upstairs windows were always left open at night to catch the evening breeze, we all do this because of the heat, but they were closed which means that the inside of the villa must have been like a furnace. But then one window blew out so the air got in, the whole villa seemed to explode including the gas cylinders. It was so hot, he looked at his watch, anyway I have to go and my sorrow for your family.

Sarah if you want to know anymore as I said I live over the hill about a half mile away. So look it's the first house on your left, you can see the roof, it's the red roof. You can come round later my wife and I will be in from 6.30pm onwards. If we can help you please call round, we can get you something to eat and have a drink.'

'Thank you Pepi.' She watched him drive away and then wandered over to the swimming pool area, which was in a mess even she could see there were blood stains all over the floor which had now turned a dark brown colour. There was blood smeared all over the place. And now you could see the blood trails had gone brown leading to the back door or what was left of it. However, there were smudge marks with no finger prints which in itself seemed ridiculous because if Tom or anyone else had carried out the killing, there would be finger prints, yet there were none. They must have been killed in the pool because the blood smudges indicated the bodies had been dragged along the ground from the pool.

Yet the Spanish police said that it looked as though there was a family dispute and that Tom would have probably killed his family after a family argument. Then he set the villa on fire, but how could he have killed all of them at once because he was incapable of killing a fly. How convenient they were burnt to nothing, there were no clues as to how they had been killed only that they were burnt to death. So how come there was all this blood, this made no sense to her, no sense at all.

She was lifting pieces of timber and broken tiles from the roof and was looking for clues and signs. Then Sarah noticed the three old derelict buildings which were about fifty to sixty yards away. Looking around again she did see the back kitchen door was still almost intact yet the key was on the outside of the door, it had obviously been locked and anyone inside was locked in, you can't lock a solid door from the outside when you're inside. Someone had clearly locked the family in. Someone had kicked the door in, probably a fireman. You could plainly see the door had been locked by the lock bolt being out and the wood had shattered, but leaving the lock on show. Sarah took all sorts of pictures including the lock.

After seeing the old buildings again she was now curious, she slowly walked towards the buildings taking her time. She walked on the right side of the small track because coming down the hill you would veer to the right of the track if you were right handed. But now she was looking at the right side all the way up to the middle derelict house. About half way she noticed something white in the track. Bending down to see what it was she realised it was chewing gum. Seeing it had been recently discarded it also had a couple of teeth marks still in the gum. Taking out her forensic bags she selected one and picked the chewing gum up with her tweezers and popped it into the bag putting the date and time but not before she had taken pictures of the gum in the grass. She carried on until she got to the doorway of the old building in front of her. All the time being careful where she trod. First she looked inside taking her time to look around. It wasn't as though Sarah had no experience of such things. At one time she had worked for a year in the FBI forensic department. And now after looking around she very carefully entered the old building, whilst taking photos.

There was a small wrapping paper torn in half which she picked up and kept with the words Gomme a Macher written on it, which was in French but she knew what it meant, chewing gum as her French was impeccable, along with her Spanish. What she did notice when she entered the old building was that there were definitely signs that someone had been behind the old window. That's because there was a depression in the dust, and by the look of it probably from trainers, she reckoned a size ten mans footprint and recently. You could see the look of the pattern on the floor area around the window. On the inside ledge where the window frame should have been there was an indentation in the dust, well two indentations which could have come from a tripod. She duly took more pictures of the inside. The window was overlooking the whole of the pool area and to an experienced shooter anyone in that area would have been an easy target, a sitting duck. Sarah pretended to look through a scope on a rifle. She figured it would have been a perfect place to shoot everyone if indeed that's what happened to her family.

She started to shake with anger. So why didn't the local police pick up on this. It was all too rushed. There were no other foot prints so no one else had even searched the house. The police wanted to bury the enquiry they wanted no bad publicity as the main holiday season was just starting. They simply couldn't care less. They all wanted to sweep it under the carpet, or so it seemed to her way of thinking. Sarah also took lots of photos with her mobile phone, especially the view from the window overlooking the swimming pool, which also took in the back of the villa. She found nothing else, so walked back down the slope again. All she had found was the chewing gum and a wrapper. Now there had to be someone else there. She took one last look around and in the burnt out kitchen she saw what looked like the back end of a burnt trainer. She picked it up and looking at the pattern she went back up to the old building. Sarah bent down to inspect the marks in the dusty soil it was obvious this was the trainer which was worn by the person in the old ruin. It was obvious to her what happened. The killer had earned his wages. And then dragged the bodies into the house and set fire to the villa. He must have changed his clothes after throwing the clothes he had worn into the villa to burn the evidence. She knew the police wouldn't do a thing about it. Then she had an idea.

To say the family had a row or dispute which ended up with one of them killing all the others was just so ridiculous. There was a serious problem with this. As she got back to the burned out villa she had one more look around then drove off back to the police department to pick up Tom's possessions. A police woman asked Sarah 'to sit down in an office while she walked into the next room to collect the family's things to give to Sarah.' There were five plastic urns full of her family' ashes, that's all there was left. Sarah sat there after thanking the police woman. How she was hurting inside. Now it was like a terrible ache. Standing up, one officer helped to carry the urns back to her car. Then the urn which was holding young Helen's ashes spilled out as she tripped over the uneven kerb. In Spain kerbs are never level. Unfortunately the lid had come off now she tried to get the ashes back into the urn which was no easy matter under the circumstances.

A passing police officer asked her if she was all right, and did she need any help. She declined his offer as this was a private matter. She was now feeling a little distressed. Looking at little Helen's ashes spread over the pavement she wept again.

But now she was very angry. In her boot there was a cardboard box with a few of Tom's things, she took the sides off the lid of the box and used the sides to pick up the ashes. Whilst doing so she saw what looked like lead fragments, only a small amount but she tried to keep them separate. Human remains do sometimes leave traces of lead, a fact of life. However, she thought they looked a little different just like bullet fragments. When Sarah got back to the hotel she asked for a fine sieve from the kitchen. She decided to check the other four urns. After she checked them out she found the same type of fragments. Thinking hard what else could it be, but her gut instinct knew they were bullet fragments. Now she was pretty certain she knew they had all been shot before being burnt to nothing.

What the hell was this all about because it certainly didn't make any sense at all? They were just an innocent lovely family unit. It was obvious to her they had all been shot. So her family had been brutally murdered, but in god's name why. Who would want to kill her gentle family? They were not a violent family at all, just a hard working unit. There must have been a reason why someone would kill them, whatever the reason it couldn't be a valid reason. No matter how long this took she would find out the reason why and then serve out her own justice. It wouldn't bring her family back but by God she was a tenacious individual.

Ed Warren was a tall distinguished slim looking man with glasses and a small white goatee beard. He always seemed to be tanned yet always being a dedicated detective of the old school who never missed a trick. Now he was aged fifty seven and not long to go before he took his retirement. He had just arrived home after another gruelling day at work as they were always short staffed and the recruitment was not going too well either. The new candidates this year were not very good. Tired, he sat down in his favourite chair, his wife Glenda said 'hi honey,' she could see he'd had a hard day it was written all over his face. Ed had a kind face and she felt lucky they had been married now for thirty-two years. She brought him a cold beer, as he opened the ring top he had a call from Sarah.

'Ed I'm so sorry to call you but I urgently need your help.'

'Of course Sarah, how can I help you, you sound a little stressed?'

'Ed, can you arrange for a DNA test on some chewing gum, there are clear teeth marks on the gum, it's long shot but it's worth a try, and could you also arrange for some lead fragments to be checked to see if they were from bullets.'

'Hey Sarah, look slow down a little and tell me how you are. So what have you found and are you okay. This doesn't sound so good to me, are you in any trouble. I'm here to help anyway I can, so tell me the problem.'

'No Ed, I'm not in trouble, well not yet, but this situation stinks. I know my family were murdered but I can't figure out why.' She told him what she had found out and the police seemed clueless. But she did need some help as soon as possible.

'Ed, I don't trust the police over here they just want to stick their heads in the sand and let everything go away.'

Ed knew she was 100% positive about this. He'd always trusted Sarah and she wouldn't just ring him for nothing. She was serious and had obviously found out something really bad. So he arranged for the Spanish Department of Justice to see if they could find out who had been using the chewing gum if possible. It was just a long shot and would probably mean nothing with nobody's DNA to show for it. However, it was definitely worth a try, and besides the Spanish police were not shy when asking the FBI for help when they needed it. After all they had a reciprocal agreement.

Sarah handed over to the forensic police the details which had been arranged by Ed. But she kept half of the chewing gum back just in case it went missing. Also she was keeping back a portion of each bullet fragment in case of the same, she needn't have worried because Ed was with her all of the way on this, and spoke to his counterpart in the Spanish Department of Justice. They were waiting to see her when she arrived.

The Spanish Department of Justice later sent Ed Warren some details, and surprisingly very quickly. They had always worked closely with the FBI when the occasion arose because they were keen to impress, and yes the lead fragments were indeed from bullets. Ed got lucky because the DNA taken from the chewing gum belonged to a Frenchman called Eric Bezier who had been a regular in the French Foreign legion for about twenty-seven years. Eric Bezier had been arrested three years previously in Benidorm where he received a caution for an assault on a woman in a cocktail bar. The local police had taken his DNA because there was an incident regarding a drink, but it was nothing really serious. However, the woman insisted she wanted to prosecute him for assault for throwing a drink all over her. Being a high class escort who tried to sell herself to him but it all went wrong. Yet it was over something and nothing, but that's who the DNA belonged to. Eric Bezier had arranged for an escort girl to meet him in an upmarket cocktail bar in Benidorm Spain, but apparently he was less than impressed with the way she looked and behaved. Apparently she'd turned up drunk according to Eric's account given to the police records.

Because of that he refused to book her causing a dispute over the booking fee which she wanted him to pay for, which resulted in an argument. The woman would not give in.

So he threw a pint of lager all over her head which made her a laughing stock in the bar. Apparently the edge of his glass skimmed past her nose. She claimed it had broken it, which was laughable but it did connect to her nose there were witnesses.

Eric was handed a caution, he also had his finger prints taken along with his DNA down at the local police station. This was the custom of all European countries when a serious incident occurred, and an assault charge was regarded as an incident. His DNA was extracted by a mouth swab. Apparently he was livid then he became a little obtrusive towards the police which went down on his report. When he was told he would end up in court if he didn't calm down, he became apologetic but it was still all on file. It was noticed he tried everything to get his DNA destroyed and his prints taken off the record and he would pay the woman her fee if she agreed to withdraw the charge. The woman had clearly seen something in his manner which frightened her and she refused to withdraw the charges. So he still had a caution and that was the end of the matter.

Sarah had quickly received the report and the fact the man was French was a giveaway. Sarah found out about his army career and asked for his army record which was a little more difficult to get hold of. It only said that he had served for twenty-seven years in the French Foreign legion. Alarmingly a lot of his career was restricted and marked down as top secret and confidential. That was all Sarah had needed to know, she had a very strong feeling, a cop feeling that this guy was the killer. But she did manage to obtain his address in Nice. She had a recent picture of this Eric Bezier. She found out he lived alone and had never been married. He was a loner. Now it looked as though he travelled a lot as the FBI obtained all his recent travel plans. It was also obvious to her he was a hit man. He was an assassin for hire who had travelled all over the world. However, he lived a quiet life in Nice on his own. Looking at the map of the South of France, the main road ran into Spain so you could easily make that journey by the road. It would be a breeze to drive through to Spain and then drive back to France.

She calculated you could easily do it in less than a day. The Spanish Department of Justice also mentioned he had flown out to Australia recently. Being there only for four days which was unusual to say the least, he had no business interest out there. Let's face it, so who flies out to Australia for four days unless it's on business. So it looked to

Sarah he could have been hired to do a job and then flew back home, job done. While he was there after only two days three people from a crime syndicate in Sydney were blown to bits in a car explosion. The Sydney police were still looking for the killer. It was a controlled explosion triggered by a mobile phone, yet according to his army records he had been an expert in all types of explosives.

There was no proof he was connected to the murders. Yet he was in the area. They managed to obtain his mobile positioning from his phone by cross angling his movements while in Australia. It was definite he'd been in the area. Sarah was told Eric had also travelled to Bristol nine days after her brother had flown to Spain with the family. Also coming back the same day, which to her meant only one thing, he had a meeting with someone then two days later Tom and his family were all dead. She worked it out they had been shot by a shooter from the derelict building, because there were tripod marks in the dust on the window ledge. The shooter at some point had a clear view of them while they were in the pool. If one had been shot then the others would have gone to help, making themselves easy targets, it would have been as the Americans say, a turkey shoot. The chewing gum along with the wrapping paper she was certain were thrown away by a Frenchman, so it seemed Eric was the Frenchman. But who did this Frenchman meet up with at Bristol airport?

She had to find out, that would be the key. She would deal with Eric later. She asked Ed 'to obtain any CCTV footage of passengers on the same flight as him. And was there anyone the passengers met on arrival there were always a few people waiting to greet passengers. And with any luck he would be on the CCTV, and also maybe on the way back to the check in later perhaps they could see who, if anyone dropped him off at the airport. It was worth a shot.'

Ed Warren had, with a lot of persuasion, managed to get the CCTV films from Bristol airport and there was this Eric Bezier walking through customs, then he was seen meeting Harry Dolan. There was also outside CCTV film of him coming back with Harry Dolan, his car number plate was clearly visible and very easy to trace. When Sarah had the films sent to her and viewed them, she seemed to recognize this Harry Dolan, but it was from years ago. She was certain he was known to her family, but couldn't remember in what connection that was.

Ed Warren sent the films over to Scotland Yard where he had a quick reply. The man's name was Harry Dolan and according to them he had a pretty bad reputation. They sent the report back about him, which he passed on to Sarah. It made very interesting reading. When Sarah had the report back regarding Harry Dolan she knew her brother would not have had anything to do with a man like that, there was nothing that she could see that would possibly be connected to her brother. Well only that Dolan had property in and around the area of the Black Swan in Soho.

She decided to fly to London to see what she could find out about this Harry Dolan and if he had any connection whatsoever with her brother. It was very strange, but there had to be a reason, it was probably staring in her face... it was.

The fear of what may happen to him was now wearing off Harry Dolan. There were times he knew that Cynthia wasn't always right but she was very accurate on most things. People were often scared after coming from a reading she had given. She did have a good reputation and it was hard not to take in what she had said. As time went by he started to become his normal self again, at least that's what his wife Joan thought. He was a lot more cheerful now, and his lucrative businesses carried on as before. Besides, Cynthia his medium friend had told him the future looked good, he also gave his wayward son Noel another bollocking about his big mouth and his stupid drinking habits.

The first port of call for Sarah in London was the Black Swan public house in Soho. She hadn't seen the pub in about twenty to thirty years. She walked in it was very busy but she recognized nobody although she turned a few heads, all male. She walked to the bar and asked if she could speak to the owner. Norman McDonald introduced himself and asked what he could do for her. Norman was a large man with a bit of a pot belly but his eyes said it all. His eyes were a sparkling light blue. His heavy dark eyebrows really stood out in a crowd and his hair had disappeared some years ago but he was as bright as a button standing at about six feet three inches tall and weighing about eighteen stone. His eyes missed nothing. He came over as honest and very intelligent. Yet he also seemed to Sarah to be a very nice man, a man who you would trust but a man's man with good manners.

'Norman, I'm so sorry to bother you, my name is Sarah Lambert. It's of a personal nature, could we have a chat please. It's about my brother Tom and his family. Please it's very important.'

'Yes lass of course, please come this way. We can go into the sitting room, it's for family only. They walked into a small room with just three easy comfy chairs, a large TV, a black cat and a coffee table. He beckoned Sarah to sit down. The cat immediately jumped up on her lap. 'Napoleon get down, he doesn't usually do that to anyone, you're very privileged Sarah.'

'Napoleon, I like that name Norman, and I do like cats.' The cat was now snuggling into her lap and purring loudly.

'What was so important Sarah? I'm so sorry about Tom and his family, and of course your great loss and if I can help in any way then I certainly will. Now don't you hesitate to ask me anything at all? I liked Tom and Laura; they were so helpful to us and the children too. And that's why we gave them the use of our Villa in Spain. Now I feel so sad about that decision.'

'Thank you Norman. It was good of you to give them the use of your Villa.'

'It was to say thank you for the easy transfer into the pub.'

'Norman, do you know of a family called the Dolans by any chance, and one in particular called Harry Dolan, if so would you know if Tom had any dealings with this man or his family.'

'Well yes sort of, that's the man who wanted to purchase this place. However, I don't know the ins and outs of it. Apparently he made the strongest bid at the closed Auction, but when Tom found out who made the bid and then he pulled the sale.'

'Really, but why did Tom do that, do you know why he pulled the sale. That sounds a little odd to me and very mysterious.'

'I can't really say why Sarah, because he never told me, only that he was not going to sell it to that man and his family. I'm sorry Sarah I'm afraid that's all I know. I have heard that this Dolan family are from gypsy descent. Apparently they own a lot of property around here. They are not a family to cross, especially this Harry Dolan. Tom didn't tell me he had a sister, but then why would he. If I can help you further Sarah, please call me or pop in anytime, you're always welcome. Tom Lambert was such a good man. Let me tell you we were gutted to hear about the fire. It's all right for us as we were well insured, anyway the Villa can be replaced....but your brother and his family can't be replaced and like I say we are sorry for that.'

'Norman thank you so much for telling me all of this, you've been a great help.'

'Oh I do hope so, we feel so guilty about it now. We wish we hadn't lent them the Villa.'

'Look Norman, Tom was my brother so believe me, he was so happy you did that for them, and he wouldn't blame you for anything, he was a good and fair man'

'Thank you Sarah, that means a lot to me.'

To Sarah it was all beginning to fall into place. It was as though a thick fog was clearing at long last. She remembered from years ago as a little girl the talk about who killed her father he was crushed under a lorry. The rumour was he was crushed on purpose, and later the lorry driver was found hanged. The coroner recorded it as a suicide. Apparently her father Henry Lambert had been a good amateur boxer when he was young. He'd stopped some member of the Dolan family killing a man and the Dolans were not the family to cross. But it was all a bit vague because she was never told the whole story, probably because she was just a small girl.

Scotland Yard in their detailed report mentioned the Dolans had a long memory. Harry Dolan in particular did not and could not lose face or he would be disrespected. To the criminal underworld that was not appreciated, nor forgotten. If nobody respected you it was about the worst thing that could happen to you.

In her mind she could remember something about this Dolan family and it was to do with her father. She could not fathom out what was said at the time because being a small child, and especially being a girl, things were kept from her. And that's the way it was back then and probably still is now. It was just the way her parents tried to protect her from the bad world of grownups. So the longer she remained a child the better she would be.

CHAPTER EIGHT

Ed Warren had somehow managed to get mobile phone numbers for both Eric Bezier and Harry Dolan which he passed on to Sarah along with Eric's address in Nice. He also managed to get a trace on his previous calls which were made to Harry Dolan. They already knew they had met up at Bristol airport. Sarah realized she had left a trail a mile long in the name of Sarah Santana. She could do nothing until she brushed out her trail and this was going to be hard to do. After a great deal of thought she decided to fly back to America leaving a fresh trail as though she was finished with all of it.

So after arranging a quiet funeral for her family in Spain, she booked a flight back to America, she would then tell Ed Warren she was going on a long holiday around America and wanted to be left on her own. And now she needed to find out what she really wanted from life. The day after landing she went into the FBI Office to have a chat with her boss to tell him she was taking maybe two or three months off to see where her future lay. She didn't wish to be contacted in that time, not by anyone. She hadn't fallen out with anyone, but wanted to be left alone for a while. No offence Ed, but I just want to be alone but I may be back in a couple of months, or maybe even sooner. All the family's things have been settled including a quick funeral. I will say bye for now. I shan't be using my phone, so please don't get annoyed if you can't reach me. I'll be around Ed, but not around.'

Ed Warren reluctantly had to let her go. She had the time owing to her and now she was taking it.

Sarah rang her best friend Elizabeth Mallory. 'Liz can you come round to see me, it's rather urgent and I really do need your help. I hope you can make it.' Within twenty minutes Liz arrived at Sarah's apartment.

'What's the problem Sarah, are you okay? Tell me how I can help you.'

'Liz this is strictly between you and me and you can't tell anyone what I am going to tell you. I do need you to back me up. What I am about to do is against the law, but if I don't sort it I will never forgive myself.'

'Oh Sarah come on, I promise on pain of death I will never ever divulge what you have to tell me. I can see you're not feeling good about this, so of course I will help you, I always will. Hey, don't forget you saved my life, and that will never be forgotten, I owe you way over big time.'

'Okay, look Liz I want you to cover for me. I want you to be me by using my credit cards and my computer, but you have to travel all around New York State, stopping here and there, and driving my Volvo estate. Can you handle that Liz?'

'Well you try and stop me Sarah.'

'You have to keep all receipts too. I've bought you a mobile phone in the name of Sally Parker, this phone is to be used only when I ring or text from England, do you understand Liz.'

'England?'

'Yes England, I'm going back to find out who murdered my family. I do have a damn good idea who did it. I have a mobile phone in the name of Gaynor Mapp. I will phone you from this number and it will only be used to ring you on this phone. Do you understand Liz?'

'Yes I do, because you want to give the impression you're still in America. Am I right, or am I right Sarah.'

'Yes you're right Liz, well no flies on you girl. It's only for me to send you messages. I will tell you when to text my real phone number which you will have and I will get in touch on this when I need an alibi, or you can use my computer to send a message to your computer as if I'm still in America. By doing these things will probably save my life or a life sentence and I'm serious Liz. You have to use your normal mobile phone; the new ones as I explained are just for me to tell you to either text or to email me.'

'Try to remember I used to be an accountant Sarah. So what are you going to do?'

'I have to seek revenge on the evil men who ordered the deaths of my whole family. Liz, you are the nearest I have to a family, you realise that don't you.'

'Yes I do, just tell me what to do and I'll do it, you know I will.'

'I'm supposed to be taking a couple of months off to get my head back in order. I want you to travel around so don't stay anywhere more than three days or maybe four. But do enjoy yourself please. So just treat this as a holiday so make out you are me and I'm on holiday. Have you got all this Liz or I can write it down for you Look when this is over we can destroy these two new phones, but please, and this is so important, please keep all the receipts for petrol, meals, motels or anything. Spend what you want to; don't just sit on my money. I'm taking out five thousand dollars as an emergency for you, but you have to use my credit cards, here they are and don't go mad' she laughed.

Sarah spent a week touring around up-state New York and then she booked a flight to Nice in the name of Clare Edwards, somehow, someway she wanted to meet up with Eric Bezier.

Landing in Nice at 3.45pm on a Thursday afternoon, then after clearing the usual dreary custom rituals and the smiling faces of the men, she walked out into the fresh air. It was unusually wet but still very warm. The rain had moved on but she could still smell the wet, a smell she liked. The taxi rank was a few yards away, as she reached it, a taxi driver immediately hopped out to put her case into the boot. It was a little different to the New York yellow cab drivers who normally sat there while you struggled with your cases. Opening the door for her the driver gestured to her to get in. She asked him to find her a hotel near the address of Eric Bezier which he did. In fact it was only ten minutes from Nice airport, yet it was also very near to where Eric lived, very near in fact just about a hundred yards away.

The driver stopped his cab where he carried her case into the hotel then he gave her his card. She gave him a generous tip and smiled, 'thank you Madame. Oh, please call me if you need a cab.'

Sarah was impressed, that's what the Americans called service. Now she wondered what had happened to the service back home, and how things change. Not long ago people used to imitate us she thought, but now that's mostly gone.

The hotel was a nice little hotel overlooking the harbour. It had lovely potted plants in Terracotta pots outside the main door you could see it had been freshly painted in a mid green. A not too obscure sign in green and white said Welcome to the Delphi Hotel. The whole place was spick and span. The Taxi driver had made an excellent choice for her. He was worth a good tip.

Sarah decided to check in for a week under her new name of Clare Edwards. Handing over her passport with that name to the receptionist was the custom in France. Her room was at the front with a small balcony with a lovely view. The room had a double bed with typical French settings, a little old fashioned but clean and wholesome with its own en-suite. After a good night's sleep she woke up early as per usual. Taking in the view again she decided to go for a walk before breakfast. She'd been walking at a nice slow pace along the harbour passing all the little restaurants. There were Italian, French, Moroccan, and Chinese. She decided to stop somewhere and have a coffee with a brandy a very French thing to do. About a hundred yards away there was a nice bar and restaurant virtually underneath where Eric lived, she wondered on the off chance if he used it. Anyway she would pop in for the evening time trade and maybe get a chance to see him, but right now she decided she wanted a strong coffee. Sarah saw there were three steps into the restaurant and coffee shop. Seeing the small bar with the coffee machine she walked the few yards left to the bar. The small area served about forty people with smallish round tables with cafe chairs, it was all decorated in green and cream with old wooden polished floors and on the wall was a menu for the day. Yet it also boasted an evening menu.

The time now was 8.36am. As she entered everyone looked up, all were men who appreciated a nice looking woman at that time in the morning. After all it was a rare sight that early. Sarah also took note of the CCTV cameras which were installed in most public places now since the terrorist attacks, especially in most cafes and restaurants. Picking up a local paper from the bar she sat down at her preferred table to read. The waiter came over bringing with him a nice smile and his note pad. She ordered a short black coffee with a brandy. After about ten minutes the door opened and amazingly, in walked Eric Bezier.

For a very brief moment he stopped, looked at her then carried on to the bar. It was obvious he had spotted her and she could see he was interested. Sarah was also an expert at body language. As he sat at the small bar at the back there was a large mirror. She could see he was checking her out. However, she did find him an attractive man and he obviously liked her.

She saw him chatting to the waiter who then came over to her and asked 'if she would like a drink with Mr Duvall who was sitting at the bar.' Hmm Mr Duvall is it she thought.

'Yes that would be nice as I don't know anyone in town,' she replied in perfect French, the waiter was very impressed.

Sarah was wearing a pair of tight blue shorts showing off her tanned legs and had a nice white T shirt with a yellow Gucci shoulder bag. She was also wearing a pair of sling back sandals, and her hair was at shoulder length. Her dark very expensive wig worked well. And her glasses suited her. Anyone would say she was in her mid thirties or even less.

Duvall came over and introduced himself. 'Hi, my name is Claude Duvall may I sit down.'

'Please sit down and thank you for the drink. I'm new to this place as yet I don't know anyone. I'm thinking of buying a place in Nice near the harbour, in fact in this area. Oh sorry I forgot my manners, my name is Clare Edwards. All my friends call me Eddie,' she laughed.

Duvall, was dressed casually in dark blue chinos and wearing a faded blue denim shirt. He was also wearing flip flops and a pair of Ray Ban sun glasses on his head. He had a day's stubble and looked very relaxed. As he sat down and crossed his legs he spoke to her. But she thought him an attractive man; she could also see he was a very dangerous one. Because it showed in the way he moved, just like a cat. 'Well' he replied 'now is a good time to buy, as the property market has fallen a little, probably due to the terrorist's lunatics, there are a few bargains to be had at the moment.'

'A nice flat would be great' replied Sarah 'but not a huge place you understand, just somewhere comfortable would be good for when I take my holidays, which I have to say are very often these days as work has now become such a bore. I don't need to be there as much as my business runs along nicely without me, thank god.'

'What is it you do may I ask? Are you re-locating to France?'

'Oh I'm not sure. I have several employment agencies in England which are doing very well, but mostly in America. I do have a good team to run them for me, but they do get paid well. So Claude what is it you do, if I may also ask.'

'I used to be in the military. I also worked for the government. Now I work on a need to only basis as an advisor, so just like you I do take frequent holidays. Please don't take this the wrong way, but if you like I could show you my flat, there are a couple for sale in my block if you're interested in taking a look but mine isn't. I love it here, but hey it's up to you. If you would like to have dinner with me tonight, we could meet up here again. They also open the back as a restaurant and the food is to die for. I could introduce you to some friends. How does that sound to you? I'm not trying to seduce you either. Trust me, you're safe with me, I promise.'

Sarah looked him long in the eyes and said. 'Well then Claude, shall we say 8pm this evening in here.'

'You have made a good choice Clare; it's very hard to book a table. I'm known in here so I can arrange that.'

'Yes ok Claude, you've talked me into it, so I will see you at 8pm.' She got up to leave, 'oh and thank you for the drink.' She had covertly filmed the meeting from a hidden camera in her bag. She also had a tiny camera in her glasses supplied by the FBI. When she got back to her hotel, she texted Liz on the new phone she gave her in the name of Sally Parker. 'Liz, start my alibi for today. I will be in touch.' Then within five minutes Liz texted back 'have done so, good luck Sarah. Love Liz x'

Sarah had brought with her an array of clothes, not too sexy but sexy enough. She knew what a man looked for. After all she'd been undercover for years with the FBI and had actually acted as bait on more than one occasion. In fact on many occasions to ensnare a few men, it was entrapment if you like, but it was her job. She was determined to get into Eric's apartment, she desperately wanted to question him and then she was going to kill him once she had proved it was he who had killed her whole family in Spain.

Eric watched her leave and thought to himself she was a lovely looking woman. She had the most beautiful figure on her and a great arse which would put a teenager to shame. However, he thought he had picked her up too easily and that worried him slightly. Because that sort of woman was not easy to pick up she was far too attractive. Another thing he also detected something in her eyes, it almost looked like fear, or maybe excitement. But still if she was new to the area as she had mentioned, then it would be a little disconcerting for her. Maybe he was overreacting, he would find out later this evening he thought to himself, would she have the fish or the meat, he thought she was a meat eater.

Sarah had walked all around the old city of Nice. Where she wondered at the beauty of the buildings, which was a cross between French and Italian. In fact the town at one time belonged to Italy. Nice is close to the border with Italy. Looking quaint the small streets were lovely. Also there were wonderful looking little restaurants of all nationalities, the fish market was amazing. She actually liked it here. One thing she didn't think a lot of was the beach which was very pebbly. Still tonight she would hopefully find out the truth. She had brought with her some Sodium thiopental, the truth drug. She also had some Rohypnol and some Ketimine so the three together can paralyse the recipient given the right dose, and it also makes the tongue very loose. Still she had a choice, her family had no choice. They were shot down in cold blood. Now hopefully she would find out why, it wouldn't be too long now.

She kept the Rohypnol and the Ketamine drug in eye drop bottles and the Sodium thiopental in a small syringe. It would be easy to drop some Rohypnol in his drink because it was odourless. She would just see where the evening took them but she had to get into his flat, she would play it cool. After walking around the lovely city, she arrived back at her Hotel at 3pm and decided she would sleep for a while. But first she set her mobile phone alarm and fell asleep. At 6.30pm she woke up to the sound of her irritating alarm. Sarah took a long shower then dressed, after looking in the full length mirror she looked the part of the seductress to a tee, wearing four inch black sling backs with a nice close fitting black dress just knee level, around her neck she wore a simple gold chain.

She had a nice long black jacket to wear over her shoulders and carried a Gucci bag. Now she looked lovely but not too sexy. Her bulging breasts were open to view but not tartly, yet enough to make any man want to see all of them. She also had some nice gold twisty earrings hanging down about two inches from her ears. Her walk screamed confidence.

Eric was already in the bar when every man's head turned round to see this lady who had just walked through the door including Eric. Quickly standing up from the stool he met her as she was walking in. She was folding down a dark blue umbrella as the weather was showing the world an early summer's rain again. Taking her coat from her shoulders and a bag she was holding with the words.

"Au Bon Marche" 1852 from the famous Paris store he hung her coat from the coat rack with her bag. Carefully, Sarah had placed in the bottom of her large bag a rope with a noose already at the end of it; she covered it up with a head scarf and the umbrella. And then he sat her down at the bar. Eric was very impressed with this woman. She was also a rich lady, at least that's what he thought. As they walked through to the restaurant the waiter asked them rather snottily if they had a reservation. Eric replied 'of course, it's in the name of Duvall.' He had booked the table this morning after Sarah had left. The waiter showed them to their table. It was in the far corner next to a window; the effeminate waiter called Charles came over and lit the two large candles and handed over the menu to Eric with a wink and a sly smile.

He recommends the John Dory which was caught less than two hours ago. There was not a lot on the menu, just seven different meals. Yet surprisingly the restaurant only had seats for forty people, however the seven meals that were available were superb. Sarah had the fish. The evening went well, very well. Sarah's John Dory, was grilled with garlic butter which was served with shallots and green beans and thinly sliced parsnips then served with small sauté potatoes.

Claude had the fillet steak served rare with just sauté potatoes, pan fried fresh field mushrooms and eight asparagus spears dipped in garlic butter. Sarah had a three-year-old French Chardonnay whilst Claude had a six-year-old Chateau-Gruaud Larose red. The meal although simple was superb. The wine was exquisite, everything was wonderful. The night went very well indeed, there was nothing in the way of innuendoes from Eric, or Claude Duvall as he called himself. For the first time she looked at her watch and the time now read 11.25pm.

'Hey this evening has just flown by Claude. You know, I have really enjoyed your company and you have told me so much about the French way of life here in the South of France which I have to say is completely different from the mad crazy Paris set.'

'Paris, dear God you can keep it Eddie. It's full of snobs, bigots, and racists. They all think they are the centre of the world. Yet they have no time for anyone only themselves. Parisians let me tell you are not liked much by other French people.'

'It's strange that you say that Claude but I never felt comfortable in Paris. It's too noisy and it's not that clean anymore and as you say the inhabitants are not friendly at all or perhaps that's just me.' Their talk had been mainly about living in France in Nice and the price of properties; she would still like to view some. She also asked him about the people's attitude to foreigners, the price of cars, wine, and much more. She found him very articulate, surprisingly good company and also very worldly. She also found him open and friendly and he was a very attractive man. Yet the effeminate waiter Charles thought the same. In another life she may have found Eric irresistible. All the time she was answering him and speaking to him in French. He was well impressed with her language skills.

'I may well sell my flat in Paris if I really fit in here Claude, or perhaps rent it out, but for the moment I'll let things roll along for a while as there's no rush. I like to feel we can become good friends at least,' she smiled at him.

'Of course Eddie and likewise' he looked at his watch and said 'let's finish off here then you can take a quick look at my place. Only at night do you get to view the whole area which is all lit up from my balcony, it really is spectacular at night. Let's face it an estate agent can't show you that can he. By the way Eddie, there's a flat just under me to the right, it's up for sale for 267,000 Euros. It's owned by a Dutch lady but she's now returned to Holland. She's had the place for seventeen years. Anyway if you like, we can have a night cap and then I will walk you back to your Hotel, is that ok with you' he smiled. 'Oh and no strings attached, trust me, mind you I can't answer for you though.' He laughed.

'Oh I don't think I ought to do that, I hardly know you Claude. And anyway I have my reputation to think of' she laughed. 'Okay if that's still all right with you, but listen, I can't be too late as I have to drive to Villafrench tomorrow to look at some properties there. I'm meeting a real estate agent, so okay but just the one drink.'

'Great you won't be disappointed Eddie. Well I hope not.'

'Anyway as a matter of fact I looked at your apartments this morning. I did see the sign for sale on two of the apartments. Now they do look very nice so it would be good to see the view from the balconies at night. And as you say a real estate agent can't do that, shall we go Claude.'

Claude beckoned her into the lift making sure he wasn't too close because after all, he didn't want to spook her. But he did want to get closer, really closer. In fact he hoped he would take her all the way. She did notice the distance which pleased her, she felt there was no pressure. The lift stopped on the 5th floor the door opened where he gestured with his hand to let her go first.

As she got out, he overtook her and then opened the door marked 27. He beckoned her into his apartment. Holding the door open for her he turned the lights on it was rather lovely. The whole place was bright, clean, spacious and very modern, well for France that is. In France it's either ultra modern or many years in the past.

Taking her coat he placed it on the coat hanger in his hallway putting her bag beside the hanger along with his jacket. She did take out her Chanel small crossover body handbag which had the other drugs which were especially for him. Again he had his shirt button undone a little further, it was very warm for the time of the year and he wanted to get her in the mood, his chest hairs were now trying to escape out of the rest of his shirt. She had noticed this movement and smiled to herself it was working out well, he was getting nice and relaxed she thought that was excellent.

Eric quickly walked over to the balcony doors to open them to reveal the wonderful view. 'Eddie, come you must see this view. Yet all the apartments have this same view although I'm a little higher than the one for sale.' Holding his hand out to her, she took it as she stepped out onto the balcony. Now the warm evening air kissed her face. It had stopped raining some time ago, she smelt the evening which smelt divine. Eric wasn't wrong, because the view was lovely, it was very spectacular.

'Eddie what would you like to drink he asked her politely.' The balcony had two wicker chairs with big fluffy cushions which he placed on the sofa kept indoors from the rain. There was a drinks trolley and the balcony had small lights along the floor. You could see the harbour with its lights. The small restaurants were lit up beautifully. In the distance you could see Nice airport about ten or twelve miles away and that too was lit up. It too was lovely. They both watched planes landing and taking off, it was surreal. Eddie commented on the view. However, she was planning another view for people to see, come the early morning light.

'Really Claude all I want is just a coffee please. I have a very low tolerance to alcohol but you have what you like.' She saw the drinks trolley on the balcony 'you make me a coffee and I'll make you a drink, so what would you like Claude. Oh let me guess on this one. I reckon you're a three finger whiskey man, am I right.'

'You're a very good judge Eddie, a whiskey it is, but make it a Jim Beam with two fingers please, the Americans can sometimes surprise us all' he laughed out loud. He never laughed again. Eric went into his kitchen to make the coffee. But it was real coffee after all this was France. Feeling pleased at how the evening was progressing he was certain he would get her into his bed.

Sarah opened her bag and took out the eye drop bottle then shook a few drops of Rohypnol into his Jim Beam. But she still poured three fingers into his glass.

'Do you want cream with your coffee,' shouted Eric.

'Yes please, but not too much though.'

'Ok Eddie, I'll put some in a small jug so you can help yourself.'

It was at that moment she heard Frank Sinatra crooning from the speakers. Not loud but nice and soft. In another time this would be romantic, the song was called, *'In the wee small hours of the morning.'* Amazingly it just happened to be one of her favourites. That was a song that her late father played a lot as he was a massive Frank Sinatra fan. But then she felt a few little tears running down her cheek because she realised why she was here. More to the point what she was about to do, but it had to be done tonight. The voice of Sinatra also reminded her of Kenny her beautiful husband and wonderful soul mate who was now dead. Now she wondered what he would think about what she was going to do. But sadly he was now dead and she was a realist. She knew he had no way of knowing. Eric came in with the coffee. He had rolled up his sleeves to just under his elbows. And yet another button had been undone on his shirt. However, he saw Eddie was crying, she looked so very sad.

'Eddie, what's the matter. Have I offended you in some way, please tell me why are you crying.'

'I'm so sorry Claude, it's this music, my Father used to play this song a lot he had all of the Rat packs records but especially Frank Sinatra's. That song just reminded me of him. Because he was a great father and husband. Sadly he's now dead, and so is my mother.'

'Hey look, I'll turn it off. I thought you may like a little music to end the evening with.'

'No please don't do that I love Sinatra.' She poured herself a small Jim Beam there was one for him too.

Putting the coffee down on the small coffee table on the balcony he put his arms around her shoulders. 'So you don't drink,' he laughed 'Eddie let's have no more tears.' He picked up his drink and said 'let's drink to the future whatever it may bring and I know you will love living here, I just know you will.'

'I hope you don't mind me changing my mind about having a drink Claude, the music swayed me. Anyway you're such good company, but yes you're right, let's drink to the future so bottoms up,' as she drained her glass. Then she looked at him as if to say beat that then if you can.

'Right, it's like that is it, well here we go' he did the same and emptied his glass too. Eric had been drinking Jim Beam for years but a few minutes later he thought this stuff is strong, or is it me. He came and stood next to her and put his left arm around her waist. Sarah leant her head on his shoulder in a romantic way. He thought to himself yes I'm in, but I won't rush it. Not just yet.

Sarah looked over the balcony. Now she had the small syringe in her right hand, this syringe was full of Sodium Thiopental (the truth drug), 'this view is so stunning. Hey Claude, what is that lovely building over there? Look way over there can you see it too.' By now five minutes had passed and suddenly he had a job to stand. 'Hey look at that building Claude.' She looked at him 'are you okay Claude, you look a little worse for wear,' she laughed.

Yet he couldn't fathom out what she was saying. Her mouth was moving and a sort of echo came out of her, he tried hard to listen. But then suddenly he laughed.

'Hey what's the matter with me? I feel drunk, but why do I?'

'Claude you're not drunk at all, mind you the wine you had was very strong but it was very good.'

'What, say again, what are you saying Eddie? What are we looking at, where is it?'

'Look to your right Claude, to your right, the one all lit up with different colours.'

As Claude turned again to look he was feeling a little wobbly and now he had to hang on to the balcony rail. He was very unsteady on his feet. Suddenly, she plunged the syringe into his neck, just under his left ear. It made him jump back, he wondered what it was, he fell into his wicker chair and five minutes later he didn't move, he couldn't move. He knew something was very wrong he wanted to sleep. Now he saw her coming towards him with something in her hands, she seemed to be wearing surgical gloves

'Hey you look like a doctor.' He slurred his words, and then he laughed again.

In her hands were garden ties which she had hidden in her bag, along with a length of nylon rope about fourteen feet long with a noose on the end of it which had also been hidden in her shopping bag. She took his shoes off and then his socks, then his trousers and his underpants, his shirt was next.

Eric was now in a dream state and had some idea of what she was doing and started to smile. But when he was fully naked she tied his hands behind his back with the garden ties then she tied his feet together. She looked at his naked body and thought, this man is put together very nicely. If he had discovered the noose she would have explained the rope and noose was for sexual pleasure, a bondage game as she was really into all that stuff, like self choking. Standing over him she asked his name.

Eric couldn't understand what was going on.

'What is your name, Eric tell me what your name is.'

'Oh you silly girl, why it's Eric,'

'Eric what' she asked him nicely. So who is Claude Duvall?'

'Eric Bezier of the foreign legion, late of the legion, Claude Duvall is my working name. '

'What do you do now Eric? What work do you do now? It's very important you tell me.'

'I'm in waste disposal.' Eric couldn't understand this questioning from this strange woman.

'Where do you work from Eric? What exactly is waste disposal, how do you do it? Who is Claude Duvall, is it you or someone else, so who is it Eric?'

'Yes, it's me silly. Both names are mine' he laughed. 'People, I remove people I've always done it for the French government. Now I contract my services to whoever can pay me, it's simple. Claude Duvall is my working name.'

'Eric you have just been to Bristol in England to see a man called Harry Dolan, tell me why? What did you do for him? You need to tell me Eric, it's very important. I work for the French government and we need to know about Harry Dolan. Now it's urgent you tell me as we have lots of money to give you, but first you have to tell us the truth. And we will check it's the truth Eric.'

'Well ok if there is lots of money then what do you want to know, just ask me? I was paid to waste a family in a villa in Alicante which I did. I burnt the villa down after I killed them.'

'How many people did you dispose of, did you shoot all of them Eric?'

'Yes I shot all five of them. That's what Harry wanted me to do; he paid me £15,000 a person.'

'Why did he want them killed Eric. So what did they do to Harry Dolan, because it doesn't make any sense? Tell me why he had them killed.'

'All I know is he absolutely hated them. He hated them because he lost face. Anyway I never ask, all I need is for them to pay me and that's it. And then my job kicks in. I always finish a job, that's always been my trade mark.'

'So is that it, you killed them, and then burnt the bodies in the villa. You did a good job on that visit Eric, is that right?'

'Yes I keep telling you yes. Hey why the questions, do you need someone wasted Eddie?'

'Yes Eric, I need you wasted. You murdered my family, they were all I had and now you're going to die as well. You can't move now can you, but it will soon be over for you. You will die easy compared to them. Now you'll be going over your own balcony in a minute.'

Eric was now inwardly panicking. He was confused but starting to get the message. There was no way he could move his body because it had shut down and wouldn't work. He tried again to get up but he couldn't. Then she came to him with a nylon rope. The weight bearing was 450 pounds; it had a noose at the end of it. Eric weighed about 190 pounds.

Sarah placed the noose around his neck, and then very carefully and slowly she pushed his wicker chair next to his balcony. Taking a dishcloth she placed it into his mouth and then bandaged his mouth with a torn tea towel from his kitchen. And then she lifted his legs up to the balcony where she lifted him over the balcony. The rope was bound round the strong rail, she looped it a couple of times so she could slowly play the rope out until he was hanging there by his neck. Eric couldn't make a noise as he was gagged. His eyes were now wildly panicking as he knew what was happening but could do nothing to help himself. She tied the end of the rope to the bottom of the steel balustrade and slowly slipped him over, where he was now hanging naked, gently swaying in the breeze in the warm night air, the time was now 2.27am.

Eric was panicking and his heart was beating like a drum but he couldn't do a thing about it. Yet he knew he was going to die he was unable to even speak. Now he could feel his eyes beginning to burst and his ears were feeling as though they would explode. But the last thing he heard was *'In the wee small hours of the morning'* a sound floating through the warm night air as he slowly but quietly started to choke to death with his eyes bursting his ears were screaming and still the sound *'In the wee small hours of the morning,'* played along. Slowly she let the rope play out.

But he wanted to wriggle, to move, to shout, and to make her stop but he couldn't move. Now his life began to spin round in front of him just like a movie and he didn't much like what he saw.

Sarah let him down until the noose tightened its grip around his neck. She could see panic and fear in his eyes. She hoped he was in pain and thinking about what he had done to her family, she hated him because he was getting an easy death. Now she saw he was really in pain she was pleased, he started to gasp and she thought his head would explode his eyes were now bulging and the blood vessels were starting to break, his tongue was bitten through and he had almost swallowed the dish cloth. He felt his lungs were bursting. Then suddenly, he gave up and he died. The music was the last sound he heard as he died in great pain. Eric he had bitten through his tongue and his left cheek, a fitting end for a cruel assassin.

'Good night Frank' she said as she turned off the music, 'thank you, you sang really well tonight.' Satisfied he was dead she looked at him one last time as he gently swung in the warm air she was pleased. She started to wipe any trace of her being there with some bleach she found in his kitchen. The time was now 2.55am. She took another careful look around his apartment and then she closed the door. Quietly she walked down the back stairs. Once outside, she slowly walked back to her hotel not once looking up at Eric. Now once in her room she changed then she picked up her already packed case then she slipped out of the hotel. Wearing a short dark wig, jeans, trainers and a dark blue jumper she used a walking stick to help with her disguise. She also wore some heavy rimmed glasses to help the effect. The FBI had taught her well about how to disguise herself in a hurry.

The time was now 3.45am. She had to book into the airport at 5.20am to get her flight to London. She knew all along it was Harry Dolan but just needed proof and now she had it from Eric Bezier, alias Claude Duvall. She also had it on her mobile phone recorder. She had recorded all the conversation with Eric as proof if needed. But now she would seek out this man Harry Dolan. She desperately wanted to know why he'd had her family murdered. She couldn't understand how anyone could lose face and if so why the hell was it so bad that Dolan had her family murdered. Now she texted Liz again to say 'moving on now, love Gaynor x.'

It simply didn't make any sense to her, it was beyond her understanding at this stage, but she would find the answer and would seek revenge. There wasn't any choice because proving it would now be impossible for anyone. After she had read Dolan's police files he had never been convicted because he kept the best defence lawyers on a permanent retainer. All that mattered to her was she had enough proof herself and that was all she needed to carry on. When you know you know. It would be a futile exercise to tell the authorities what she knew because that would only bring in expensive Lawyers and this would take years to prove if ever she could. She had seen this happen over and over again in America especially with Mafia lawyers. They could keep delaying court appearances for years and even forever. And all it took was money and by all accounts Dolan had plenty.

Harry Dolan had a long record of using top lawyers to get out of situations. So she was going to make sure he would never do that again. His time was rapidly approaching. No she had done the right thing and now she would go after the instigator Harry Dolan. Who was next on her death list? She still had one hell of a job to understand why he could do such a thing over him losing face. It was sick stupid and insane, and yet totally evil.

Sarah had now got in touch with the Spanish Legion and the local Police to say she was no longer looking for anything or anyone and wished for the file to be closed. She was going back to America for good, and thanking them for their help.

Now she would start to dish out the justice herself she already knew what the outcome would be, but the participants had no idea yet.

She was a highly trained agent, she could use any weapon of her choice and she was deadly in un-armed combat. To break a man's throat was easy for her also she could rip a pair of balls out of a man, and if need be, to kill a man with a single blow to the lower part of the nose with a hard blow with the heel of her palm, thrusting upwards that could push the bone into the brain. A hard blow that way could kill in an experienced hand.

CHAPTER NINE

At 6.37am that very morning a lady who was walking her two Pomeranian dogs towards Eric's apartment block. She happened to look up as a couple of seagulls flew past her then upwards. But one of them had dropped something. Something splashed against her legs. Her dogs barked because they saw some birds flying low and it spooked them. She thought these damn seagulls crapped on my legs. They ought to do something about them. Then she looked up and saw the body of Eric, at first she thought it was a dummy that some drunken idiot had hung over the balcony. Shit it was probably unruly students. And they too were a damn nuisance at the best of times a waste of bloody space. Now she was standing underneath the dummy. But she saw there was body fluid which had splashed over the pavements. Disgustingly it was still dripping, suddenly she was repulsed by the sight, and then some more smelly body liquid had splashed onto her shoulder. She waved her fist at the body accusing it of crapping on her legs. She immediately called the Gendarmes.

The police thinking it was some sort of terrorist attack immediately closed the area down even before they got there. Now the local police sealed off the area as the local police station was only a few yards away. Anyway, after all who knows what these latest maniacs would do. The local cops were running around blowing whistles, shouting, cursing waving their arms about and being typically bolshie French. All they managed to do was place some flimsy barriers across the main road and stand there like they were important, until the big boys arrived which they did in record time.

When the anti terrorist squad arrived they were concerned that the whole building was booby trapped. They managed to get it all checked out then they got everyone out of the building before they finally arrived at Eric's door.

There were elderly people still in their pyjamas wondering about complaining and business men still half dressed and wives with towels around them having been hauled out of their showers, it was a total French balls-up. They finally managed to get a master key to Eric's apartment from the janitor an hour later, after placing mirrors under his door and a small endoscopic camera they decided it was not booby trapped. Now satisfied, two members of the elite squad slowly opened the door and went inside. But not before they told everyone to stay clear while they checked the place out. Now all they could smell was bleach? They called for the forensic guys to come on up.

There were two police officers standing looking over the balcony at Eric Bezier who had now turned a nasty purple blue sort of grey colour. He did look like a dummy and he was still dripping body liquid all over the pavement below. After checking the whole place out they hauled him over the balcony to lay him on a stretcher. First thing that caught their attention was the small syringe embedded in his neck. It was obvious he had been murdered, but the question remained, why? It was their job to find out. The police checked out his past and they found out he was an ex legionnaire he was highly thought of by the legion. They searched his apartment but found nothing. As a matter of fact the place had been wiped clean of all prints hence the smell of bleach as they entered the apartment. This looked as though it was a professional hit and now they needed to find out the reason why. It was an unusual murder. But however, it looked like a revenge killing. Because he was in a real mess and there was his entire bowel contents still dripping all over the pavement below.

The national news had a tip off. The enraged woman with the dogs rang them and for a small reward. The newspapers managed to get hold of the story and some pictures of Eric. Some were recent and some while he was in the legion. There was also a picture of Sarah in the restaurant with Eric because in France now there was CCTV in all the public places, but she knew that, and that's why she was in a dark wig. Her picture was also on the news.

Police were saying they wanted to trace this woman in connection with Eric Bezier, sometimes known as Claude Duvall and if anyone had any information regarding the woman then they were to contact the police without delay. Because it was a matter of state security and to withheld information was a crime against France.

Harry Dolan had now got back to his old self. Now he was feeling good as he went about his daily business. Yet he wasn't even thinking about Tom Lambert and his family. Now it was of no concern to him anymore. He had read about it in the papers of course but he had no conscience about it and let's face it business is business and life moves on, the world doesn't stop when someone's dead. Harry was at work when he turned on the TV to check on the races at Cheltenham, and then the news came on. First there was a news story about a man in Nice, the South of France who had been hanged from the balcony of his apartment by his neck, he was an ex legionnaire. At first the French authorities were wondering if the death of the man had anything to do with any terrorist organisation. But crucially that was soon dismissed. It was now being treated as a murder investigation. There was a very recent picture of him alongside that of a woman who was wanted in connection with the death, she may be able to help them with their ongoing enquires.

The French police had made his day with the news. Harry looked at the picture of the dead man but then he quickly realised the man was Duvall. They gave his real name as Eric Bezier. However whatever the man's name was or had been he was extremely pleased he was dead. All connections to the deaths had vanished. Anyway now pleased as punch he poured himself a large Irish whiskey. He took a big drink and sat back to relax, so much so that he fell asleep feeling happy and content. After ten minutes Harry was dreaming he was in a very expensive restaurant in Paris eating alone but enjoying the meal, the wine was superb. When suddenly a young attractive woman walked up to him dressed in black and white then she smiled at him but he couldn't see her face although he knew she had smiled at him and he smiled back at her. But he was puzzled he couldn't focus on her face.

And then she stabbed him in his face with a huge knife, he struggled but could do nothing. 'Don't worry, don't panic' a voice said to him, 'here comes the ambulance, here comes the police, here comes the priest, and here comes your wife', all of them arrived quickly. All of it was in slow motion, and then suddenly three nurses took him into the ambulance. Two held him down and the third one took his trousers down and fondled him while the next thing he knew she smiled at him. Then she placed a plastic bag over his head and he began to suffocate. It was all in slow motion again, he was so scared that he actually fouled himself.

Suddenly the dream vanished because he was woken up by his office girl Tina shouting 'Mr Dolan, Mr Dolan, please wake up you've had an accident. Oh my God please wake up Mr Dolan, please,' she was holding her nose. 'Oh the smell,' she started to gag. She had found him sitting in his comfy chair but smelling like an overflowing rancid sewer. He had a look on his face as though he was about to die of something really horrible. But he smelt as though he would too.

Harry woke up to find he had emptied his bowels in his trousers while he'd been dreaming. Now he looked petrified, but the office girl Tina had quickly made an exit, she had run to the loo to be sick because the smell was gross. She could smell him on her hands and she was now throwing up as she ran to the toilet. She started sobbing. She came out of the toilet and rang his wife Joan and told her what had happened.

'Really? Oh dear how unfortunate for you. Harry doesn't usually do that sort of thing, oh dear. Look Tina I'm very sorry to hear that, but I have to go as I have a dentist appointment. Look can you please deal with it. Come to think of it, there must be some rubber gloves and sponges somewhere. There must be plasters and toilet rolls, disinfectant, and stuff you can use you know plastic bags bin liners etc. Hey look you're a good girl Tina so sort it out. I have to go right now. Oh look my Taxi is here. So you will have to deal with it that's what you're paid for isn't it, so just do it, by Tina.'

After putting down the phone Joan thought yeah I should be so lucky. She just carried on eating a large slice of carrot cake from the fridge until it was gone, and now she settled herself down with a large gin and tonic to watch the afternoon's crappy soaps on the television. She'd completely forgot the conversation she'd just had with Tina. After finishing her drink she decided to slip into town for some tea before Harry came home smelling like a pig in actual shit.

No she didn't want to be here when Harry came home stinking of something nasty. Anyway it was not her problem. She looked at her hands and said out loud OMG they'd just been manicured this very morning. Good god, she shuddered at the thought.

Tina was now horrified she wasn't paid enough to clean him up. And so she grabbed her coat and walked out but not before being sick again.

And now the smell was all over the place. Then suddenly Harry came stumbling out of his office slowly dribbling shit while making his way to the toilet. He went to say something to Tina, but thought better of it and anyway nothing came out of his mouth. Then the guilt had started to affect him again hence the dream.

Tina never returned to work.

CHAPTER TEN

Ed Warren had sent Sarah the details of the Dolan family, who belonged to it, who was in charge of it and a list of their misdemeanours. Sarah sat down in her hotel in Notting Hill to study the details. But it was long, very long and she was not impressed by the reading. She stayed in the hotel until she quickly found a small basement apartment to rent in Clapham with a large garage. Sarah could see that Harry Dolan always demanded respect from all the family. Yet from a police point of view he was clean which was incredibly laughable. Now he was always involved in most things but it was hard to stick any individual thing on to him. His three sons were a menace as well, that wasn't surprising considering who their father was. The file on the three sons was not good either. The file on Jason Dolan was not as bad as the other family members. But he was marked down as being gay which was underlined. And so the overall picture that came over was not good, they were an evil lot. They were a nest of shit house rats.

The eldest son Noel, who was now aged 36, ran the strip clubs and brothels in and around the Soho area of London. Now he was fast turning into his father Harry. The second son Alex who was 34 was in charge of the betting shops. Where they now had five shops all around the London area and he was another chip off the old block often in trouble for fighting. Always getting off because his dad had the best Lawyers money could buy. They also intimated witnesses whenever they could. The last son Jason who was 31 years old was in charge of the luxury mobile homes in and around the Epsom area. Altogether there were 65 mobile homes to look after. Every home was rented out to dubious people and some to family members of their gypsy family.

Strangely the three boys all seemed to look the same. They were carbon copies of Harry. There was no mistaking them for brothers and they all stuck together no matter what.

So if one family member was harmed then all of them felt harmed. This was instilled in them as children, it was their mantra. They had to get even no matter how long it took to sort someone out.

The mother Joan was from an old Romany gypsy family called the Biddles. Unsurprisingly she had been tainted by Harry Dolan and had turned into a nasty moaning fat lump of a woman. But after being married for forty years her husband had taken the best out of her. What was left was just a fat mess. Joan used to be a lovely looking woman but now she was about four stone overweight with an eating problem. She had an overactive knife and fork. So when she was not eating anything she constantly smoked her face off and ate cake like it was going out of fashion. She thought nothing of hitting out if anyone disrespected any member of her family. She had not had sex with Harry or anyone else for at least twenty years. And yet she knew Harry was always shagging the girls at work, but if she stepped out of line he would simply beat her, having now done so for the last forty years. So she learnt to keep her mouth shut. Or as Harry said he would stitch her lips together. There was no doubt if he was in the right mood he would do it.

At one time he had a man beaten a man up for laughing at him in a pub. Harry had a bad back at the time and did have a strange walk about him. So he arranged for his minders to break the man's legs with lump hammers. And that happened twenty-two years ago. The man still walked with a twisted leg. Harry told him 'you have to show some respect.'

Although Joan always dressed beautifully and had what she wanted, she wasn't happy. She always yearned for her old life in their old mobile home. She knew perfectly well if she and Harry went through a divorce this would in effect set the families against one another. Because to them marriage was for life. Divorce was out of the question. Gypsies married for life, you had to make the most of it. And there were oaths and money exchanged many years ago, this could not be altered. Joan was now stuck in this loveless marriage until the end. So she found comfort in her food, lots of food. They also had separate bedrooms and had done for years. That would never change.

Sarah picked out the eldest son Noel Dolan who was in charge of the strip clubs in and around London. Apparently there were five clubs in total and one in particular was the Lone Star Club and restaurant. There was also a pole dancing club which was a den of iniquity. That was a place where he met his friends. That's where drug deals were carried out. It was the HQ for want of a better word. Noel had his own little gang of friends where he acted as boss. Apparently he was worse than his father. A brutal enforcer and being cruel to his girls was not unusual, but the norm.

Now aged 36, he'd still not married although he had a string of women hanging around him all the time. Power attracts some women, usually beautiful women. However, the thing was Noel could be charming and at the same time become very cruel. Being a real Jekyll and Hyde character who didn't have any real close friends but as long as he had money in his pocket and his pick of the girls he was happy. Most of all he liked to show he was the boss and if one of his strippers rejected him for any reason he was not worried about giving them a slap, or even worse, much worse. Sadly his girls were terrified of him, but the money was good. It was known if any boyfriend of any girls who worked for him disagreed with the working hours or anything for that matter he sent a crew round to sort out the boyfriend. Noel would not tolerate any interference from anyone. Any interference he set to work on the girls himself.

He still lived with his parents in their large house. Where he had his own apartment within the house, it was very large. The house was in Park Street Mayfair. That was including his own two car garage for his Porsche and his E type Jaguar. Both cars were post office red and in beautiful condition. His apartment which had three bedrooms and a roof terrace overlooking London was immaculate. It was a view to die for from his terrace and the views over Hyde Park were fantastic.

Harry had acquired the house some years ago from a Banker who became desperate for money after losing his high power position. Having agreed to pay the Banker only half what the house was worth in cash and the rest would be paid off in twelve months.

However the Banker had a nasty accident, he fell under a tube train and was killed instantly. There were no relatives whatsoever and Harry never paid a penny back. Some witnesses said there were two men who were standing very close to the Banker. However, the Banker was apparently a well known gay man, and at the time that's why he had lost his job. His boss found him with two rent boys in his office. He was caught after his boss and secretary returned to finish of some important business connected to the city. There and then, he was asked to resign immediately or be removed. So he resigned with a paltry pension and a rubbish payout. So now he needed to down size his house. The house alone was now worth in the region of four million and growing. Harry had been asked many times to sell it. He said to one man, a Russian oil man that he would not sell for ten million and the Russian replied okay I will give you eleven million. The estate agent was very upset as his commission would have been enormous. Harry told them simply, to 'piss off.'

CHAPTER ELEVEN

Sarah had been told in the police report Noel Dolan was in charge of the strip clubs. According to the report, the Lone Star Club was Noel's HQ. That was the place to find him as he was a regular boss. Yet he always arrived at work at 10am most days except when he went to the races with his cronies.

Noel also held the auditions there for girls who were good at pole dancing, or thought they were. New girls who could strip were mostly from the Eastern European block and worked really hard but for less money. They had the most wonderful bodies and of course were very popular. They would easily do anything for money, anything at all. If you wanted bunny, dish out the money. That was the motto. Nothing was for free.

Harry Dolan, Noel's father had a large house in Gower Street in Euston, a stone throw from the Lone Star Club and the other clubs in and around the Soho area. He let the house to his son, and Noel in return then let the rooms to the girls. But God help any girl who missed her rent. There was never an excuse good enough not to pay. Not even if they had in some way been hospitalised the rent was to be paid on time. Sometimes the girls secretly took back clients to their small rooms for sex. There was always a doorman in the hallway to oversee any problems because some clients could turn nasty. And the doorman was simply a deterrent, but they took note in a book of who came in with whom and there was always extra to pay if the girls brought back a client. One stupid doorman was caught taking a back-hander from some of the girls. He also had a few freebies thrown in, but he was caught and taken away, he was never to be seen again. Some said he went back up north, but everyone knew he went south.

One girl called Natasha, who was a lovely Ukraine girl, had the tip of her nose cut off as an example to the other girls. That was for trying to sneak in a client at 4am in the morning.

When she was confronted she denied she had done so. One of the other girls had told the doorman, who in turn told Noel, who in turn had her disfigured for lying to him. She was dropped off at the A&E and warned if she opened her mouth she would end up as pig food on Noel's father's farm. But there was no farm but she didn't know that. Terrified she kept her mouth shut. She left and was never seen again. There were more people that had gone missing over the years. While there were no serious checks as to where these people went to.

There was another young girl. A Polish girl aged just nineteen who was a stripper with a gorgeous body who had laughed at Noel's father Harry. Because of drink he had failed to get an erection. The mistake she made was telling the other girls he was useless in bed and his manhood was the smallest she had ever seen. She was taken out by two of Noel's minders and had her face disfigured with acid. She was unable to ever laugh again. Then she was despatched back to her native home in Poland, she was also never seen again. But the list went on and on. Yet there was never any proof that Noel was involved, all this confirmed to her what a despicable animal he was.

Sarah would have no problem in dispatching him. Now she wanted to clear this nest of vipers. Now she would destroy them the same as they simply destroyed other people. Life meant nothing to the Dolans except of course their own. Where they ruled by fear of disfigurement and death, and retribution no matter how long it would take. There was another case of a young girl from Scotland who withheld money from Noel Dolan. He personally cut her left ear off and sent her back home on the pain of death if she opened her mouth about what happened. She was also gang raped by his cronies and the event was filmed. If she ever spoke out he would make sure everyone who knew her would see the film, including her parents.

Sarah had to figure out a way of getting into Noel's apartment to be with him. With no one else knowing she was there. She had to find a way, he was 36 she was 49 but could easily take 10 years from her looks. She would try the seductress way but the timing had to be spot on with no witnesses.

She sat down to think of a plan, it was not going to be easy but she would find a way, in fact an idea, a simple idea, had already begun to form in her head.

Noel Dolan was 6ft tall with wide shoulders. He had dark curly hair and a menacing look about him. Some people considered him to be a handsome man who dressed very smartly, some would say he was a sharp dresser, he always wore a suit and tie and his shoes were always highly polished. He had the sort of hair that didn't need combing as it always stayed in place; it was thick and wavy, a little curly like his fathers and his two brothers. His head was square and the jaw strong. To some women he was attractive but to others he never looked right in a suit. Arriving on the Monday morning at 10am as usual, he opened the office in the Lone Star Club and then he swore when he realised he would be very busy. That's because he had to go through all the VAT returns which he hated to do. Someone had to do it; someone had to hey diddle the books. But after one and a half hours he decided to take a stroll, he needed some air. Just as he stepped out into the street he spotted a very attractive lady about the same age as himself give or take a couple of years who tried to open the door to the club, but he always locked it. He was the only one in at this time because the staff didn't arrive until 6pm.

'Yes, can I help you' he asked her.

'No, not unless you work here' replied Sarah.

'Ah yes you could say that, I own the club, so now how can I help you?' He could not stop himself from looking at her breasts; she also had the most gorgeous legs. The looks didn't go unnoticed. Sarah was dressed in a dogtooth tight knee length skirt with black and silver sling back heels. Her blouse looked as though it was cream silk with an open dark blue light raincoat. She was also holding a small blue and white spotted umbrella as it looked like rain.

'Well, I have heard you need some bar staff. I'm looking for a job. I have worked bars all over the world. I have also done some stripping before, but I guess I'm too old for that now' she said smiling.

To old, well that's a matter of opinion and in my honest opinion you're not too old, you're not too old at all. So whoever told you that must be a blind man. You look amazing to me, and yes we could do with some bar staff, but we have more than enough strippers and pole dancers. Someone like you just might be able to keep my girls in line. Look if you fancy a challenge that is, so what's your name?'

'Call me Gloria.'

'Well glorious Gloria, come on in and let's give you an interview if that's ok with you. We might as well get down to brass tacks before we open and see what you've got.'

'Ok but I reckon you have already seen what I've got' she said. 'I hope the money is good as I also hear they need some bar staff at the pub around the corner, the Black Swan. I was just about to go there and see what they are paying the staff.'

'Oh don't bother with that place Gloria, the staff never stay more than a week or two. That's because the owner can't keep his hands off them, and the money is rubbish. I can promise you we pay a hell of a lot more than what they pay their staff, that's guaranteed Gloria, well if we get on,' he smiled.

'Ok then so let's talk, there's no harm in talking, let's see what you have got for me, if anything. And I don't mean any funny business either. Mr eh, what's your name?'

'It's Noel Dolan. But you can call me boss or Mr Dolan but never Noel. Well not yet as that's strictly for my good friends, so let's go inside. Now can I offer you a drink Gloria?' He walked into his office which was very large with its own bar which had four plush stools around it, there was a large expensive sofa bed and two comfy matching chairs, a huge desk and a bank of telephones. Then on the desk there was a lot of paperwork relating to his recent accounts, also a large calculator. He beckoned her to take a seat and to get comfy. 'So Gloria, what drink would you like?' Noel had a job to keep his eyes from her breasts and those legs. He thought he could do with her right now.

'A coffee would be good but I don't really drink, especially when I'm working or having a job interview Mr Dolan' replied Sarah.

'That's refreshing to hear Gloria. So where have you worked before, you're not from around this part of the world that's for sure. I detect a slight American accent in that voice Gloria, and I don't reckon your name is Gloria either' he laughed. Hey 'not that I give a toss, just so long as you're honest and can do a good days work. And keep your eyes on my staff and your hands out the till.'

'I do have experience of that, in fact a lot of experience,' replied Sarah.

'In that case Gloria where have you worked before?'

She told him that the most recent was in Spain. She'd had jobs in America, Canada, New Zealand and now England. She used to be married, but now divorced and there were no children involved. She was a free agent and now she wanted to give England a try as she liked English people in general.

'You say you have experience of being in charge of staff before Gloria. If so how many staff and for how long?'

'Yes I have, in fact we used to have our own bar and restaurant back in the States. We sold it three years ago. We had it for eleven years and it was a very busy place. The turnover was $565,000 plus a year. We employed seventeen to twenty-five staff depending on how busy we were. When we became divorced we sold the bar and restaurant.' She could not afford to buy out her ex and neither could he afford to buy her out. And so they sold the bar, the house, cars anything of worth and moved on, simple as that. 'I would like to point out I'm far from broke Mr Dolan. However, it's stupid to use your own money to live on. I can take good care of myself especially when pushed, but I'm a good worker. You could do worse than take a chance on me so let's see what happens. I'm certainly not desperate for a job or for money. I expect to be paid what I'm worth. I will also speak my mind and creep to no one. If you can't handle that then I will be saying goodbye, and hello to the Black Swan.

CHAPTER TWELVE

Noel Dolan had a feeling he was being interviewed for a job. This woman was different and very sexy with a worldly charm to go with her good looks. 'Look Gloria, why not start tonight with a trial run, you have to know where everything is first so I won't expect miracles. All I need is someone to do as I ask and to work for me and not for them after all the money is good and the working conditions are also good. I need to trust you 100% and that's all.'

'Well Mr Dolan there's only one way to see what I'm like, the balls in your court now.'

'Okay Gloria listen. Tonight, my Father is coming over with a couple of his friends for some drinks and a meal later. Now it would be a good idea if you can serve them. His name is Harry Dolan. My Dad doesn't like to see scruffy staff, untidy or unclean, the hair has to be neat and tidy and the staff's nails must be clean. Now he also likes to see staff smile the same as myself, so are you up for that tonight? I will pay you £25 per hour, but you do have to earn it Gloria. You also say nothing to the rest of my staff what I pay you, it will be strictly cash.'

She thought for a moment. 'I have a date for tonight, but you know what, I'll cancel it I wasn't that bothered anyway. So Mr Dolan, what time do you want me to be on duty for?'

'Great, OK be here for 8.30pm and no later. I don't accept lateness believe me when I say that is my pet hate. And it's the same with my dad. Tonight can you wear a simple white blouse and black skirt with heels, not too high to start with and we can see where we go from there on? I'm sure you will give me a few pointers on how the staff ought to dress as your experience will come to the fore.' Looking at his watch he said 'I have to start work now Gloria, it's been a pleasure to meet you and we will catch up later. So just come to the door and ask for me. I will leave instructions with the doorman to let you in. Otherwise he will charge you an entry fee and we can't have that can we,' he laughed.

Sarah laughed back 'Ok Mr Dolan I'll see you later.'

'Look Gloria, you can call me Noel. I don't mind now I've met you.'

'If it's still ok with you Mr Dolan I will call you Mr Dolan. I would never use the word boss either.'

'Okay if that suits you then it suits me too.

'I have to show some respect after all you're the boss. Look nobody called me Gloria in my bar and restaurant, only my husband and no one called me or him boss. To me it's far too familiar for my liking. I will not allow the staff to call you anything else except Mr Dolan because that's the correct way to proceed. So can we leave it at that if you don't mind?' Sarah thought he came over as ok, but she knew his real story and she was not going to hang around. The quicker she got on with it then she could move on to the next son Alex. The more people that saw you the more they knew you, and the more information they had on you the more they could tell anyone who may ask about you.

Noel thought about her, he was very impressed with her attitude she showed respect which to the Dolans was paramount. His dad would like her, he already had a hard on for her himself and she certainly had the right attitude.

Sarah took a taxi back to her small rented house. She took off her dark expensive wig, and headed for the shower then had something to eat. So far she was managing to keep a cool head. It seemed a good opportunity, but she wasn't looking forward to working there. However, the father Harry Dolan was coming tonight and she would keep calm about it. Having decided to punish his sons first, then she would kill his wife. But Harry Dolan would be left until the last, that way he would suffer more and knowing he would be last, making his life a misery.

So in the meantime she sorted out a black pencil thin skirt and a white blouse, not too low but just enough to make a show of her generous breasts. Now she sorted out the black four inch heels and all she had to do now was wait. The time was 2.45pm.

Noel had been well impressed with Gloria and was looking forward to working with her. Just so long as she didn't let him down, but my, was she one sexy woman. The trouble was his dad would probably like her as well. Anyway he would see what happens. But he was pretty certain she could do a good job on the staff and that was the main reason for giving her a chance. There was a presence about her which was something he hadn't encountered before. She was a little scary but that would buck up the staff and keep them on their toes. Her body was lovely he would love to get her in his bed maybe after a week or sooner he would work his charm on her. It usually worked when he set his mind to it.

Harry Dolan rang Noel to tell him to keep a table ready for him and his two friends, because they needed to talk business in private. Now he would also like a lobster salad so did his friends and to keep on ice some nice Californian Chardonnay. The club had a couple of private booths with settle seating. You pressed a bell when you wanted the waitress. That cost you money but not for Harry Dolan, it was his money that set the club up in the first place. It had been the first pole dancing club to open for business and it had been incredibly successful ever since. Having opened eleven years ago it had been busy since the first girl slid up and down the pole.

Sarah had seen the news on TV about this dead Frenchman being found hanged from his balcony in Nice. And then she saw the picture of herself which bore no resemblance to how she looked now. She was wanted in connection with the hanging, but the police so far had absolutely no clue to who she was.

Harry Dolan was meeting his two friends tonight in the Lone Star Club. It was a business meeting and one of them had a problem with another man relating to his wife of only five years. Harry arrived at 8.15pm and was shown to the booth by Noel who explained he had a new girl who would take their orders and bring them the drinks when they wanted them. 'Oh and don't go chasing her Dad, I want to keep this one she's a good worker, so its hands off or she will leave.'

To Sarah, alias Gloria this was a great start to her mission to seek retribution. At 8.20pm Gloria arrived and told the doorman not to charge her. The doorman laughed and said, 'I know, go right on in you know where it is by now.' Walking to the back of the passageway she opened a door to the staff changing rooms. Already seven staff had assembled. Noel introduced Gloria to them all and finished off by saying 'any problems then take them to Gloria and she will sort it out if she can, and if she can't then neither can I.'

Noel was pleased to see her, she looked simply gorgeous with her dark hair and simple skirt and blouse hugging her lovely shape and her boobs looked lovely, her legs were shapely and smooth.

Sarah had noticed his sly looks at her body and thought good. Step into my web my dear.

But Noel knew he wouldn't be able to rush Gloria into his bed, he would have to wait for the right time and he knew it would come soon enough. Now she was a woman worth waiting for.

Harry was engaging in conversation with his friends as he walked in to the Lone Star Club and restaurant and walked them to his favourite private booth. Harry sat them down and then he pressed the waitress button. Within two minutes Sarah knocked on the door then walked in she said 'good evening gentlemen. I'm your waitress for this evening so what can I get for you?'

Harry looked at her as though he had seen a ghost. Now he just sat there. His friends said 'Harry you look as though you have seen a ghost, what's the matter with you?'

'Sir, can I get you a drink' asked Sarah, and asked them again for the drinks order.

Harry looked at her and said 'have we met before, what's your name? Noel did tell me but I've forgotten it. I'm sorry about that I have a lot on my mind right now.'

'It's Gloria. So can I get you guys a drink? I have just explained I'm your waitress for the evening.'

'Look Gloria can you just bring us a large bottle of Irish whiskey and a bucket of ice to start with then we will have the California Chardonnay. Noel has it on ice and please can we have the lobster salad too, say in the next fifteen minutes.'

'Certainly sir,' she said, and then turned and walked away to get the whiskey. She was amazed at how much father and son looked alike, they were like twin brothers.

'Harry said Christ she's a real looker isn't she. I wouldn't mind giving her one.'

The other two laughed 'yeah, you and us as well Harry. Do we have to get in a line behind you, or can we all just join in. You know this booth would be ideal,' they laughed.

'You know, that would be great? I'll ask Noel if that could be laid on and if you don't ask you don't get am I right lads?'

'They all laughed and the other mate Shaun the Hog (he kept pigs) said 'you know what lads she's lovely, where did she come from, and I loved her accent too, it's very mid Atlantic.'

'It's best we leave this one well alone lads or my son is going to get the hump, and you don't want to upset him now do you Freddie.'

'Damn right we don't Harry.'

'Noel said she's a Brit with an American accent, her husband apparently was American. Anyway let's see how we get on and I reckon Noel is after a slice of that. Maybe its best we leave that one all to him judging by the way she is. I reckon he will have his work cut out to get into that one,' they laughed. 'But mind you I will ask him if he could lay it on for us guys,' he used his mobile to ask Noel what the chances were the reply was not very encouraging, 'seems the answer is a firm no lads.' They all laughed out loud.

Noel had also told Gloria not to fraternise with any of the clients, not ever, and especially his father Harry. She was special and he wanted to trust her and for her to keep the other girls in order. It would hardly work if she was doing the opposite. Noel told her that her role was like a PA to him and her wages would be reflecting on that. In fact she was now on £35 an hour. She took that advice on board. But then she knew she would get into his apartment. She knew he wanted her and it was a matter of time that's all. That would come the next evening, with a full moon. The evening had gone really well for all concerned and at 2.45am Noel closed the club saying goodnight to the staff then asked Sarah if she needed a lift home. She didn't need one, 'see you tomorrow' said Noel, 'oh did you enjoy your first night, was it what you expected,' he smiled.

'Yes I did enjoy the evening and your Father is a rascal and so are his friends, but they all enjoyed the evening. I'm really looking forward to tomorrow evening so goodnight Noel.' She leant over really close to him and kissed him gently on his cheek. She deliberately pushed her breasts into him and she could feel he had a hard on. And then she slowly walked away with a smile on her face. Got you she said to herself you greasy bastard.

Sarah woke up at 11.48am, tired but pleased now she wanted to work out how to kill this Noel. It was going to be scary for all concerned. Now she wanted to leave a message to Harry Dolan and she wanted him to be terrified of who was coming for him. She wanted him to be unable to sleep and she wanted him to panic. First she would visit the betting shop where the other brother Alex was working, because she decided he would be next. She did not want this to drag out - she wanted to kill them all as quickly as she could. Sarah didn't want to hang around. She needed to get rid of these low life people, it was something she had to do and then get back home to America. She figured if she quickly disposed of this family the police would be thrown into disarray and while the confusion was taking place she would be gone. She knew if she didn't even try to kill them then she would never forgive herself.

CHAPTER THIRTEEN

Alex Dolan was a big man 6ft 2in tall with a bad attitude. However, he had a brilliant brain on him hence he was in charge of the betting shops. There were also a couple of pitches at the race tracks. But his temper was legendary. Being able to use himself he was a bully boy and thought nothing of slapping women around and anyone he thought he could hit when the mood took him. He had been brought up seeing his father beat his mother up, now he was doing the same. Alex had been in many a fight in his time. He was now only 34 but had slowed down a lot. His flat over his betting shop was lovely. Alex lived over the main betting shop in Charterhouse Street, Holborn. Having had various girls in his life but he also had a long suffering wife called Pamela. And she too was from gypsy stock they had two children, a boy called Charlie and a girl called Kathleen.

Pamela wanted for nothing in the way of clothes or cars. However, love was not on the list as Alex hardly saw his wife and his two children. They had a luxury mobile home in Epsom and his wife lived there most of the time with the two children who went to school in the area. Some weekends Alex spent a night or two in the home there. Yet gypsy women were very loyal and seldom became divorcees, it was not something gypsies do.

Sarah had donned a disguise of a much older woman as she walked into the betting shop called Beeches she pretended to check out the races along with all the other punters, she used her walking stick to stump along. After five minutes she saw the staff step back as a large man, the double of Harry and Noel with dark curly hair walked in from the back of the shop. She saw the frightened look on their faces as he inspected the till drawers. Then he started saying hello to various punters he paid out £978 to a punter who had won an accumulator bet and the guy was over the moon. The look on Alex's face was like thunder which put him in a real mood for the rest of the day.

There had been one incident when a regular punter, an old man who was aged about seventy eight won an accumulator bet the full amount was £21,000 paid in cash and the man was ecstatic about the win, all he kept saying was he could now go to Australia to see his son and he was jubilant. Alex Dolan was raging after paying the old man the money. Later that Saturday night he had his cronies knock on the old man's door and they beat the poor man into a coma and took back the money. Alex paid them £1,000 each. The old man never recovered and died seven weeks later. Obviously the money was never found but the police had a good idea what happened, but good ideas do not solve crimes.

Sarah figured out Alex was about seventeen stone and would take some killing. Being as strong as an ox this would need some planning. Never seemingly to keep still for a minute, he was almost hyperactive. This would be a challenge for her. However she still had the skill and she had the time, but first she was going to deal with Noel. Tonight would be as good a night as ever. There was also going to be a full moon.

Regarding Alex, she just had to know who she would be dealing with so she would come back for Alex another day. In the meantime she had to figure out how to get rid of Noel, but she had half an idea already. She would use the same technique she used on Eric the Frenchman. So that way she knew it would spook Harry Dolan which was what she wanted. She wanted him to know the grim reaper was coming for him and his family. She was going to kill him last in the knowledge that all his family, like her family, had been wiped out. But she didn't want him to know until the last minute. She would make sure he would die in great pain. And now it was just a matter of time.

Sarah turned up on time at 8.15pm where she had a word with the staff. Asking them to help her as well because she was new and still finding her way around. Noel arrived to say a few words because there had been a conference at the John-Albany Hotel, thirty men or even more would in all probability descend on the club as they had done so the previous year. Last year they had spent a shed load of money, so they had to give them a little leeway in their behaviour.

But they were not to accept any groping and swearing. Big Charlie the doormen would deal with all of that. He hoped they all have a good night and then he asked Gloria to step into his office. Sarah, alias Gloria followed Noel into his office. 'Close the door Gloria, I have something to say. After work I would like you to come back with me to my apartment because I have some important issues I wish to talk to you about, its work related so I can't really talk about it here. Before you say anything I am not going to try and seduce you, I promise you.'

She laughed 'oh that's a shame.'

Noel thought maybe he had missed his chance on that one, 'no really Gloria, I need to speak to you for a while and to be honest we won't have the time tonight as it will be very busy so keep your eyes open for fiddles and the odd bit of groping like the girls doing hand jobs and such like.'

'WHAT, are you serious Mr Dolan?'

'Yes very serious, they certainly did last year and they were charging £75 a hand job and some even got under the table with them. God knows what they charged for a blow job but keep an eye out will you? I don't need a police visit again or get done for keeping a disorderly house and all that rubbish. One of the Russian girls was caught having a threesome in the gent's toilets. In fact she did it twice and charged each man a hundred pound each. Needless to say she has now moved on. We think it was her that informed the police and they came down on us like a ton of bricks. So we had to shut up shop and it cost me a load of money. I had three parties booked in that night too.'

'Ok Mr Dolan I'll see you later, and getting back to your apartment I hope there will be no funny business. I do hope you understand that.'

'Gloria please I have given you my word, but I do need to talk with you. I'll see you later, and now I have to show my face about, so you enjoy the evening.' The evening went well, very well. Being incredibly busy they took almost twelve thousand pounds, she did see some fiddles going on but this was not a career move for her. Just a means to an end and it did not disrupt her thinking at all.

Noel locked up the Lone Star and walked along with Sarah. He had ordered a cab for the short journey home to his apartment which was just less than a mile away. When Sarah entered the apartment she was shocked because it was lovely. There were lovely paintings on the wall and thick carpets. The living room was huge with three sofas and various mirrors. And the fireplace was huge with logs all stacked up ready and waiting for the first sign of winter. Around the living room there were lots of photographs of family members from long ago sitting next to Gypsy caravans and their black and white cob horses. On show there was some very expensive china here and there. They were kept in expensive handmade Mahogany cabinets. The kitchen was beautiful, it was very large with an enormous dining table and eight chairs, there was the customary bar with eight stools next to the kitchen then off the kitchen there was a pool room and a darts board plus a football table. 'The best bit though' said Noel as he saw her looking around 'is the roof terrace, you have to come and take a look.'

'Okay, you lead the way.' She said.

Noel went to a small narrow Mahogany antique sideboard in the hallway next to the stairs leading up to the roof terrace. There he opened the left hand top drawer and picked up a key. She noticed there were a few more keys in the drawer and all were numbered with names on for various locations. And then he held his hand out for hers.

Sarah let him take her by the hand as they climbed up a flight of stairs leading to the roof and stepped out onto the beautiful terrace. Now you could see all of London lit up at night - it was breathtaking. You could see all over Hyde Park it was beautiful.

The floor tiles were lovely and the parapet going all round the terrace was painted a dark red, there were flower pots in the corner some with exotic flowers. But an outside telescope could take in more of the incredible view all around the terrace. The garden furniture was lovely and obviously very expensive, almost like it was out of a Hollywood film set. The loungers had thick seating and there was also a built in Barbeque area with gas piped into it. There was a bar with eight stools they were fixed to the floor. The bar at the moment had its shutters down.

'This place is immaculate Noel, so does your mother clean it for you, or do you have a cleaner?'

'My mother' he laughed 'OMG no, she doesn't do a thing, she just eats, drinks, shops and cooks but cleaning no way. We have a cleaning company that calls in every two days, why, are you looking for a cleaner Gloria?'

'As a matter of fact I could do with one as I don't get the time these days.'

'Let me get you their card, hang on I have one in my wallet. Look, here it is, they're called Your Clean Easy. I think it's a Polish outfit as the girls are mostly Polish and some have even worked for me. Listen Gloria I have to laugh, does my mother do the cleaning that's a good one.'

'Thanks for the card I'll ring them tomorrow. Why are you laughing at your own mother for Noel, that's not a nice thing to do.' For a moment she saw a flash of temper quickly flicking in his eyes then it was gone.

'Gloria my mother is just lazy. She's a woman who does nothing all day, she doesn't get up until lunch time and then she drinks, eats and has various friends round then goes out shopping, and that's her life. Please don't lecture me on my own mother again, and not only that, she has a housekeeper Mrs Wilson who lives in a small two bedroom flat which is next to the front door and she seems to hear everything. She says she's as deaf as a post, but she isn't, she could hear a mouse fart from across the road.'

'Ok fine your mother is nothing to do with me she looked at her watch. Anyway I have to be going.'

'Oh look I'm sorry I've upset you. I'm sorry Gloria but you don't know the full story, so maybe one day I will tell you if you manage to stick around for a while, let's just have a quick drink.' There was a beautiful full moon. You could almost feel the moon it seemed so close, and in another life it may have been romantic. 'So would you like a glass of wine' he asked her. 'By the way there are only a handful of people who have seen this view before Gloria. Can I get you that wine now?'

'Yes Noel that would be lovely. I bet you say the same thing to all the women you bring up here but listen I insist I serve you, so let's have no buts about it let me do this. I'll bring the bottle up from the kitchen and two glasses. Now you take a seat out here with me and we can talk.' She smiled as she touched his face then kissed him very lightly on his lips. So sit down and wait for me I won't be long.'

He never realised it was the kiss of death, he thought she desired him and tonight he would have her, he was feeling so hard for her and it didn't go unnoticed by Sarah.

'Honestly Gloria I have hardly brought anyone up here. I promise you I haven't.'

'Yeah right' she laughed 'it's your life and you can sleep with whoever you want, it's nothing to do with me, anyway I'm no angel.'

That was music to his ears. Now he knew he would be able to get into her. He just had to time it right. There was a good feeling about her the moment he had set his eyes on her. But she had sex written all over her and those legs were the best pair he had ever seen and beautifully tanned too. He would enjoy her this night and it's so kind of the moon to make a big appearance too. That sets the scene brilliantly, or so he thought.

She quickly skipped down the flight of stairs to get the wine and two glasses. But first she took a quick look in the sideboard drawer there were various keys she thought this could be interesting for later. Once back in the kitchen she opened her bag which was in her much larger bag containing a nylon rope with the noose at the end of it. Now she had left in the kitchen, she took out the already loaded small syringe full of Ketamine and the eye drops bottle which was full of Rohypnol. She selected a bottle of Merlot and two large wine glasses. Listening intently in case he came back down the stairs she dropped a few drops of the tasteless Rohypnol in one of the glasses. Then as she came back up to the roof terrace she put the wine glasses down on the outside table. And then she slowly poured out the wine and gave the drugged glass of wine to Noel.

She said all excitedly 'hey, look at that view out there, it's so lovely, you're so lucky Noel, really lucky, how I wish I had a view like that from my roof. Look at that moon, it's so romantic, it's just so wonderful.' She held her arm out to touch the moon, look I can almost feel it Noel.'

'Yes I know Gloria, it makes you think of your life and where we're going. So anyway now you have to close your eyes and make a wish on the moon. Go on make a wish do it now but don't tell me what you wished for. If you do, then it won't happen, that's the saying and maybe it's true.'

Sarah laughed, 'ok I will make a wish, but a secret wish, I won't tell you either. But what a lovely place, it's a place to die for' she said as she smiled at him. 'Noel, is it true you have to be stark naked when you make a wish on the moon? I read that somewhere or it doesn't work, have you heard that one? Apparently it works better it there are two people naked then they make love to seal the wish.'

'Yes I have heard that one,' he laughed 'maybe that's true, but hey what a strange thing to say, a place to die for' he laughed, 'it is a beautiful place. But all this cost a heap of money, my dad's money. He also lives next door with my mum he has done so for years. But he would never sell this place and I rent this from him, but of course at a reasonable rent.'

'So you're not married Noel, have you ever been married at all?'

'No never, anyway if we both make a wish we both have to be stark naked then make love and I'm up for that if you are Gloria.'

'Yes I am' she laughed 'so let's do it.'

He took a large mouthful of the Merlot, swallowed and looked at the glass again. 'Jesus I needed that. I don't think marriage is for me Gloria I can't stay faithful for long that's my problem. But as I get older I do wish I had some kids but the business keeps me busy and I don't seem to have a lot of time for real romance. Besides I have never met anyone I wanted to be with 24/7.' So he took another drink. 'Wow I feel a little woozy, Jesus what's in this drink, it's very strong, is yours strong as well.'

'Funny you should say that, but no I'm okay, but you're not. I did spike your drink Noel' she laughed.

He laughed as well, he looked at his glass and said 'yeah right, but the problem is I have been working too hard lately. I have to sit down before I fall down.' And then he fell into one of the expensive sun loungers and just lay there, looking at the moon and the stars. Looking at the moon he said 'that looks like home to me' he slurred.

Sarah sat down on the lounger next to him she said, 'hey have you already forgotten you too have to get naked and then close your eyes and make a wish? So go on get your clothes off and I'll do the same.'

Struggling to get his clothes off he eventually managed it. Now he lay on the lounger with a surprisingly large hard erection poking up at the moon.

'Noel you have to close your eyes and make that wish and no peeping. Here take another drink.'

He drank the remainder of the wine. 'Hey you have to get your kit off Gloria.' Closing his eyes he felt very tired as he made a wish. His eyes were tightly closed as she came towards him. And then she quickly plunged the small syringe full of Ketimine into his neck by his left ear right up to the hilt.

He turned and shouted out in pain 'hey what are you doing,' he tried to get up but he couldn't move his legs, and his arms felt like lead weights. His mouth seemed to be stuck then he just lay back unable to move any more. Staring at the moon with a smile on his face but he felt so incredibly tired now.

For one brief moment she felt a little guilty. Then she thought of her brother Tom, his wife Laura and the three children, there was no one who felt for them, only her. Remembering the police report and all the things he had done to young girls and the people who had gone missing made her job a little easier. No one bothered to ask about the young Polish girl aged just nineteen who had acid in her face and could no longer smile. And the beatings he had dished out to other girls. Noel was a nasty terrifying man who would soon be a forgotten piece of work. Now the only one to mourn him would be his family for now. But it would soon be their turn. She had to move fast now, she had no way of knowing how long the drugs would last as everyone is different when it come to drugs. Now he was completely paralysed and naked. Noel just lay there, in a fuzz of nothingness.

Quickly tying his wrists together behind his back, she tied his ankles as well with the garden ties. Now he had some vague sleepy idea what she was doing but could do nothing to stop her and he didn't care either he was so sleepy. Now he was just laying there naked looking at the moon.

Placing the noose carefully around his neck with the nylon rope from her bag she secured it to the base of the strong TV Ariel base. The nylon rope took a weight of 400 pounds and he was about 200lbs.

She went down to the kitchen to get a dish cloth to shove into his mouth then she tore a linen kitchen towel in half with a pair of scissors to wrap all around his face satisfied she ran back up the stairs to finish him off. Yet somehow he had managed to crawl away to the far corner of the terrace. Standing over him he made another attempt to crawl away. She simply dragged him to the edge of the parapet. Stupidly he smiled at her but then using all her strength gained from her gym workouts, she lifted his legs up to the edge of the parapet. Bending down she lifted him up by gripping him under his arm pits lifting him up then sat him on the edge of the parapet. No one could see her. She wasn't overlooked at all. Slowly she played out the rope to let him down until the rope went tight. She left him to swing naked in the breeze. There was noise's of him choking and spluttering then making gargling noises. Then he was sick through his nose the noise was not pleasant but she hoped he was suffering. And then a few seconds later there was no more noise, he was obviously dead.

The time was now 4.18am. Picking up the two wine glasses and the bottle she went to the kitchen, put on a pair of surgical gloves from her bag, she washed the glasses and the bottle of wine. Then found some bleach and wiped the place clean from top to bottom. Now satisfied, she thought ok Alex Dolan you're next on my list, two down and four to go - it won't be long now. Walking back up to the terrace she took one last look at Noel, he was very still and very dead. The world was not going to miss him, he would be hard to find as he was slowly swinging naked between two large houses. But now it was no longer her problem. On the way out she opened the sideboard drawer and looked at the keys, there was one for the main door and one for next door, his Father's house, she took the keys and left. Leaving his apartment at 5.23am, she was now wearing heavy rimmed glasses she walked with her folded down walking stick. Taking an old coat from his wardrobe she wore that as a disguise as she shuffled down the street.

Harry Dolan woke up screaming his head off. He was having a terrible nightmare. In his dream he could see a woman in black and white but could not understand what that meant to him.

A woman was standing over his sons with a large rope. There was a rope for him and his wife too. But it didn't make any sense. He was trying to see her face, he knew he had seen her face before but couldn't remember where. Every time he looked at her face, she seemed to turn into a ripple in a pond after he had thrown in a stone. Now he couldn't focus properly. He screamed out 'Who the hell are you?'

'Harry, wake up, are you ok' asked his concerned wife who had been sleeping in her own bedroom 'you seem to have had a nightmare. Harry will you wake up.'

Harry woke up in a cold clammy sweat. The time was exactly 4.18am. But now he looked terrified and lost to his wife Joan.

'Jesus, what a dream that was, it was about the kids and some woman with a rope with a noose on the end of it. What the hell is that all about' he shouted.

'Oh look Harry, it's just a bad dream' said Joan 'go back to sleep' the time was now 4.35am. Then after a cup of tea made by Joan, he went back to sleep. Something was wrong and he couldn't shake the feeling off. But it stuck to him and then he saw Duvall laughing at him, he was dreaming again. When he finally woke up he had a feeling of terrible doom hanging over him.

Sarah had now arrived home to her apartment where she took a shower and afterwards fell asleep. She had never given out her address to Noel or anyone else at the club, only a false one. Now she broke up her cheap mobile phone that she rang Noel on and dropped the bits down a drain on the way home. So now, she was a missing person but she still had her original phone in her own name which had to be switched off or she could have been tracked down. Also her other phone to contact Liz back in America was switched off too. She looked completely different to how she looked before as she had turned back into herself. Her main job now was to get rid of Alex. She purchased another pay as you go phone in another alias.

When Noel had failed to turn up for work, the staff made calls to Harry to ask where Noel was. Harry was completely baffled as Noel was never late, not ever, so he rang him himself. There was still no reply so he went next door and let himself in only after ringing the bell. Harry knew something was wrong. Noel would never stay in bed. It was just not like him. Opening the door to Noel's apartment the first thing he noticed was the very strong smell of bleach all around the place which he found very strange. Then he looked in all the rooms shouting out his sons name, nothing. Deciding to go onto the terrace, he found the terrace door was locked but he did have a key, so he went back to his apartment to get it.

Joan his wife knew where it was and said 'I'll come with you.' They both returned to Noel's apartment where they searched it once again only to still find nothing. Strangely his bed had not been slept in. They opened the roof terrace door. They could see there had been some activity that had taken place, they could see that because the place had been disturbed and his clothes were on the floor. Noel for all his faults was a clean and tidy man, so where the hell was he? Then Harry saw the rope, it was tied around the base of the large TV Arial base and it was very tight. But he immediately knew what had happened. Looking over the edge he saw his son slowly swinging in the light morning breeze completely naked. Turning to Joan he said don't look but she was already looking. The sight before them made them ill. Even the local pigeons had crapped on his head.

Now throwing up, he couldn't help himself then Joan screamed and screamed. The sight was not a pretty sight. To see your son hanging in the breeze like that was a terrible thing. Screaming loudly, Joan broke down as Harry called the police. Now he had no choice. Joan was just screaming, crying and wailing. Suddenly she began beating him in his chest saying she blamed him. She always did blame him for being a feckless father and husband.

Leaving her to scream he tried to walk away from his responsibility. But his pain was immense. Harry didn't know what to do. Looking around the roof terrace, he said to Joan 'don't touch anything, the police always say that, so don't touch anything. Come away now Joan. We have to leave Noel until the police arrive, we can't do anything for him now. We can help him by trying to catch the bastard who did this to him.'

CHAPTER FOURTEEN

DCI Reggie Arnold was a veteran of 35 years policing and his assistant DS Trevor Bailey were sat with about forty other police officers listening to some whining drivel about working standards and health and safety matters and all the bollocks that goes with it. The speech was being given by a tall thin man who uncannily resembled a young Tommy Cooper, minus his bulky appearance. But he also had a speech defect. He was what the lads call a brown breader....brwouwn bwed? He was of those.

His name was Rupert Brindle. He came quickly from the law society as a stand in for the usual bloke who was suddenly taken ill. Presumably he was the only one who had offered to speak. Coppers were not the best of audiences, because they were very cynical and critical at the best of times. DCI Reggie Arnold had listened to a lot of speeches in the last thirty-five years of policing, but this one was the worst. Apparently they all had to be there on pain of being disciplined if they didn't. The trouble was they were all trying to take the piss out of the man called Mr Rupert Brindle the trouble was the name came out as Wupert Bwindle when he said it. You couldn't make this it up. Rupert Brindle said 'good morning police officers, I will be as bwief as possible I understand you need to be chasing cwiminals. My name is Wupert Bwindle.'

DS Bailey, who was DCI Arnold's new sidekick, suddenly burst into laughter and was now laughing a loud manic hysterical laugh which then managed set all the room off. Rupert Brindle thought he had them in his hand, he thought to himself. Well I'll enjoy this speech because it wasn't as bad as he thought it would be. Yes he was enjoying this....so far.

The whole room was now in tears. All the men and the women were mostly seasoned Detectives with their sidekick's rookie detectives. There was no way this Rupert guy was being taken seriously, and to top it all he was higher up on the stage in the conference room which sometimes doubled as a dance and entertainment area.

But the howling laughter was now concentrated on Rupert's shoes as he had the biggest feet anyone had seen, they must have been a size 18 or even more.

One Detective shouted out (no one quite knew who) 'he's got Clown's shoes, look clown shoes.' Everyone looked, and then as one.... everyone rolled about laughing. Rupert Brindle stood there looking a little upset and confused scratching his head which simply made everyone laugh even more.

'You, hey you what's so amusing.' Rupert pointed his finger at Trevor Bailey. 'Come on what was so funny so tell me what your name is.'

DS Trevor Bailey said 'who me sir?'

'Yes you. What is your name?'

DCI Reggie Arnold glared at his sidekick, he had told him earlier on 'to behave himself.'

DS Bailey looked at his boss and said 'What?'

'I asked you for your name officer?' shouted Rupert Brindle. He wasn't letting this go.

'It's Trevor sir, DS Trevor Bailey.'

'Well Twevor Bailey, tell me what's so funny?'

At the word Twevor the whole room erupted into hysterical laughter again, some people had to leave the room, mainly women as the ladies toilets were just opposite the room in the corridor.

DCI Reggie Arnold had also now lost all self control. He was now in hysterics.

'Hey, why are you laughing?' He pointed his finger at DCI Reggie Arnold, 'so come on, what's your name?'

'Err sorry sir, its DCI Reggie Arnold.' He looked angrily at DS Bailey for making him laugh.

'Well Weggie Arnold let's all share the joke shall we?'

At that remark the whole place now turned into an uproar of laughing and giggling and several more had to leave the room.

Rupert Brindle stood there holding his head in one hand while gestating with his other to all calm down. But at that moment, thank goodness, DCI Reggie Arnold was called away on his mobile by his boss DCS Ronnie Stewart. DCI Arnold was taking DS Bailey with him. They were told by their very pleased DCS Stewart to get round to Harry Dolan's house because apparently someone had murdered his son Noel Dolan.

Looking as pleased as Punch, because whoever did it took a thorn from DCS Ronnie Stewart's side which had made his day. Saying 'and before you guys go round' at the same time he opened his famous whiskey drawer 'we drink to the perpetrator, well done. It's a good day.'

'DCI Reggie Arnold said 'well for one I'll drink to that!'

DCS Stewart said 'there is Karma after all. So you two get this down your necks and get on with it, between you and me, somebody has done the world a favour this day, so let's raise our glasses. After all lads there is a God.'

The two police officers arrived in record time. Harry Dolan was already on his step waiting for them. But he shouted out 'well well, you two fucking clowns took your own sweet fucking time.'

'Sir we are just around the corner at West End Central as you well know. We realise of course you're distraught sir as this is your own son, but we are here now and we did come as quickly as possible, so I hope you will co-operate with us.'

Dolan shouted or rather screamed. 'I fucking know he's my son, what am I stupid or what? I'm his Father, or rather I was.'

DCI Reggie Arnold had arrived with DS Trevor Bailey to this abuse. In his 35 years in the Met he understood how upset Dolan was. He'd seen it many times before. Dolan just needed to let his feelings out, to show his anger and to vent his frustration on someone, and they just happened to be the first to investigate the death of his son. 'Can you tell me where he is Mr Dolan? Oh and have you moved or touched anything since finding your son. I do need to know sir.'

'No we haven't, his mother has taken to her bed as per fucking usual, she hardly gets out of the thing. And anyway a fat lot of use she is. We found him today at lunch time. He hadn't turned in for work which has never happened before. You know he was a good worker and a lovely person and the fucking pigeons had even crapped on his head.'

DCI Arnold almost choked, he thought a nice person? That's a wheelbarrow full of bollocks because he was a hated person. The two police officers asked to be left to do their job and Bailey asked Harry to go and make a cup of tea and to leave them to it. They looked at the body of Noel and realized someone had done their homework. This was in a way a sophisticated murder, even though the body was now in a state. There was pigeon shit on his head and some on his shoulder. In fact they saw a row of the flying rats on the roof with their heads now bobbing up and down with curiosity.

DS Bailey had a job not to laugh at the birds. He said 'maybe he had upset the wild life as well sir.' Noel was slowly turning around in the breeze with the tension of the nylon rope, his body was naked and very grey and his face was purple grey with blotches all over his once handsome face. They noticed he was hanging between two buildings but there were no windows so no one saw anything or heard anything. The body was not a pretty sight. But his mother must have been in bits when she found him there with Harry.

'You can't help feeling sorry for the parents but it took a long time for the hangman to catch up with Noel, because I know of three killings he ordered. But we couldn't prove it, and also girls he maimed said DCI Arnold.'

'Sir this took some planning to execute the murder, it seemed to make a statement of intent, there must have been a good reason why Noel Dolan was found hanged like this. However, he must have had quite a few enemies he was a much disliked individual. In his short life he had brought a lot of misery to a lot of people, and he gave out a lot of pain too,' said Bailey.

DCI Arnold thought this looks like a revenge killing. Having seen many murders and experience told him this one was well planned, now he was certain of that. If you wanted to kill someone you just did it. This took some planning as it was a difficult thing to do to hang another man and it must have taken some time and people to carry it out, or did it?

DS Bailey could see the place was well cleaned. Because after the murder it was spick and span, but the murder scene itself was very untidy. Now to DCI Arnold that meant one thing. It was a message.

'Sir' asked DS Bailey 'what do you make of all this?'

'You tell me Sergeant. So give me your theory?'

'I think sir; this seems to indicate a message to someone, and maybe to Mr Dolan. Also the whole place has been cleaned with bleach including this area. The terrace is untidy not like the rest of the place. Now I could be wrong sir, but this mess up here seems to be a deliberate attempt to tell someone something, to draw their attention to, but I can't as yet think what.'

'I think you and I are on the same wavelength, and to me it does seem to leave a message, I think you're right Bailey.'

Harry came up with a tray of tea and biscuits. DCI Arnold started to ask all sorts of questions. Harry hadn't got a clue who had killed his son and neither had Joan. However, she was now unable to stop crying and had to be sedated in her bed by her Doctor.

DCI Arnold asked Harry 'if he knew of anyone that Noel could have upset, or who would want him dead.'

Harry said 'he was not responsible for his son's dealings, and he had no idea who would want to harm him as he had done nothing to hurt anyone, as far as he was aware.'

DCI Arnold knew that was a big black lie as they were one of the most hated and feared families in and around the London area. Noel had hurt and maimed a lot of people, mainly girls over the years as well as the men who had worked for them. Some had disappeared altogether, including girls. They had intimidated witnesses of forthcoming trials and were well known for getting at jurors, bribing and then also threatening them. There were also one or two police officers who had been got at in the past and DCI Arnold was sure they would again in the future. So you couldn't believe a word Harry Dolan said, or his dutiful wife. She just did as she was told, or else.

DCI Arnold called in the forensic people. Where they eventually came to the conclusion he was murdered. He looked as though he had been drugged, that conclusion was reached due to the small syringe imbedded in the left side of the neck where he was found hanged. They did offer their sad condolences to Harry and his wife. Underneath they were not surprised he had been murdered. Noel was a nasty, or had been a nasty piece of work.

Who could have killed him? No one ever came up to his apartment according to his father and mother but he didn't kill himself, someone had to have been invited up. They could all smell the bleach and knew the murder had been planned by the look of it and all evidence had been wiped clean. There was no doubt it looked like a professional job. It was well planned.

DCI Arnold with DS Bailey visited the Lone Star Club with Harry. Now they wanted to question the staff. There was one notable absence, a new woman called Gloria. She had only been there for two days but no one could really say much about her only that she had a slight American accent and was a stunning looking woman. Harry told DCI Arnold she was working there on a trial basis and she had served him herself the night before last. She seemed to be very professional and friendly. Everyone liked her as far as he knew although she had only just started in a supervisory role. Yet she seemed to be a good worker and also very attractive.

Harry gave them a good description, 'she was about 5ft 8 inches tall, slim and with dark shoulder length hair, and she also had great legs and a nice figure. She wore thin glasses and weighed about nine stone. She was a about a size ten, she was all woman though.

'That was not a lot to go on, London is full of lovely looking women,' said DS Bailey.

'Really is that right,' said Harry, 'well that's encouraging to hear because whenever I go out, all I see are mostly middle age fat slovenly women wearing those disgusting leggings and most of them seem to have a fag on and their ears are stuck to huge mobile phones while probably trying to get an appointment to join Weight Watchers. I don't know where you two hang out but it's not the same place as me and I live in a good area. Like I said, I only saw her once and she was a nice looking lady.'

'I presume she wasn't wearing leggings then Harry?'

'That's very funny, very funny' said Harry.

DCI Arnold asked the staff if they had seen anything unusual about this woman and did they know where she lived.

Everyone said they had seen and heard nothing. One of the staff members, a woman called Rita who once had a fling with Noel and had hoped for a more lasting relationship with him.

Sadly she ended up being very disappointed. 'The boss had a hard on for Gloria,' said Rita. 'It was obvious she could tell because his attitude towards her was sickly gooey. Noel was always like that when he wanted to shag someone. He always had been. But once you let him in, he buggers off until the next one.'

DCI Arnold said, so I take it your talking from personnel experience Rita.'

'Too right, and I'm sure other girls will tell you the same. Anyway she was the last to go that night. The two of them were waiting for her to leave. I left just before them but I turned around on the corner to watch them leave together. They hailed a London black cab and got in. It was obvious he was taking her home to his place or to hers, but probably to his apartment.' Rita still missed the grub screws they used to have (sex on a table). It just wasn't the same with her lazy husband.

DS Bailey contacted all the taxi operators that worked that night. Luckily he came up with the taxi driver who was a London Black cab driver but crucially he had a CCTV in his cab. Later, when they looked at it you could see this Gloria woman was sitting very close to Noel but talking. However, she was showing her legs in a provocative way thought DCI Arnold. But that was about all. Until that is they got out at his apartment. It was only a short journey to his place, less than a mile so there was not much to show for it, he could see she was in a mood to seduce him by the way she moved with him.

'This Gloria was the last person to see Noel alive was she,' asked DS Bailey, 'we have to find her, but no one has a clue where she lives. Anyway who is she, where did she come from and where did she go? Is she dead too? Did she do it, if so she must be very fit to lift the guy over the parapet to hang him like that? Noel must weigh about fourteen stone at least, or maybe she had an accomplice?'

'Sir' said a probationary policeman who was standing there with his hand in the air bobbing up and down like he was still at school trying to get the attention of the teacher. He was trying to get the attention of DCI Arnold. He'd been guarding the entrance to the club, 'excuse me for saying this, but can I have a word sir?'

'Ok if you must, but is it relevant to the case constable?'

'Sir, yes maybe it could be. Look there is a case going on at the moment in the South of France in Nice, there was a French guy who was found hanged from his balcony in the same way only last week sir and its almost identical. There was also a rag rammed into his mouth. And there was a woman with him who the French police want to have a chat with, post haste sir. Yet it was all over the news, they thought it was a terrorist situation. I'm surprised you haven't heard about it sir.'

'Really constable, for your information last week I was on holiday in Portugal. I saw no TV, this is news to me.'

DCI Arnold turned to Sergeant Bailey. 'Go and find out about this French killing that happened last week in Nice. If this is true then we may well have a killer woman running loose and we better find her and pronto. We've all heard about killer clowns, but a killer woman? Jesus, that's got to be much worse and less predictable and take the constable with you, well spotted PC 458.' The constable looked like the cat that had got the cream. With the help of PC 458, Sergeant Bailey got in touch with their French counterparts in Nice. The French police sent over all the details of the hanging in Nice including photographs and they in return received all the relevant information regarding the information so far about the murder of Noel Dolan. There were definitely similarities in both the murders. In fact they were identical in every way. To DCI Arnold it had to be the same person or persons, no doubt at all in his mind. But they could not inform the press, well not yet as it was too early to marry the two together.

DCI Arnold had the most up to date information. Being informed that the man in France was a guy called Eric Bezier who had a large amount of Rohypnol, and also a large amount of Sodium thiopental in his system. The latter was supposedly a truth drug. But the small syringe was still embedded in his neck when they found him. Now that was exactly the same as Noel Dolan.

'Bailey, this had to be the same killer who certainly knew what they were doing. And also the place had been wiped clean with bleach. So what was the connection or had there been one if any, there must be a connection somehow, there had to be, but what?'

'Yes I think your right sir, there must be a connection,' said Bailey 'and I reckon its staring us in the face somehow.'

'So what was the motivation, there normally is one, find that and we crack the case Bailey.'

DS Bailey agreed totally.

DCI Arnold had managed to get the movements of Eric Bezier from the French Police. Now they found out he had flown to Bristol so when all the information was collated together, lo and behold there was Harry Dolan seen picking up this French guy from Bristol International airport and also bringing him back. The French police had good information that this man Eric, went under another name of Claude Duvall who was known in some quarters as a hit man and a very good one, but with no proof....as yet.

They also found out this same man was in Spain for a short while. They had his mobile signals for the last two weeks. They had the hours given to them from the mobile phone company. Then he was back in Nice, where he made a call to Harry Dolan's mobile. The curious thing about this was that Harry Dolan had met this man for less than twelve hours in Bristol. The other odd thing was that a family from Soho who used to own the Black Swan public house had all been lost in a fire in Alicante and the chances were that Harry Dolan knew this family. Eric was there at the same time and then hours later back in Nice which was an easy drive along the main coast road all the way into Alicante. So there could well be a connection. Astonishingly it almost looked as though Harry Dolan had this family killed. Then again the idea seemed absolutely crazy thought DCI Arnold. But then again he knew all about the Dolans, they had been a thorn in the side of the police for years and literally got away with murder before and more than once. There were over the years people who had gone missing who had strong ties with the Dolans. Where did they go, no one knew anything? Harry Dolan's middle name was ...revenge.

DS Bailey said 'Sir I think we should pull Harry Dolan in for a grilling about this French guy. Because there must be a connection down the line on all of this, so why did he meet him? Now it's strange the way the French guy died. Being the same way Noel Dolan has died. And so the same thing happened to his own son, it's bizarre sir, there has to be a connection, there must be one, you couldn't write this up.'

'Yes Bailey' said DCI Arnold 'so let's get him down the station for a chat and that's all. But I guarantee he will bring his brief with him, he always has done in the past.'

'Maybe we can get him off guard sir at his home while he's grieving.'

'That's what I like about you Bailey, you're all heart.'

'I know sir I'm a fool to myself at times. My mum always said that about me.'

DCI Arnold laughed, 'well let's get the airport CCTV pictures, ok they are not brilliant but you can clearly see the two of them together. Dolan's picking up the Frenchman and also taking him back, that's cut and dry as far as I'm concerned, so go on give him a call....now.'

'Mr Dolan, good morning this is DS Bailey here sir, sorry to bother you in your time of grief but we may have some news. Look sir we have some new information regarding this woman called Gloria, we think you will be able to recognise her from some photographs, or rather some CCTV pictures. So can we pop round and have a quick word? We need you to take a look at some pictures of this woman as quickly as possible. We may be able to distribute her pictures at all the ports and airports, so are you in now sir? We really understand your situation but we do have to move quickly on this, as I have just said you may be able to recognise the woman concerned or maybe not, but we do have to eliminate her from out enquiries Mr Dolan. Can we come round now, let's say in thirty minutes give or take a few minutes. Are you still there sir?'

'Yes, yes, that's ok come on round now, let's try and get to the bottom of this, but don't ask my wife please, she's in bits at the moment. She can't even put a sentence together, she's still all broke up.'

'I do understand sir, we'll be there in thirty minutes, sorry for the distress but we'll be as quick as we can. Just five minutes of your time that's all sir' said DS Bailey.

Mr Ben John-Paisley QC was sitting behind his plush red leather bound desk writing a few memos for Mrs Brown his secretary of some thirty years who was sitting on the opposite side of his desk, pen in her hand and writing pad on her knees, the old fashioned way. Ben felt his mobile vibrate in his pocket, he looked at it and could see at once it was Harry Dolan. Mrs Brown winced as she heard him groan. He never liked dealing with Harry, but once you dance with the devil you have to finish the dance no matter how long it took.

He'd known Harry Dolan now for thirty-five years. Harry also paid him a handsome retainer which helped to put his two daughters through Law school. Knowing full well he was a criminal with a dubious line in crooked deals. But some said he could make things hard if you upset him and he was the not the forgiving type. Now it was better he did his best for him at all times.

'Harry, it's been a long time, how are you? The old bill, what do they want I wonder? Of course I will be round in five minutes after all we are neighbours. Mary and myself are so very sorry to hear about Noel, he was a bit of a lad but nice with it,' his eyes halved closed as he looked at Mrs Brown, as he said it because they knew what a horrible shit Noel could be, or rather he had been. He was all charming when he first met anyone but could bite quicker than a Cobra. 'So the police want to have a nice quiet chat do they, hmm they always say that. I hope you haven't already said anything to them Harry, they are a canny lot and DCI Reggie Arnold and myself go back a long way. He's a very good cop, also a very clever one. I don't know about this DS he has with him, a Sergeant Bailey you say, no I haven't any experience of him, he sounds like a pup to me.'

'Ben get your arse round here now its urgent said Harry.'

'I'm on my way. By the way old chap, have you any of that whiskey left. You know the Irish one with the red and green label? Good, pour me one will you it's the best I have tasted. I need to clear my throat, oh and my regards to Joan. I will see you in about five minutes.'

'Make it sooner Ben for fuck sake,' replied Harry.

'Mrs Brown, can you postpone any calls for the next two hours as I have to pop to the neighbours. I don't care how urgent anyone is, I will be engaged with Harry and if I need to be any longer I will phone you.'

'Certainly Mr Paisley, oh and do try and remember you have to see Lord Hawthorne this afternoon at 2.30pm, so don't come back pissed like the last time. And don't deny it because I was there can you remember?

You also fell over the waste paper basket and ended up looking up the skirt of the young office girl as she went to help you up, you frightened her, you silly old man, that's why she left.'

'Oh don't be so dramatic Mrs Brown, if I remember it correctly it was a real treat for an old man such as myself and she did have lovely legs and a nice, how do you say it, ah yes a thong thing.....hmm really quite lovely.'

CHAPTER FIFTEEN

When the two detectives arrived, Joan Dolan showed them into the huge living room where Harry Dolan was sitting with his solicitor and well known QC Mr Ben John-Paisley of Paisley and Wright. They were the large well known legal firm in London.

DCI Arnold said 'good morning Harry. That was quick of you to arrange for your brief to be here.'

Harry laughed, 'you did say a quick word didn't you, so if it's going to be that quick then my brief here Ben can listen as well, that's in case you speak too quickly and I can't keep up with you lot. After all there are two of you so I thought it would even it out a little.'

'You always were one step ahead Harry I'll give you that,' laughed DCI Arnold.

Mr Paisley asked him to get to the point and indeed make it quick as his client has a lot to do today, so please get on with it. 'DCI Arnold as you know, we have locked horns before, so will you get to the point and don't hang around with silly tricky innocuous questions.'

DCI Arnold laughed, while DS Bailey sat stony faced. 'Okay Harry, sorry Mr Dolan. Look can you please tell me why you met this man, a French man at Bristol International Airport. But then a few hours later you took him back to get a return flight? His name was Eric Bezier, but sometimes known as Claude Duvall.'

Harry hunched over to talk with his brief for a few moments then said 'yes Inspector, I did meet Duvall at the airport and it was of a personal nature and none of your business.'

'Why did you meet him Mr Dolan, it could really help us in our enquiries?'

His brief said 'my client does not have to answer that DCI Arnold so why the innocuous question?'

'We are trying to establish if your client can help us. Look we need to know if this woman seen with this man was the same woman who briefly worked at the Lone Star Club, now she's also gone missing.'

'Are you insinuating that my client Mr Dolan has got something to do with her disappearance Inspector,' replied Dolan's brief,

'No, no of course not, however, she may well be involved in the murder of his son Noel. She is also wanted by the French Police in connection with the murder of this Duvall chap. So let's face it the murders were exactly the same. The CCTV shows quite clearly Mr Dolan met Duvall/Bezier; we want to see if there is in any way another connection. So look, it's quite obvious you know this man.'

'Yes I do, and I did meet Duvall. That was the name he gave me. The woman is not known to me, I'm afraid I have never seen her before. But yes, you're quite right I did meet this man at the airport because he rang me a few weeks ago about purchasing a mobile home in Epsom. The guy told me he loved racing and owned a couple of race horses. Now there was a mobile home for sale which happened to be mine. He also asked me if I knew of anyone who could stable his horses, and he asked did I do that sort of thing. I told him no, I didn't do that because I haven't got a yard.'

'You don't have to say any more Harry' said Ben.

'Well I am helping these pillocks.

Look he told me he was absolutely sick and tired of staying in crap hotels which charged the earth so he wanted a place near the race course. He couldn't stretch to buying a real house so looked at buying a mobile home, and that's all. I told him the price and he thought it was a little expensive but he would think about it. I told him to make his mind up soon because it would sell easily and it was up to him. In fact he was supposed to ring me last week. Now I know why he didn't ring me. Anyway I have now decided not to sell, and that's all there was to it. So let's get down to business DCI Arnold, have you any idea where this bitch has gone? If she murdered my son I want her in court.'

His brief Mr Paisley asked 'so is there anything else you need to know DCI Arnold, as you see my client has helped you with your enquiries. So will there be any other questions? My client has a lot to arrange, the funeral of his son for instance. If you don't mind I will show you to the door.'

Once out in the street, DS Bailey said 'well that was convenient to say the least so what's he got to hide sir? Maybe he knows we are on to him. What the hell is the tie up between the two murders and this woman? I never slept last night thinking about it and I know Dolan is involved somehow, but how, or maybe Noel his son is the link, but now he's also dead.'

'Look' said DCI Arnold 'we have to find this woman, she is obviously the key. So did she murder these two men or did she have an accomplice? There has to be a reason, let's face it, there's one in France and one in London. Harry Dolan is connected to the murders he must be in some way. Yet he has lost his own son, this doesn't make any sense. You say this Duvall chap was also suspected of being a hit man. Well if that's the case maybe Harry employed him for a job. And perhaps you're right about this family in Alicante but the report as far as I know is that they were killed in a fire.'

'Sir I have a gut feeling Harry Dolan knows all about this but how do we get him to open up about it because this goes a little deeper, he's in this up to his grubby neck.'

'Bailey, the dead man and his family in Spain were Thomas Lambert, his wife Laura and his two sons and daughter and they used to own the Black Swan. Now the funny thing is, which has just occurred to me, it was just the sort of place that Harry Dolan would like to get his hands on, and after all he has businesses very near the pub.... the Lone Star and the betting offices. Also Harry and Noel were within walking distance from the pub. But surely you can't kill someone for not selling a pub to them can you? Maybe he employed the French man to kill them for some reason.'

'Well sir,' said Bailey. 'I bet it's not the first time he's used a hit man. Just take a look at all the people who have suddenly gone missing over the years. Now this mystery woman has suddenly vanished too. I'm willing to bet Harry Dolan is somehow behind all this and yet his son was murdered. Perhaps something went terribly wrong.'

Alex and Jason turned up together at their parent's place where their mother broke down again. Alex was saying if I find out who killed my brother they are going to suffer a worse fate than Noel did.

'Well' said Jason 'we can arrange a hit once the person is found, but who did he upset this time?'

'What do you mean who did he upset this time said Alex.'

'Well come on Alex, he was always in a mood about someone. As you well know he had a bad temper, he always had it in for someone. He did screw up that young Polish girls face not that long ago. Have you conveniently forgotten that balls up? Maybe it was a revenge job?'

'Jason who's fucking side are you on then? He was our brother. Try to remember all the Dolan family at the funeral are going to be asking awkward stupid questions. What are we, clueless idiots? We have to find out who killed him because the police are not going to bother are they? Let's face it Jason, all of them hate us, always have done over the years, because they can't pin anything on us they'll not lift a finger.'

'Hey you two don't start to argue' said Harry. 'Noel wouldn't have wanted us to do that so come on, let's have a drink to his memory.'

'Yes and you too mother' said Alex, he whispered in her ear 'I will find this person mum and so help me God I will destroy them.'

Harry poured all of them a large whiskey and said 'to Noel' they empted their glasses in one.

'This will be a full gypsy funeral. We had better get the booze organized boys.' The funeral was arranged for burial at the Epsom & Ewell cemetery. The Dolans had already booked and paid for 24 burial plots many years before. The funeral would be held at 1pm, there would be a horse drawn black carriage with two black stallions with all the red and white frills. There would in all probability be about a thousand family members and friends, maybe even more attending. The wake would be held at the Epsom racecourse function suite and it would be a day to remember. Gypsy funerals are something to behold and are normally attended by several families. It can also be a place where many an argument and old scores can be settled with fists and if there is no punch up then it's sometimes deemed a failure. A gypsy funeral should be talked about for months afterwards, and even years everyone has to dress up and to arrive in great style if money will allow. It was good to see various Rolls Royce's, Bentleys, Porches, they were just the norm. All who attended had to wear as much jewellery as possible, it was all about respect and without respect you're nobody. There was the old, but beautifully preserved Dolan family Caravan pulled by a brown and white cob which was beautifully decked out in flowers. The caravan was about a hundred years old maybe more, the wheels were red and yellow, same red as the body of the caravan and the roof was a dark green with another horse following behind as a spare.

This funeral was a large event as the Dolans were a well respected but feared family. The day went well with the normal drinking, fighting, horse trading and gold dealing going on.

There must have been about 1200 people there and the whole event was handled with care and sympathy. As the main spokesman Harry's cousin Gerald said, life must go on so all of you eat drink and have a good time. Now then everyone raise your glass to Noel Dolan, and his family.

Standing in the crowd there was one woman, a very attractive woman. Sarah had to be there. She wanted to see the other four people on her list, the next one Alex, then Jason, then Joan and finally Harry. Watching as the cortege slowly went by she stood back behind a tree watching through her small covert binoculars. Sarah also noted the large oak tree which was next to the freshly dug grave. Strangely it had a low strong branch which was hanging virtually over the actual grave. But this gave her an idea which would have a sort of poetic justice. She smiled as the idea came to her. To put the idea into use would be rather difficult as this man Alex was a large man. All her strength was needed and more to do away with him, but she would do it. The oak tree had a strong circular bench wrapped around the tree. The winding tarmac driveway was only two yards away, which would let a car stay for a while. There was a very old fashioned black painted street lamp by the side of the driveway.

Noticing Alex had no woman with him although there were plenty hanging around him. Sarah knew they were no contest compared to her sophistication. All of them were wearing far too much make up and were encouraged by their parents to get in with

Alex as he was a very wealthy bachelor. Most of them looked like tarts. However gypsy girls were nothing of the sort they were all mostly virgins. Sarah just wanted to catch his eye and he would see the difference in the way she was dressed. Somehow she wanted to deal with him at the grave site. It had to be when no one else was there. Having dressed in a large black hat, black dress with simple pearls and a fairly low cut neck and four inch black heels she looked beautiful. She needed to get out of the way of Harry Dolan. But she needed to attract the attention of Alex. Now she felt a little vulnerable in case Harry came over. She could see he was on the other side of the hall with his wife Joan accepting condolences from people. So she had to be very careful and to make her move quickly while Harry was busy. This would not be easy as there were so many people at the wake and Alex was talking to most of them.

However, she would leave it until later when he had spoken to most of them. But an opportunity did arise but much later, and she took it.

Alex Dolan was slightly drunk but not too much, he never ever got drunk. It was sometimes a sign of weakness his father had told him many times. 'Look' he said 'you have to get the other man or woman drunk but not yourself.'

The afternoon was now drawing to an end and it would soon be early evening. People were now starting to leave and he'd ordered a double whiskey. As he stood at the bar the rest of his mates were pissed or sitting down with the women in their lives. Standing there waiting for his drink a woman dressed in black was sat at the table opposite him. Elegantly, she emptied her glass. But he watched her with curiosity. Alex hadn't seen her before. Now she smiled at him as she put her glass down. Noticing she was on her own he walked up to her and asked her if he could get her a drink.

'Oh I was just about to get myself one, yes that would be nice thank you, a whiskey and soda would be good, an Irish please, that's very thoughtful of you. My name is Christine, and you are?'

'Hi my name is Alex, Alex Dolan and today we have buried my brother. He was only 36; it was such a sad waste of a life. No one should die that young, no one.'

'I'm so sorry to hear that Alex. How did he die, was it sudden, was it expected, you're so right it's such a waste of a young life.'

'His name was Noel and we think he was murdered.'

'Murdered? Really how terrible for you. But how come he was murdered. Are you certain? What are the police doing about it?'

'We found him hanging from parapet of his roof terrace. It seemed somebody had doped him first. What a cowardly thing to do, to drug someone first. They found a syringe with a drug in called Ketamine, it was to make him sleep. As for the police they don't give a damn.'

'Alex, did Noel upset anyone? Was he depressed or maybe was this some sort of revenge attack?'

'We don't know, but we do know he would never have killed himself in this way.'

Harry Dolan was a man who missed nothing and neither did his wife Joan who was still in tears. She dabbed at her damp eyes then commented on the woman that Alex was talking to, 'who is she Harry? Go and find out.'

'I don't know as yet but she seems to be familiar said Harry. 'I can't say I know her. She seems to be on her own and Alex is making a play for her by the looks of it. I was going to go over but then I may put my foot in it. Anyway he seems to be doing okay by himself' he laughed. It was then he had an odd feeling about her, something wasn't right, it just seemed that she was not the type Alex usually went for. He could plainly see he was playing up to her, he would defiantly find out about her later.

'Anyway Christine' said Alex 'let's not talk about Noel's death. Why are you here today and what's your connection with us gypsies? I have to say you do look very attractive. What is it you do can I ask, and where is your man? You surely can't be on your own, a nice looking lady like you.'

'Well Alex, I'm afraid I am, my husband died two years ago. I'm now unfortunately on my own. The reason I'm here, and you have to promise me you will keep this quiet about what I do or I will be asked a lot of questions.'

'Ok I promise not to tell anyone, but now I'm curious' replied Alex.

'Look Alex, the reason is, I'm a writer and I am writing a book about a gypsy family which I can't talk about yet, it's bad luck to do so. Look don't worry it's a work of fiction. I do need to get some simple information. I took the opportunity to take a firsthand look at the goings on at a gypsy funeral. I need to speak with someone who is connected maybe it can be you.'

Crossing her long legs she managed to show a glimpse of her lacy stocking top. And it didn't go unnoticed by Alex; he'd already had a crafty look at her generous breasts and noticed the flirty way she was behaving.

'Christine you're not attached to anyone. I mean you have no man here looking after you. Look there are some rascals here looking for the odd woman or two, you do have to be careful.'

'Really well I never. I shall have to get me an escort to see me to my car then. So can you recommend anyone for me Alex?'

'You could do worse than to allow me to escort you to your car young lady, if permitted of course.'

'Thank you Alex, look as I said I am writing about a gypsy family. I needed to see this funeral for myself as you don't get the chance very often. Can I ask you something Alex?'

'Certainly ask away.'

'I would like to take some pictures with my camera of the cemetery when everyone has gone so I can get the atmosphere right. Now would you be so kind as to meet me here. Let's say the day after tomorrow, because tomorrow I have an appointment with my publisher. If we say at 7pm when it will be quiet, we will have the place to ourselves but please keep this between you and me.'

'Ok where shall we meet?'

'Let's meet on the bench, the one wrapped around the tree next to Noel's grave. Then you will see my car it's a black Range Rover. Look if you can't that's okay maybe some other time. I just want to capture the moment to get the atmosphere right and have someone with me as it's a little creepy on my own Alex. Will that be okay for you?'

'Ok, of course it will. Christine, I'll see you the day after tomorrow at 7pm. I'll help you all I can, I have to go now and mingle some more.'

When Alex had returned home he had a call from his father Harry. Alex 'that woman who you were talking to at the funeral who is she?'
Alex told him the story so far and why he would be meeting her again. She was a writer and needed some good advice. So maybe he could help with her research. He was going to meet her again in a couple of nights.

'I've seen her before somewhere Alex I'm sure of it. What does she do again?'

'A writer Dad, she's a writer. That's what she told me.'

'Well I would like to take a closer look at her if you don't mind Alex. But there is something not quite right about what you have told me. Noel was with a woman with a similar description. The one who worked for him called Gloria and now she's gone missing. Alex, this could be her. I have a bad feeling about this woman. Are you meeting her again? Maybe I can also help her with questions regarding her research.'

Alex had been asked by Sarah for his thoughts on a gypsy funeral. She wanted to know how it was all organized. She needed to know for her new book, she needed him to be there with no one else around. But just the two of them and then perhaps they could have a meal afterwards and she would pay. She told him he could name the restaurant. She also needed someone to sit with her as it was a spooky place on your own. Especially being a woman he readily agreed to be there. Sarah had rented a black Range Rover with a tow bar which had a winch. She had also switched the number plates of another Range Rover. Inside the back of the Rover there was a rope with a noose at the end of it. Now that had to be done before she was seen by anyone else.

There was a screw top bottle of Shiraz and two glasses with two spare in case of breakages packed into a picnic case from Fortnum & Mason. At 10am two days later she had returned to the cemetery and parked besides the oak tree with some flowers in case anyone noticed her. She quickly measured out the distance to the tree and its overhanging branch from the driveway picking her spot perfectly. Later on she changed into a pair of jeans and a dark top with trainers. There was some hard work to do.

Now she was filling her small syringe with Ketamine, and the eye drop bottle was filled with Rohypnol, everything was going to plan. Alex had to mingle at the wake so she told him to meet her there at 7pm. Alex was hooked on the line and tonight she would add another Dolan to her list. It would be the turn of Jason Dolan next. He worried her as he was the quiet one. As yet she hadn't found out much about him, but she would, she always did her homework because it was so vital.

Alex thought to himself this woman was a bit of all right he might get lucky tonight. The restaurant they would eat in was the Woodpecker Inn about five minutes away from the cemetery. Booking a table for 8.30pm he also booked a double bedroom. The table was the one in the corner out of the way. A writer is she, he thought, well that's certainly different and he was looking forward to it. Now he looked at his watch, the time read 5.05pm. Harry wanted to come to meet her. Alex said 'no he would sort it himself and he didn't need a chaperone with him.'

Sarah arrived next to the tree at 6.00pm. She stepped out with a bunch of flowers and looked around the cemetery. The night was still and no one was around. Opening the back of the Range Rover she arranged the rope for easy access. She would need to be quick. Realising he would be trying it on she would go along with it. Now the small syringe full of Ketamine was in her pocket in a tube to stop it from breaking. In the other pocket was the Rohypnol in the eye drop bottle. She also had the picnic basket on the circular seat it was open and ready to go. All she had to do was sit and wait, she didn't have to wait long as the time was now 6.47pm. Seeing his car a dark blue Porsche slowly driving towards her she became a little tense, because as it approached she saw a movement in the passenger seat. There were two men in the car, one was Alex and the other was Harry? He'd persuaded Alex he should be there.

Alex pulled up and they both got out of the car. But she knew she was going to be caught.

Harry walked towards her he said 'writer are we? Christine is it? Right you bitch what's your real name and don't you make a move. Because we're going to teach you a lesson you murdering bitch. You killed my son now you're going to have the same done to you.'

Alex quickly took a look in the back of the Range Rover and shouted 'dad the bitch has a rope with a noose at the end of it in her Range Rover.'

Harry shouted out 'bring it here she's going to be wearing it tonight.' Now he foolishly walked up close to Sarah. Harry Attempted to grab her round the neck. But she quickly stepped back which for a second unbalanced him. She grabbed his left wrist with her right hand pulling it down hard. At the same time she grabbed his right hand with her left hand and pushed up his wrist twisting it underneath to his right but really hard which almost broke his wrist.

Harry screamed and looked stunned. Sarah was quick, and yet so strong she half twisted, letting go of his left wrist she drove the point of right elbow hard into his throat. Now he stood there holding his throat making a choking noise and his eyes filled with water from his tears.

She moved in so close she could smell his whiskey breath. Quickly kneeing him hard in his balls; they felt like a bag of jelly. As he fell back she quickly moved forward and chopped him another vicious hard blow to his throat. By now Alex was almost upon her. Standing up straight she let him come on to her. Then as he was almost on her she dropped onto her right knee and struck him hard in his balls with her right fist. Alex bent down and grabbed her hair hard at first, and then he laughed because he felt nothing. Pulling her up to punch her he suddenly stopped and relaxed his grip because a terrible ache began in his lower stomach. Stopping now he held his punched balls, there was an agonising sickening feeling in his stomach.

Sarah stood up and now using both her hands chopped him hard in both ears with the flat of her hands (the heel of the palm,) he heard a terrible bang inside his large head. And then she chopped him twice more but viciously hard in his throat but now he had a job to breathe.

Quickly she took out the syringe and rammed it into the left side of his neck where it was embedded up to the hilt. But now he was trying to get his breath. She poked him viciously hard in his left eye with her thumb. Alex let a loud yell as he was now in a world of pain. Now he was half bent up trying to breathe whilst also trying to see. There was an awareness of something in his neck and he very quickly started to feel a little unsteady.

Taking the rope, Sarah placed the noose end around his neck pulling it tight. And then she quickly used garden ties to secure his large arms behind him by his wrists then doing the same to Harry, also secured their legs as well. Holding both men's noses she tipped the Rohypnol down Alex's mouth doing the same to Harry still holding their noses as they tried to breathe some air. Both had to swallow.

Alex was now choking, she was satisfied he had swallowed a large enough amount and for good measure she chopped him really hard once again so hard this time she broke his windpipe.

Alex was now confused and in a lot of pain, he became disorientated then semi conscious.

Harry Dolan was now secured by the wrists so were his ankles. But he too had swallowed a dose of the drug Rohypnol.

Sarah threw the end of the rope which had a weight attached to it over the old branch twice, which hung over Noels grave. Now grabbing the end she secured it around a lamp post at its base twice. Next to the tarmac stood the Range Rover with its tow bar and the winch. Switching on the winch Alex was slowly being dragged along the ground until he lay on his brother's grave amongst all the flowers just under the old oak tree branch. Sarah stopped the winch to talk with him.

Alex was vaguely aware of what was going on, he tried to speak. Sarah went over to him and said 'you're Dolan number two and your other brother is next and then your mother and finally your father. Remember your father had my family murdered all five of them. So now I will kill all five of you, and with you gone that leaves three more so I'm executing all of you. Goodbye Alex'

She walked back to her Range Rover, switched the winch back on but very slowly she wanted to see justice.

Alex was hoisted up and struggled hard but with the drugs he didn't manage to struggle much for too long. Now he was swinging from the branch over his brother's grave. Making another futile attempt at wriggling it was no use while the branch above him started to bow a little more. The branch creaked loud in protest at the seventeen stone weight but it held. There were a lot of leaves that had fallen down over his brother's grave. Sarah thought it was poetic justice to see the two brothers now very dead and the father unable to do anything about it.

The rope was now secured tightly around the old lamp post base making it secure. She did it a few more times round the base standing next to the driveway. Stuffing the flowers she bought down the front of Alex's trousers as he gently swung in the breeze, gave her some satisfaction. The flowers had a card which said, rest in peace.

Walking up to Harry Dolan, she managed to prop him up against an old gravestone she whispered, 'for now you live, but I am coming for you very soon. There is no hiding place, because I'm the dead man's sister.' Looking back at Alex, he was no longer struggling because he was dead.

Harry was trying to focus but the drug had a serious effect on him, he felt useless.

It was now beginning to get dark; there was the sound of an old owl hooting and a few fruit bats flying about. Now the moon was starting to make an appearance. It was a crescent moon which started to come into view....a few stars had now begun to sparkle and there was a slight chill in the air.

The grass was now feeling a little damp. Suddenly the old street lamp which was by the driveway made a clicking noise as it slowly came on giving out a sort of waxy yellowish glow.

Now satisfied, Sarah took the car keys from Alex and his mobile phone with a lot of numbers which perhaps could be useful. She took Harry's mobile as well. She took a look around the area where she had been, but making sure she left no clues. Then looking back she saw Harry was out of it. She wanted him when he came round to see and feel Alex. So she cut his wrist ties and also his ankle ties. Satisfied she got into her Range Rover. Switching on the engine she headed out of the cemetery for home. She would change the number plates which were held on with Velcro straps back to the originals. But the whole time she had worn strong surgical gloves.

Harry was unable to understand what had happened but he soon would do. When he finally became compos mentis he saw in the waxy light from the street lamp his son Alex, gently swinging from the old oak tree. But he was now very dead swinging slowly in the chill night air over the grave of his son Noel. He screamed out, a loud animal like scream. Now he could see the bloated face of Alex in the soft yellow light, his tongue was hanging down from his mouth and his eyes had burst. Holding on to Alex by his feet he hugged them for the last time. But his body was cold, so very cold and now Harry was howling like a wounded dog. The time was now 3.57am.

Opening Alex's car door he found no keys as they had been taken. His mobile phone was missing along with his sons. Seeing a faint light about half a mile away he realised it belonged to the caretaker's cottage. He could see it was built next to the driveway to the cemetery. He started to walk but slowly as he was still confused. As he got nearer the light became brighter the outside light was on over the caretaker's cottage door. Now he was banging on the caretaker's door really hard until the lights from the open doorway and hallway lit up the gloom.

'For God sake, whatever do you want at this time man. The time is only 4.23 in the morning' said Mr Logan the caretaker.

'Just get the police will you, please phone them now. My son has been murdered, please phone this number.' It was DCI Arnold's mobile phone number. Harry pushed Mr Logan aside as he had seen a phone on the small table in the hallway.

'Hey you can't do that, this is breaking and entering' shouted Mr Logan.

'Well tell it to the police who I'm ringing now you idiot, hello DCI Arnold?'

'Yes who is this at this time of the morning?' By now Mrs Logan had come from her bed to see what all the noise was about.

'Harry say that again, your son Alex has been hung....where.... the cemetery....stay where you are, we are on our way.' DCI Arnold rang his sergeant. 'Trevor get your arse out of bed and get to the helipad. There has been a murder, another hanging, this time its Alex Dolan and he's been found hanged from a tree branch over the grave of his brother Noel.'

'What?'

By the time he had got to the helipad the helicopter was waiting with the rotor blades spinning and DCI Arnold was already there, 'good morning sir this is weird, so who the hell is doing this?'

Joan Dolan, Harry's wife had tried ringing him but Sarah after harvesting all the information and numbers from the two mobile phones had turned off their phones. Now she had Jason's phone number and some details, such as his email address and actual address. She also had Harry's email address, this will come in handy she thought, and maybe she could use it. On Alex's phone there was the address of their villa in Marbella and also the phone number. By now Sarah was well gone she was now planning to finish off Jason, he would be the next port of call.

CHAPTER SIXTEEN

Jason had a phone call from his father, 'Jason I want you to go to Spain, go to the Villa, no one knows where it is. Remember son don't say anything to anyone. Get the first flight available.'
'What, how come Dad, what's happened.'
'It's Alex, he's been found hanged over the grave of Noel so if they can get to him they will get to you son and we think you're next on the list. Well we know you are, so don't argue just go. We haven't the time to talk about it so just go please. And don't worry about the business we will take care of that, please son don't argue, do it now this minute. I don't want to lose you as well son. But listen you have to beware of a strange attractive woman about 5ft 8in tall that may approach you, we know it's a woman, I saw her.'
'Dad I have things to do I can't just get up and go.'
'Yes you can and you will, even if I have to put you on a plane myself.' Son I really can't talk at this moment in time about Alex you have to go like NOW. Harry knew she would come after Jason even though he was gay, not many people knew, but Harry always knew so did his mum Joan. It was a well kept secret, gypsies don't like gays. She wouldn't find him in Spain.

Jason caught the flight to Malaga near Marbella at 3.15pm the same day. He didn't even pack a bag just hand luggage. There were already some clothes in his room in the villa in Marbella. He rang no one, but he did have a few friends in Marbella and he knew the clubs and bars really well. He did take his laptop with him. Arriving at the villa at 6.47pm, Jason emailed his father and said that all was well and how long did he have to stay in the villa for.

Harry emailed him back. 'For at least a month son until we can clear all this up, the police are on to it and now we have a sighting. We will get her, but I hope I can get to her first.'

Jason checked his clothes situation, he needed some more clothes and he also had to eat. Obviously there was no food in the fridge so he made his way to Manuel's restaurant and bar. Which was just a short walk from the villa he ordered an Argentinean steak with a salad and a bottle of the house red.

He didn't like the idea of being here for a month on his own, but he did know some people and he couldn't go to a club looking the way he did. Clothes were the order of the day starting tomorrow and he would get the Jeep started which they kept in the garage at the villa. It was an American Jeep. They had it maintained on a regular basis, the same as the gardens and the pool.

The property was maintained by a family who had looked after it for years, the same as the other villas in the area. There was also a golf course within a mile and although he was no golfer, he did feel safe. This whole thing was a nightmare and why would someone kill his brothers, and why would they come for him? He thought his dad had done something bad. Now he was not saying what it was, because he couldn't think of anything he had done. However, what his brothers did was a mystery and he didn't move in the same circles as them. Jason simply didn't believe he was going to be killed.

Sarah rang Jason's home. He lived on the mobile home site, but no one answered so she tried his mobile, again no one answered the phone. She had an idea he had gone. But she knew where he would probably go. Spain because she knew Harry had a villa there, it wasn't rocket science. Jason was a seemingly nice man who had never really been in trouble with the police. Yet mostly he kept himself out of London and all the usual places that his brothers went to. For years he managed to keep the fact he was gay to himself as his brothers would go ballistic if they found out. But he was sure his mum and dad had some idea, but nothing was ever said by them as far as he was aware?

CHAPTER SEVENTEEN

DCI Reggie Arnold and DS Trevor Bailey were quickly dropped off by the police helicopter in the field next to the well kept cemetery. They were met by the local police and the caretaker Mr Logan who took them to the grave of Noel Dolan and there was Alex strung up by the neck. It was not a pretty sight. But already a crow was sat on his shoulder looking at his face. DS Bailey shooed the large bird away. DCI Arnold had told the local police officers to tape the area off and to let no one in, only funerals that were arranged. 'Luckily there were none for that day,' said Mr Logan.

DS Bailey asked Mr Logan if he had seen or heard anything or did anything unusual happen apart from the obvious. And was there any unusual activity at all?

'No nothing at all, everything was normal until early this morning when this man Mr Dolan started banging on our door.' Harry was sitting on a bench drinking a cup of sweet tea made by Mrs Logan. He was holding his head in his hand looking spaced out. Now looking a lonely pathetic figure but he didn't look so dangerous anymore thought DS Bailey.

DCI Arnold called Bailey over. 'So what do you make of this Trevor. Look it's obviously the same person who's been doing this, so what's this now, three so far and I don't think they are going to stop now. By the way, don't feel sorry for Dolan. He looks down and out but trust me he's now a wounded animal, which makes him a very dangerous one.'

'Sir, Dolan has another son Jason. But now he has to be warned he may be on some sort of murder list. He needs to disappear for a while until we find this mad person.'

'Oh, and one thing Bailey this person is not mad, but very clever and cunning.'

Harry Dolan was shattered, he felt destroyed. He'd now lost two more sons; he told DCI Arnold what happened he told them. 'I can't believe what happened, it was a woman on her own, a woman with an American accent and she beat both of us up. She was some sort of un-armed combat expert. Look she took out my son and look at the size of him and then she hammered me. Christ a bloody woman. I can't believe it. A woman did this to us. So who the hell is she?'

DS Bailey asked him for a description.

'She was about 5ft 8 to 5ft10 inches tall, attractive very sexy, wearing blue jeans with a dark top and trainers weighing about 10 stone. Maybe she was a little lighter but she was fast, very fast. She was driving a black Range Rover. In fact she was the same woman Noel had employed at the club. Yes the very same woman he was certain of that. That bloody woman beat us up,' but he could not believe a woman could do that. 'Hey look at the state of my neck. So what sort of a woman would do this, some bitch she is' replied Harry after giving them his description of Sarah.

DCI Arnold thought Dolan was rambling and not making a lot of sense, it was the drugs. On and on he kept saying it was the dead man's sister.

DS Bailey saw the bruises on his neck to confirm his story.

DCI Arnold also found it hard to believe a woman on her own could have done this to a man the size of Alex, yet even Harry was not small. She had expertly wound the nylon rope around the bottom of the lamp post. Still how the hell had she hoisted Alex so high off the ground?

After they very carefully inspected the area around the murder scene, DCI Arnold noticed some car tyre skid marks on the grass verge. Realising she had used the Range Rover to hoist Alex into the air and using the back of the Range Rover which probably had a tow bar and a winch at the back of it. Then when he was high enough she simply untied the rope and wound the rope some more around the lamp post where it was held firmly in place and tied with a knot at the base of the lamp post. That was a clever shrewd move. This woman was something else.

DS Bailey wanted to know why was this woman was killing these people, there had to be a reason, good or bad they wanted desperately to find out. They asked Harry again what did he know about her and had he done anything to upset anyone. Which in hindsight was a stupid question, there must be queue a mile long of people who he'd harmed in the past.

DCI Arnold told DS Bailey as a long shot we have to go and find out about the London family that were burnt to death in Spain. They all seemed to be linked as they were all in the same area together at the same time as the dead Frenchman was in Spain. Let's see if there was any connection with Harry and the dead family. The fire may have had something to do with Harry because he met the Frenchman in Bristol. Two days later the family were dead. Dolan had been in touch straight after with the Frenchman who apparently worked as a hit man. There was no proof of that but that was the information given by the French police.

'I'll go round to the Black Swan pub and ask about Harry. So maybe they can help us with our enquiries sir.' Said DS Bailey,

'Yes' said DCI Arnold, 'its best we check it out. The French police also found a secret bank account apparently belonging to this Eric Bezier. On the day he met Harry there was a deposit of £40,000 between the time he met Harry and the time he left. Four days later there was a further £35,000 making £75,000. All deposited in that same week as the Lambert family were burnt to death. Now it sounds to me like a payment for a hit and I reckon it was Harry.'

DS Bailey told DCI Arnold he had found out that the dead family who were burned to death in Spain used to own the Black Swan in Soho London. DS Bailey had now seen the new landlord and asked him 'if he knew anything about the fire in Spain.' The landlord told him yes 'he did because he owned the villa which was burned down. Tom and his family had the villa for a month free of charge because they helped them move into the pub with no hassle.' Norman McDonald also told DS Bailey about the dispute between Tom Lambert and Harry Dolan as Dolan wanted to buy the pub but Tom Lambert threw his offer out. Dolan was unable to purchase the pub.

'This is the connection we have been looking for Trevor. Well done.'

'And sir, listen to this he also mentioned Tom Lambert had a sister called Sarah who came round asking the same questions and when he asked the landlord to give a description of the dead man's sister she fitted the description perfectly. That was apart from her short blonde hair, including the American accent of the missing woman called Gloria. Now this was all starting to fit into place. Yet it seemed that if Harry had for some reason ordered a hit on Tom Lambert's family then the sister finding out the truth would in all probability now be after him for killing her family. Farfetched it may seem, but he would find out who she was and where she had been.'

What he found out shocked him. Then he realised how good Sarah was in a tight situation. He thought she could have easily been wearing a wig, because being blonde was not mentioned by anyone else.

DCI Arnold had the forensic guys round but he knew there would be nothing to find. Because this killing like the rest was well planned and professionally carried out. However, he found it hard to see how a woman could have committed these murders. Alex Dolan was a big strong man, an ex knuckle fighter. Weighing about sixteen or even seventeen stone, how could a woman hang him from a tree on her own like that because it just beggared belief? If it was this woman on her own she couldn't have weighed more than ten stone? What the hell was going on, it didn't make any sense at all.

When they finally let Alex down there was a small syringe which again was imbedded in his neck, everything fitted the same as the other murders, that was the only thing that forensic could come up with. The murderer left no DNA or any significant trail. This was done by a true professional.

After enquiries, DS Bailey found out that Sarah Lambert had moved to America when she was just eighteen years of age because she married an American air force policeman called Kenny Santana. They moved to New York and later she became a police officer in the NYPD. She was head hunted by the FBI and moved to the FBI. Apparently she was highly thought of but she also fitted the description of the woman wanted in France and now here. But where had she gone?

Her name was Sarah Santana. There were flight details of Sarah landing at Heathrow then she apparently caught a connecting flight to Alicante Spain. They had to find out where she had gone.DS Bailey had a strong feeling she was one canny woman and they would have one hell of a job to find out who she really was. But from other experienced police officers he was told he would get no help from the Americans, they always kept their cards close to their chests.

DS Bailey contacted her office at the FBI where she was moved to. He was told she was on extended leave believed to be somewhere in upstate New York or even further. As she was on leave it was her prerogative go wherever she wanted to go. She had also left specific instructions not to be contacted. She just wanted to be alone to collect her thoughts about what she was now going to do with her life. But no one could verify where she had gone, at this moment in time she was a free agent and free to come and go wherever she wanted to go. Apart from that, they couldn't or wouldn't offer any more information. Sarah was a highly thought of member of the FBI. All they did was give the barest of details about her and could not help any more as they did not wish to contact her because she needed time to come to terms with her grief. It was best she was left alone to decide what she wanted to do with her life, apart from that they could not help any further.

Sarah thought to herself, Jason has gone to Spain, that's good she had him all to herself now. After all she now had the details of Harry's villa in Marbella and Jason had gone AWOL. She thought she had better get to Spain to check this out. Only this time she would be Nadia Aslam, a Muslim woman. She had the passport which the FBI had previously arranged for her on a covert job back in Orlando America, and it was still in use for the next eight years.

She had the Hijab and the Burkah and other clothes a Muslim woman would wear. Who would be looking for a Muslim woman? But she was now more than a little concerned the police had started to take an interest in her and it was obvious they would be checking out the airports and ports. Thinking back she had made a mistake by going to the Black Swan and giving her real name which was obviously checked on. But she wanted to kill Jason quickly and then get to Joan and then of course Harry Dolan. Now that was her prize and her end game. He was the bull's eye!

DCI Reggie Arnold and DS Trevor Bailey called round to Harry Dolan's apartment in Knightsbridge. Speaking to Harry he told him 'it would be a good idea to move Jason away to somewhere safe and that would also help the police.'

'No need to worry on that one, he's been moved to Spain to a Villa and you're the only one who knows this. Even Joan doesn't know and she's in a right state about all of this, she's been sedated and can't get out of bed. Mind you Inspector she's useless anyway and too fat to move. Maybe it's best she stays in her bed out of the way, she gets on my nerves at the best of times.'

'Look we realise your upset Mr Dolan and we're very sorry for you,' said DCI Arnold.

'Inspector Arnold, we have lost two sons we are not going to lose a third one. What are you doing about it? You're bloody useless and so is your daft sergeant standing next to you. Look at him, he's a right plank. I bet he couldn't find his own arse in the dark. I can't sleep, the Doctor has put me on these tablets to stop me becoming depressed and now I feel so hyper I want to kill someone. I want them to suffer, to die, it was that bitch.... she said to me I'm the dead man's sister and she's coming back for me. Why don't you go and find her, she must be out there having a right laugh. Why can't you find her, the pair of you should wake up.'

DCI Arnold asked him to give him the address of the Villa in Spain because she may also have the address.

Harry looked at him as though he was mad, saying, 'give you two planks the address? Are you fucking serious, you must be both insane, you lot can't keep your traps shut, so the less people know about it the better.' Harry flopped into his chair and promptly fell asleep, it was the tablets.

There was a middle age nurse hovering about who was paid to sit in with the Dolans and dish out the tablets. Her name was Beryl and she was also there to keep watch, because it was also a suicide watch until her replacement arrived. Now she looked at her watch and saw she still had three hours to wait. She said. 'look officers, he's out for at least two to three hours, he's just had a sedative tablet and he's not his normal self so you had better go as he's not going to wake up now.' All she had to do was watch the TV; there was nothing else she could do. She was bored out of her mind but the money was better than working on some awful hospital ward, so she made herself comfortable and read her book. The telly was rubbish again, it always was in the daytime, she looked at her watch maybe she could snooze a while.

DCI Arnold and DS Bailey went to let themselves out but the housekeeper opened the door then she closed the door quickly behind them.

However, they both felt sorry for the Dolans for losing two sons, but it was beginning to make sense the reason why now. Perhaps it was Sarah Santana who was doing the killings. But then after all she had been trained by the FBI in all sorts of tactics and she could use herself if the need arose. She certainly did when she single handed battered Harry and his big son Alex.

Wondering where she had gone DCI Arnold was sure she was using another alias. He was certain of that and there was no use asking the FBI again, they were a law unto themselves. They looked after their own as they were doing so now, that wasn't hard to work out.

In a few pubs in Soho there were some people who were glad to see the back of the Dolan brothers though Jason was not that well known. But Alex was a cruel bully. The betting shops suddenly seemed a little brighter. To a lot of punters the news was brilliant because Noel was an evil man who liked to hurt girls or have anyone hurt who got in his way. The Lone Star Club had a far better atmosphere now he was dead, in other words they would be no loss to the human race, and life goes on, only this time much better than before.

DCI Arnold had all the airports, the ports and all the usual stuff checked out twenty four hours a day until he said stop. Yet so far Sarah had not been seen. And as for the Range rover there were thousands in and around London. Plus half the gypsy families alone owned one.

He knew that was going down a blind alley. Now he tried to put himself in Sarah's shoes, what would she do? She would go after Jason and kill him the same because if it was correct that Harry had her family killed.

She would also make him suffer by taking out the three sons, and then his wife and then finally Harry. He was absolutely positive about this. The address of this Villa where Jason was staying was becoming elusive to find but Harry would not budge there was no way he would tell the police where it was. Obviously it was bought with illegal earnings.

DCI Arnold thought, there again Harrys villa could be anywhere in Spain. But he reckoned the kids would not have liked to be out in the Spanish sticks. So no it would be in a popular resort, probably Marbella as a lot of English criminals lived out there. He figured it would be in that area, he figured right. If Sarah Santana had got hold of this address in Spain then Jason would be in a very dangerous position. Back here in the UK the police could give him protection, in Spain he was very much on his own, he was a vulnerable young lad and in a place on his own. He thought that was a very stupid move by Harry Dolan.

CHAPTER EIGHTEEN

Jason had woken up in high spirits he was going shopping and tonight he would go down to the gay club called Sisters. He had been there many times and he knew a few of the local gays and you could get a decent meal in there. At one time you used to be able to. The music was always good and it was also a friendly place. In Marbella there are some amazing shops, bars and restaurants, already after an hour he had spoken to three people he knew. All of them were all chatty they all said the Sisters club had new management and it was better than ever, and the DJ was gorgeous.

Now the holiday season was almost in full swing there was a mood of excitement in the air. Everyone seemed to be laughing and smiling and it was great to be back. Jason hadn't been here for the last two years. He had bought some clothes, shirts, T shirts, trainers, flip flops and trousers plus two pairs of jeans and some underwear, a new shaving kit, also a new wash bag, he was ready to party.

John-Slinky-Peters had not seen Jason for a couple of years. Now there he was leaning against the bar at Sisters chatting to the barman George, when in walked Jason wearing a new pair of black skinny jeans and a white T Shirt with a large gold chain. He had his man bag with him and he was now into the part of the gay swinger. John Peters was called slinky because that's the way he walked, slinky.

'JASON you old tart,' shouted out Slinky Peters 'where the hell have you been, we all thought you had died,' he laughed.

'Slinky, OMG are you still around I heard you were in Japan in Jail. How did you get out or was this all bullshit. But you look a lot younger than the last time I saw you. What's the story come on tell me.'

'Well, first let's get the drinks in I'll tell you all about it. I did have a spot of bother. You know those Japs are a mistrustful lot. I was going out with this Jap business man, who was well minted, or at least that's what the liar told me, but when we arrived at his apartment it was a slum.'

'Slinky your outrages,' laughed Jason.

'Listen, it was virtually made from cardboard and paper, you could even hear the next door neighbours cat fart I kid you not. Later some of his friends came round and they all tried to bang me so I had to fight my way out. I just went through the cardboard walls and ran off. I had no idea where I was but I left my passport, wallet and other things in my bag at his place so I was arrested for assault and they kept my passport until it was all sorted out.'

'So how did you get away, did they arrest you, were you in a jail or what Slinks, tell me you Tart.'

'Yes I was in a cell because I couldn't afford a hotel, have you any idea how much a hotel cost. I used the police cell as my home until it all got sorted out. And then after three weeks they gave me back my things and let me go as long as I never returned to Japan...yeah right, as if I would.'

'Slinky you were always a loose cannon' laughed Jason 'anyway it's good to see you.'

'Same here too Jason, he hugged Jason and kissed him. 'Look would you like another drink, it's not cheap in here, well the drinks aren't' he laughed 'it's the clients that are cheap in here dear' he laughed.

Jason told him about his two brothers who had been murdered. And that everyone thought a woman was doing it, but no one knew why or who. It was crazy, his two brothers are dead and it hurts.

Slinky held him in a tight hug and said 'look darling you are amongst friends good friends now and we will look out for you, so don't you worry anymore my love. It doesn't sound like a woman could do this though.'

'I know this sounds farfetched Slinky. Apparently it was a woman. My dad reckons she's after me and I haven't a clue who she is or what she looks like. I need to be beware of a tall attractive woman who apparently is the killer. This place Marbella is full of attractive women all year long. It's crazy I have never hurt anybody at all in my entire life. To be honest Slinky I know this sounds really bad but in a way I'm not that bothered.

I'm sorry to say my two brothers were not nice people and I never got on that well with them. Violence was their middle name and they were cruel to everyone. Now they did have enemies and I don't have any as far as I know, none at all. I have always kept well out of the way of them.'

'Jesus Jason, we all love you, I can't think you have a bad bone in your lovely body, you're such a kind man and you would never hurt anyone, so you just relax and let's have a good time.'

Jason lifted up his glass and said 'hey lets all drink to that Slinky.'

Sarah Santana landed in Malaga and the name on her passport read Nadia Aslam. She was dressed in a black Burkah and carried a black back pack with her. She had no problem with customs.

She hired a taxi to take her into town and asked the driver to stop at a large department store. She paid him and walked into a large department store. Once inside she changed into holiday clothes in the ladies toilet but still went as Nadia Aslam. She was now dressed in blue jeans and trainers with a yellow and white striped T shirt but still had a wig on. This time it was dark with pink streaks, it gave a sort of punkish look which looked nice. She also wore thick rimmed sunglasses. Walking into the coffee lounge she checked out the street map to find out where Jason's villa was located. She quickly found it.

After giving it some thought she decided to use the name Clare Edwards again. Now the Muslim disguise would be her escape route if needed and she had an idea it would be. She also decided to hire a scooter instead of a car. Deciding instead to purchase one for cash from the classified adverts so there was no trace. It was a means of getting away quickly, and you also wore a helmet which would disguise your face.

The time was 9.35am. Slinky Peters woke up next to Jason who was still sound asleep. God his throat was so dry. He slowly sat up then carefully swung his legs over the side of the bed which was as big as a lawn and padded his wobbly way to the kitchen.

He had to have a coffee, his head was slamming around from the wine but first he took a swig from a coke bottle then punched the button on the electric kettle. When it had boiled he made enough coffee for two large mugs and checked the fridge for milk, good there was plenty. And he also noticed plenty of red wine. It was hot in the kitchen as the sun had been on the windows since early dawn so he opened the kitchen window to let in some air.

He could hear the sounds of the morning and then looking out of the window he saw a person sat on a black scooter. He could tell it was a woman. Yet even he could see what a great pair of legs she had. She appeared to be reading a map. Laughing oh well good luck with that then he thought. As it was a well known fact women couldn't read maps.

Jason had crept up behind Slinky and put his arms around his waist and kissed him on the neck saying to him 'what are you looking at Slinks?'

'Oh that woman over there, the one on the scooter, maybe she's come to see you' he laughed.

'What about her.'

'Oh I always wanted one of those scooters, I still do, and they're good to get about the town on, also cheap to run and lots of fun, so maybe soon I'll get me one.'

'Yes you're right and you're in the open air too. And don't forget they would be easy to park,' when they looked again the woman on the scooter had gone.

Sarah left her cheap Spanish hotel she had checked into under the name of Clare Edwards. Finding the Villa was a simple enough job, but by now she had seen enough and she knew that's where he was. Her intuition was right; she now had to decide how and when she was going to kill him. She wanted him to hang the same as his brothers. Stopping outside the Villa on the other side of the road and next to a small wooded area, she had seen what she needed to know.

Later that night she parked the scooter at the top of the road and managed to walk unseen through the wood where she came to the side of the road opposite Jason's Villa. The lights were on, but she waited and then at 8.33pm. Jason walked out with Slinky holding hands. She followed them but at a distance. Within ten minutes they walked into a club called Sisters. So she gave it another ten minutes and then walked in, she managed to see the pair of them now in conversation with three other gay men.

Ordering a gin and tonic at the bar she sat down to observe Jason and the man he was with, both of them were drinking red wine. She figured out he was a strong man and looked a decent man. Her family were nice and also innocent but now they had been wiped out by his father. How could she let Jason cloud her judgement? Little Helen her niece was just sixteen and a lovely little girl but she was murdered then her body burnt to a crisp, the same as the rest of her family, no he had to die and then Joan then Harry, who would be the last to die.

The five gay men were all laughing at silly things and just having a good time. Guessing the two of them would not be home until the early hours; she finished her drink and walked out. Discretely heading back to the Villa the time was now 11.45pm.

George the barman had noticed her and thought she was a lovely looking woman, with great legs too. She had asked the barman if a guy called Tony Willis had been in this evening. But he said sorry he had never heard of him. That's because he didn't exist, she gave a fictitious description of this so called man. Simply wanting to deter anyone from checking on her later, her mobile phone was a good ploy too, she held it as she walked out, it was to throw anyone off the scent if need be.

Arriving back to the Villa within ten minutes she checked it out in case of burglar alarms. There were none. It was a lovely evening as she walked round the back to see the swimming pool which was huge. The moon's reflection shone brightly in the water and it seemed so surreal. Looking up to the bedrooms she noticed that the main one with a large balcony was virtually hanging over the kidney shaped swimming pool. She guessed it was Jason's bedroom. Using all her skills she managed to easily open the back door to the utility room. Quickly she went up the stairs to find she was right about the bedroom, and the balcony was overhanging the pool. Now she decided this would be the place to do it but how?

It had to be as soon as possible as the other man could be a problem but she knew that she could handle it. She didn't want to hurt anyone not connected to her cause, and she could do without it, but then a plan began to form in her head.

The two friends were having a great time in Sisters; they all had several dances together and exchanged hilarious stories. Jason was so pleased he was a gay man, but he found women lovely too but boring as hell at sex. Having tried normal sex it did nothing for him, he knew he was a good lover but with women he just didn't feel the same. After meeting up with the other gay men they arranged to meet up the following night, where the banter was light hearted and funny. They decided they would meet for a party at the Villa but swimming trunks were not allowed.

Sarah opened the fridge door and took out the nearest bottle of red wine, there was six bottles altogether. So she unscrewed the top of one of them and tipped some wine into a glass. Pouring a large amount of Rohypnol into the bottle, she tipped the wine she had taken out down the sink. Screwing the top back on, it looked as though that bottle was already open, they would use that bottle first to pour out the wine with. That way if the two of them drank from it they would be asleep or nearly asleep and a lot easier to deal with. So she decided to go along with this, she wanted to do it quickly then get out and back to England.

Jason was laughing at Slinky who was falling about due to the drink. Jason was too as he had a lot of wine, by the time they arrived back at the villa it was 2.35am. Sarah watched them walk up the drive with their arms around each other, they stopped to kiss and walked on; they opened the door and went into the kitchen. Jason opened the fridge door and asked Slinky if he wanted a drink of red.

The voice from the toilet shouted out 'please, but make it a small one.'

'A small one, no thanks Slinky I only do large ones,' and fell about laughing the same as slinky. Jason opened the drugged bottle and poured two glasses of red.

Slinky shouted out 'take them to bed Jason. We can drink them in the bed while watching telly.'

'What am I, your servant you cheeky sod, okay I'm on my way then I'll turn the TV on. I think there's a film on Sky. Dirty Dancing I think.'

'Ha ha, we already did that early on' laughed Slinky.

'I know we did.'

'Just turn the TV on Jason.'

'Okay keep your hair on. Anyway it's on now, so hurry up you old tart.'

'Listen, you're going to be wearing that wine in a minute,' laughed slinky.

Jason was laughing as he was sitting on the bed when Slinky came into the bedroom. Jason had a glass in each hand, he gave one to Slinky and put his own by the side of the bed on the bedside table, 'well cheers' said slinky 'let's drink to the summer.' Both drank a large amount from the glass and within ten minutes both men were out for the count.

At 3pm Sarah started to make her move. Opening the back door to the utility room she crept up the stairs with a nylon rope with a noose at the end of it. As she came to the bedroom door she could see the pair of them fast asleep. Acting quickly using garden ties to secure them. She gagged Jason with a dish cloth and a torn kitchen towel was wrapped around his mouth. And then she plunged a small syringe into his neck just under the left ear which was full of Ketamine. But he never woke up and his partner was still fast asleep. Measuring out the length of rope she needed, she placed the noose over Jason's neck and pulled him to the balcony where she secured it to the bottom of the metal balcony railing. Lifting up his feet and then his legs, she took him under his arms then lifted him up to the railings. Using the top rail as a brake for the rope she let him over the balcony until he was swinging from the balcony naked. Watching him she thought well he never felt a thing, she heard him choke and then he was dead very quickly. Much too easy she thought, but he did seem as though he was a nice lad, but so was her nephews and her poor little niece. But nobody cared about them, least of all the hated Harry Dolan. How she wanted him dead it hurt to think about him.

Then she heard the moaning, she quickly went into the bedroom as Slinky seemed to be coming around. Hitting him hard on the back of his neck with the heel of her palm she knocked him out. Then she dragged him into the en-suite bathroom making sure his arms and legs were secured. Gagging him with a cloth and a kitchen towel she came out locking the door behind her, all the time she was wearing strong surgical gloves. Now she cleaned the area with bleach found in the kitchen.

Looking back at Jason she felt sorry for him as he couldn't have chosen his parents. Now he was hanging there with the moon light on his face and his body, which lit up every time he gently swung round in the light Spanish breeze. Yet he almost looked like a painting he looked so innocent he looked beautiful just like a sculpture by Michelangelo.

How could she have left him to live? Her niece, little Helen was brutally shot then her little body was burned to a crisp. She left the Villa after making sure no clues were left. The time was now 4.23am.

CHAPTER NINETEEN

At 830am that morning the pool cleaner, a British ex pat who made his living cleaning swimming pools and a little gardening arrived at the Villa, his name was John Benton. Parking his van at the back of the Villa as usual he knocked on the back door but nobody appeared to be in. Knowing it was empty most of the time, but he always knocked on the door because it was good manners. Walking round the back to the pool everything was still. Suddenly he heard some splashing. Looking around there was Jason hanging from the neck and leaking body fluid into the pool. He heard some banging which seemed to come from the bedroom above the pool. Jason was naked and slightly swinging in the morning breeze but hanging there with a gag in his mouth. Now it was obvious Jason was dead, so he rang the police. A police officer told him 'not to touch anything they would be there straight away.'

Yeah he thought he's heard that one before then they turn up hours later. Now he tried to open the back door it was locked. But he knew there was a long ladder round the back so he fetched it and propped it up against the balcony. He'd seen lots of bodies before. John was ex-army; he was in 3 Para and had seen a lot of death in the Falklands and other places. Now he could hear noise and shouting which was coming from the en-suite bathroom. Swinging his legs over the balcony he climbed over being careful not to disturb anything but he didn't know how long the police would be. So he had to help whoever was behind the locked door. 'Don't panic I'm going to let you out.' He shouted. Reaching for the key he turned it and opened the door.

Slinky was tied by his arms and his legs behind his back with garden ties and his mouth had a gag inside it. John managed to get it off. Then the police arrived with howling sirens also followed by an ambulance. Suddenly the road was filled with neighbours and passing traffic stopping in the road, and then the heavens opened up. It just poured down with such heavy rain which soon dispersed the nosey crowd of onlookers.

When it rains in Spain it just floods the roads and everything else but sometimes for only a few minutes. Yet this would make the murder scene a lot more difficult to handle. Most of the forensics had been washed away.

John Benton had to give a statement about what he saw along with Slinky who was now in hysterics shouting, 'everyone I love dies on me' he screamed out loud 'I'm cursed, you hear me, cursed.'

The ambulance medics gave him a sedative to calm him down and to try and get him to speak coherently so the police could question him. But he could not really give them a lot, as most of the time he was pissed. He could remember nothing as the drug Rohypnol was still having a bad effect on him. His head was all over the place and he could hardly remember his own name. They made him as quiet as possible until later. But then they would question him again. It was obvious it was not he who murdered Jason. After all it would be a little difficult for a man to kill someone then tie and gag himself and then lock himself in the toilet.

John Benton looked up at Jason who was now soaking wet, not that he would feel a thing. But the rain had now suddenly stopped but some of the rain was falling from his hair then running down his body until it reached his feet where it dripped onto the garden table below with a tap-tap-tapping sound.

John felt so sad a young lad like that was dead. Because it was not a pleasant way for your life to end especially as he hadn't really had a life to speak of. The rain had now stopped for a while and the sun broke free once again to light the day. Then he noticed the sun was shining on Jason's face it made him look so young and yet also so old. It reminded him of the Falkland's conflict where he had lost a few of his friends and the unspeakable acts of pure violence perpetrated by both sides. After the police had questioned him he drove home. Now he couldn't get the images of war from his mind and he needed a drink. When you have to stick your bayonet into a sixteen-year-old Argentinean conscript's eye you never forget it, it stays with you. Some of his army mates had slotted themselves a few years after that horrible, pointless war.

Sarah now returned to her hotel. She had parked the scooter in town leaving it parked next to a line of many other scooters parked up. Then she hired a taxi to take her to the hotel where she booked a flight on line and paid for it under the name of Nadia Aslam. She took a taxi to the airport and when she arrived she used the toilets again to dress in her Burkah, she also wore a pair of thick glasses and flat black shoes. Arriving at the airlines desk she picked up her boarding pass then checked in with no trouble and waited for her flight back to London. She had a three hour wait. Yet all the time with one eye on the entrances.

When the police arrived at the Villa they initially questioned Slinky and the pool man John Benton but the place had been wiped clean of any prints. All the clues they had was the statement Slinky made about a woman on a scooter reading a map which to him meant nothing. It meant nothing to the police either. Now they had reached a dead end and were literally clueless. The downpour of rain had probably washed away valuable evidence. The police used that as an excuse to wrap up the case. It was suicide according to them, it plainly was not but the holiday makers were coming over and they didn't need any bad publicity. The police decided to ring Jason's dad to tell him because they were not getting anywhere and they needed all the help they could get. When Harry heard the dreadful news he was with his wife Joan, they were with their solicitor Mr Ben John-Paisley QC. Harry dropped the phone and then completely broke down, he collapsed and then so did Joan.

Ben John-Paisley picked up the phone and asked 'what was wrong' and the police told him Jason was found hanged from his balcony overlooking his swimming pool. The police asked if there was anything unusual about Jason's friends and did he have any enemies at all that he could think of. They thought he had killed himself by hanging. Joan had already gone into shock. The same as Harry who was now on the floor a blubbering mess.

Mr Ben John-Paisley QC ordered a private doctor, his own private doctor. He asked him 'to get round to Harry's address as quickly as possible.' Now he rang DCI Reggie Arnold and told him the terrible news 'and could he please get round to see them ASAP if not, to make it sooner.'

The private doctor a Mr James Alton had both Harry and Joan put to bed, the pair of them was sedated for their own health. There were nursing arrangements made in 12 hour shifts but this for Harry and Joan was too much to bear. They remained there for two whole days but when they came round the news was a terrible blow to them all over again. But the doctor had now given them a mild sedation and Mr Ben John-Paisley arranged for the undertakers to bring Jason's body back home for burial in the family plot next to Noel and Alex, now there were three graves.

DCI Reggie Arnold and DS Trevor Bailey were informed by the Spanish police about Jason's death and in the manner in which he was found and could they be of help to the Spanish police. There were no clues. Only that a male found at the Villa by the name of John Peters also known as Slinky who was a well known gay man, was found trussed up in the en-suite bathroom. Apparently he'd been drugged and was making no sense of the previous evening at all.

DCI Arnold and DS Bailey flew over to Spain to interview Slinky. They found the whole experience a waste of time as there was no clues at all. Only that a woman was seen on a scooter outside the villa early the previous morning and she was wearing a crash helmet, apparently reading a map. But she did have a great pair of legs. It was impossible to say how old she was due to the crash helmet. However that rang a bell with DCI Arnold, there was always a woman involved or around when these murders took place and co-incidentally all seemed to have great legs? Slinky told the two police officers 'they both went to the Sisters night club and restaurant just about ten minutes away the night before.' DS Bailey asked him 'if he had seen any women in the club,' Slinky replied 'no he hadn't, but the bar owner Clive might have served her if there had been one.'

DCI Arnold and DS Bailey walked into Sisters at 9pm that night and asked the barman and owner Clive 'did he serve a woman in the bar that night of the hanging.'

'Yes, there were a couple officer, there was one with a man and another one by herself. The one on her own was a tall lady, very classy with dark hair and a great body and lovely legs. She was not a great distance from the two lads and their three friends but she was within an easy distance to see what they were doing. I can't say if she was watching them at all but she may have done and then she left at about 11.45pm. She had a mobile phone she was talking into, she only had a couple of drinks all night and I thought she was waiting for someone but couldn't be sure. She did ask if a guy called Tony Willis had been in. I told her I had never heard of him. Now she said he was a tall man who was aged about 45, dark and good looking. I said to her take your pick as most of the guys are good looking and all ages and she laughed. Oh yes she did have a mid Atlantic accent though. So that's it I'm afraid I can't be of any more use to you, but if you fancy a drink later' he said to DS Trevor Bailey 'then we could have some fun' he smiled.

Bailey now turning red walked out with DCI Arnold following him laughing, 'hey you scored Trevor you've still got it let's face, it he never asked me.'

'Bollocks' came back the expected reply.

They followed the road back to the villa which took about twenty minutes to get back. They walked through the back door and re-enacted the murder scene. Now it would have been easy to have carried out the murder if you had the time, and someone had had the time. DCI Arnold was convinced it was the same woman who was involved with the other three hangings. He knew this was a revenge killing, he just needed the motive then he would find the killer.

'If it was a woman she had to be strong and cunning as she worked with speed and was definitely a professional and she never left a trace behind her. So who the hell is this killer woman, because now she's gone serial,' said DCI Reggie Arnold.

DCI Arnold asked the Spanish police for any recent CCTV pictures of incoming flights from England, especially from London and back again. There was only one woman that caught his eye, a woman wearing a Burkah. When he returned from Spain he checked the London airports for the last week on incoming flights from Spain and there were one or three women wearing Burkahs but they all had people waving them goodbye except for one who did not seem to have anyone with her, she had landed at Gatwick and then she caught the coach. But he did manage to track the coach back to Waterloo Coach Park where she got off and went to the ladies toilet in the station. She never came out again.

DS Bailey said 'that's a bloody good disguise sir who would have thought to do that?'

'A bloody clever woman that's who and we still have no idea where she is but we do have a name, although I doubt she is using her real name, but she has to be somewhere out there.'

'Sir we had better get the Dolans some protection during the funeral service of Jason, she will know all about that, so we can't be sure she won't try to kill anyone else belonging to the Dolan family'

'Yes you're right Bailey, but she's now after Harry and I reckon she will go for his wife Joan first though.'

'Why do you think that sir, is it that obvious?'

'Yes, to me it is. Look when you think about it, this is a revenge killing this is Sarah Lambert getting her own back for Harry killing her family and he will be the last one to die. Now she is making him suffer the same as herself. She wants to let him know she is coming for him and he will be the last one to die. I'm certain of that so we have to keep a sharp eye on Harry and his wife. Because she could come for them at any time and she is so good at disguises. God only knows what she will dress up in next. I am now getting on to the FBI to see if I can find out some more about her, but they won't give me much as the yanks look after their own very well, we ought to take a leaf out of their book on that too.'

'Why is that sir,' asked Bailey?

'Simple Trevor, we give far too much information away and we get nothing much back in return.'

Landing on time at Gatwick, Sarah caught a coach back to Waterloo Coach Station where a coach went every fifteen minutes. She was still wearing the Burkah and did have some unpleasant looks from certain people. But when she arrived at the station she walked into the ladies toilet with her case and came out twenty five minutes later dressed in a top and skirt and wearing a light green raincoat and a bobble hat. She was also carrying a large M&S bag, she was now Clare Edwards. Even the CCTV could do nothing to identify her. Within ten minutes she walked into a department store and changed in the ladies. This time leaving behind her old clothes she had been wearing and the M&S bag which contained her other belongings. Now she came out wearing a red bomber jacket, dark skinny jeans, and black trainers with a white rim. She also wore a dark wig and sun glasses, with a rucksack over her shoulder with the Burkah and shoes inside.

She had left her case in the ladies at Waterloo station, so no one could identify her now. Her main objective now would be to get in close with Joan Dolan. Now she was next on the list and she had worked out a plan. She knew the police would be waiting for her to make a move. This had to be planned out precisely to the minute. Noel Dolan had told her that his lazy mother didn't do any cleaning in their apartment, even though she did nothing all day and he too employed the same cleaning company, a firm called Your Easy Clean. The firm called in every two days, but they never had the same cleaner all the time because staff was hard to keep, and most were Polish girls and sometimes the odd Polish man.

Jason's Funeral was taking place on the coming Friday morning at 11.45am, today was Tuesday. This time Sarah wouldn't go to watch the funeral as she was obviously now known by Harry, not a hundred per cent. It wasn't worth taking the risk. She wouldn't have a chance to kill Joan at the funeral as there would be too many people attending including a lot of the police. She was getting concerned now because she had an idea they knew who she was but only by name and as far as she was concerned she was still in America, but she had one more ace up her sleeve. She still had another identity in the name of Louise James. She had obtained that name herself and nobody knew her by that name, not even the FBI.

DCI Reggie Arnold and his side kick DS Trevor Bailey however would be attending the funeral with several other policemen and women. But the women would all be under cover and watching everyone and everything that was going on. The wake would be an all day affair but Harry would be sick and tired of trying to explain to all his relatives what had happened to Jason because they didn't know and Joan would have a job to talk about it. She just planned to drink all day to blot out the pain. She wanted to stay at home but that was impossible to do. Because that would have split the Dolans apart and she had her own old family the Biddles to consider. But her Romany relatives were the genuine gypsies.

She had a job to speak to anyone now. Losing three sons to some maniac was bad enough in anyone's life but not knowing why was unacceptable. A lot of relatives who knew Harry thought he had done something to cause all this. It was obvious to most people that his empire had now started to crumble around him. Now he was nearing seventy three and going on a hundred. Yet his wife Joan was getting even bigger by the day.

The Lone Star Club was losing money as everyone had their hands in the till. The fear was fast disappearing from his employees. Feeling all alone he now trusted nobody. But it was time to get his act in order, and he planned to retire after Jason's funeral was over.

The funeral was huge with the usual two black stallions and the coach with all the trimmings. There were the fancy cars, the flowers, the fights, the drinking and the making up with various family members and then the internment of the coffin. Joan was trying to throw herself into the grave while screaming and wailing. Several family members stopped her. So in the end she was taken back in to the reception area of the function rooms and a doctor was called in to sedate her again while Harry was walking around in a daze. He was looking out for possible trouble later on, such as one of them muscling in on his businesses. Now more than ever he had to be vigilant because that's the way it is you're soon forgotten when the fear leaves people. Pathetically he was heard calling for Alex who was a vicious enforcer and could handle anyone in a fight.

People who saw this thought he was losing his marbles and gleefully looked forward to rich pickings. After all who was now in charge? His three sons now resided in the three freshly dug graves so who would Harry leave the businesses to now? The future looked dark and grim for Harry, but bright for others?

    Sarah had also been keeping a watch on the Dolan's residence as she was waiting for the cleaner to arrive. At 9.30am a woman about the same weight and height as herself turned up to clean. She was wearing a yellow jumper and blue jeans and also had a blue cap on.
    The jumper had written on it 'Your Clean Easy' in black script. She used her mobile phone to take a picture and went to a cheap clothing store to buy the same style jumper and then she found a T-shirt shop that printed whatever you wanted on the shirt. Showing the assistant the black script writing from the picture so could they copy the writing on her jumper. Explaining to the assistant 'she had damaged her work top. She would be in big trouble if she turned up for work without it, because it was the second time this had happened.'
    The assistant laughed and said 'no problem and could she call round in thirty minutes,' which she agreed to do.
    When she picked it up it was perfect, she looked exactly the same as the cleaners did, all she needed was a canvas bag with cleaning products in it. She bought the products from the local market. Now she had to decide how to kill Joan. She would have liked her to swing on a rope the same as her three sons but that was going to be difficult to do, because she must have weighed about twenty stone, maybe a lot more.
    On the day of the funeral the cleaner was due and the day before Sarah had rang the cleaning company to say 'don't come tomorrow, please leave it a week before you start again because we are on holiday.'
    Sarah knocked on the door at 11.30am the housekeeper a Mrs Wilson opened the door, she saw Sarah in her uniform and looked at her watch and said you're late, in fact two hours late. It's a good job Mrs Dolan is out as she wouldn't have liked you coming so late.'

'I know we're sorry, but the usual girl is off sick and she didn't tell us until two hours ago, sorry about that, look do you want me to carry on?'

'Yes okay then you carry on, do the kitchen and the living rooms first please, then the rest of the place.' While she was in the living room she noticed the half bottle of Gin and also one in her bedroom so she poured a large quantity of the drug Rohypnol into each bottle. In the kitchen she found an electric carving knife it was razor sharp. So she put it in her bag with the garden ties and some ducting tape but all the time she was wearing surgical gloves as all cleaners do and leaving no trace of fingerprints. Sarah was on her own while the housekeeper Mrs Wilson retired back into her small flat on the bottom floor.

'Just knock on my door when you have finished' she said to Sarah 'and let yourself out.' Walking up the stairs to their roof terrace the key was in the door lock. The roof terrace was the same size as Noel's next door and the same level. Not as nicely finished, but she could see it was never used. It would be a simple job to jump from one terrace to another and let herself in, because she now had the key.

The normal time it took the cleaner was two hours so she walked to the main door and Mrs Wilson's flat was leading off next to the main door. Sarah opened the main door then knocked on her door and slammed the door shut. She quickly ran up the stairs to the stairs to the roof terrace. She locked the roof terrace door and kept the key she doubted if anyone would notice and if so she would sort the situation out, that's if one arose. She waited until it got dark.

At eight thirty, Harry Dolan and Joan arrived back home. Mrs Wilson let them in and retired to her rooms as the couple entered the kitchen. Joan was the worse for wear and Harry told her to go to bed as he was going back out to see about some business. He helped her to her bedroom which was a way down from his and sat her on the bed. But he didn't feel as though he could help her take her clothes off because the sight of her naked was not the best sight in the world she didn't look good. He was really going out to see one of his women and he would not be back until later.

He told her he would most probably be late but she was already comatose on the bed in a state of undress. Walking out of the bedroom he headed to the front door, he closed the main door behind him and left in a taxi.

At 11.33pm Sarah unlocked the terrace door and crept down the stairs leaving the key in the door which she locked behind her. Standing outside Joan's bedroom door she could hear laboured breathing, then some grunting, then snoring. She noticed Harry was still not in. There was even more snorting and more snoring coming from Joan's bedroom, but then it went quiet again. Quickly she stepped into the bedroom she slowly and carefully held Joan's wrists, then tied them together behind her back, she did the same to her ankles. Quickly taping her mouth with ducting tape, and she plugged in the electric carving knife. Switching it on she held it against Joan's throat. Slowly she started to carve her throat like a Sunday roast holding the knife against her jugular vein while she was laying on her right side. She held a pillow against her throat as she cut into it to deflect the blood from splashing her. But the blood poured out onto the bed sheets. But Joan never woke up and it took less than five minutes to kill her. Sarah got no satisfaction from this killing but it had to be done and quickly. This was the night of her last son's funeral. No one was expecting her death as well at this time but this was poetic justice. She noticed Joan had drunk some more Gin when she got in at some time; the drugged gin had worked well. Sarah wished Harry could have been here but she wanted him to know he would be last in line and his time was almost up. To spook him she wrote on the dressing table mirror using Joan's blood, the sentence. 'I'm the dead man's sister Harry, your time is almost up?'

Sarah finished up after cleaning the area with the usual bleach, which was her trade mark now. There was a spare set of clothes which she had brought with her, so after cleaning herself up and then changing, she bagged up her old clothes and took them with her. Quickly moving down the stairs she let herself out quietly and walked to her car a couple of streets away. Now she had to figure a way to kill Harry, she already had an idea and it was not a nice idea but it would be very affective once set in motion.

Harry arrived back home at 3.15am, he simply went to bed and never bothered to look in on Joan. She was always asleep and he quickly fell asleep too. The alarm sounded at 8.30am and by 8.45 he still hadn't had his mug of tea. Every morning he always had a large mug of builder's tea made by Joan every single morning, but so far she had not appeared. Shouting to her 'hey Joan where's the tea?' Then he shouted out 'Jesus, do I have to do everything myself these days woman?' Becoming really annoyed now, he swung his legs out of bed and marched into her bedroom yelling 'you fat lazy bitch where's my tea?' As he marched into her bedroom the sight before him made him scream out loud. And then he cried but he still managed to call the police. Harry knew he was finished. He would not function on his own very well now. And in the mirror he saw the message, written with Joan' blood.

When the two Detectives arrived they searched the premises from top to bottom to make sure no one was hiding in the building, they searched all over upstairs and downstairs. There was nothing. DCI Reggie Arnold with DS Trevor Bailey couldn't believe it. The sight of Joan was bad. Her head was virtually decapitated and her wrists and ankles were tied together the same as the other murders. But there was no visible sign of a struggle. It was hard to understand how someone had got into the house and carried out this murder, and again there was the smell of bleach. After forensics had sorted out the crime scene they reckoned the drinks were spiked.

And so yet again it was perpetrated by the same person as before. Only this time they/she did not hang Joan. But looking at the great mass of dead flesh lying on the bed you could see why. Joan must have weighed about twenty two stone. She now looked like a large Bull Seal washed up on a shore. That would be a hard job for anyone to hang her. You would need a crane.

DCI Arnold had never in thirty years seen so much blood, it was everywhere, but mostly soaked into the sheets. It had also come through the thick mattress and onto the floor, spreading into a large crimson pool under her bed.

DS Trevor Bailey was also shocked, because being a relatively rookie cop he had not seen that many murders close up and the sight repulsed him.

This was a cruel way to kill anyone, especially as Joan had just buried her last son that very day. No one could expect that to happen. The person must have got into the house, but how? So they questioned the housekeeper, Mrs Wilson. DCI Arnold asked Mrs Wilson, 'did you let anyone into the house at any time yesterday morning?'

'No I let no one in because there were no callers, none at all.'

'Think Mrs Wilson, was there anybody else who came into the house at all think, please think.'

'Well yes, the only other person who came was the cleaner and she wasn't here long, just for the usual two hours and then the girl left, simple as that.'

'Was it the same girl this time, the same one as usual?'

'Err no, the usual girl was sick so they sent a replacement, she left after two hours, I saw her go.'

'What was wrong with her and what did the replacement look like?'

'I don't know you will have to ask them the reason. I just opened the door there was a woman standing there about 5ft 8in tall with the uniform on. You know yellow top with the writing and the blue baseball cap, she had heavy black rimmed glasses on. She said sorry but the other girl called in sick at 9am which had put them all out of rhythm. So you will have to ask them the reason for that, anyway she left as I said two hours later.'

'Did you see her leave the premises Mrs Wilson?'

'Yes of course I did, well I heard her leave'

'Heard her leave, what do you mean heard her leave Mrs Wilson. Did you actually see the cleaner leave the premises?'

'Well she slammed the door and I assumed she left, after all there was nobody else in here including her because I looked round the rooms to make sure she had done a good job and she wasn't there. Like I said she left. I didn't stand in the doorway to watch her leave. Anyway she knocked on my door to say she was leaving then I heard the door slam, so in my mind she left as normal. That's what the cleaner always did. I asked them to do that. Jesus I can't stand over them for two hours, not with my varicose veins, give us a break. What more can I say? That's the usual way they all leave, that's all I can say about it, there is no more. I didn't stand and watch her leave by the front door, maybe she's still hiding in the building' she laughed.

DS Bailey said 'sir, maybe she has a point. I want to try something. Mrs Wilson can you go into your room and listen to me when I knock on your door, then listen to hear the front door slamming is that ok, it won't take long. When you hear the front door slam can you come out please into the hallway?'

'Yes okay, so I'm ready when you are this is a waste of time you know. Christ I don't like silly games I have my health to think off.'

DS Bailey, to the amusement of DCI Arnold knocked on Mrs Wilson's door then opened the front door, slammed it shut then sprinted up the stairs. By the time Mrs Wilson came out then looked into the street DS Bailey was almost up onto the roof terrace. Now he unlocked the terrace door because the key was still in the lock. Then he opened the door and took the key out and locked it from the other side and then he waited.

DCI Arnold told her to wait in her rooms while he called out for Bailey. Nothing so he called again, still nothing. He searched the place until he came to the stairs leading to the roof terrace. Trying the door it was locked. 'Bailey come out now, what the hell is this, hide and seek?' Then the terrace door opened and Bailey stood there grinning. 'Solved it sir, she hid out here until the evening. She took the key out of the terrace door then locked the door from the terrace side of the door, nobody could get on to the terrace then later she came down in the early hours and murdered Joan.'

DCI Arnold was impressed, 'well done Trevor I think you're right, she had to hide somewhere. She knew Harry would be the worse for wear because of the booze, and so would Joan. I bet Joan is full of the drug Rohypnol, but well done. This makes perfect sense and the old girl Mrs Wilson would have a job to climb the stairs to get up here, it would take her all day.'

'So she hid up here, what a crafty woman and it is a woman. So look let's get on to the cleaning company, Your Clean Right, and check this out.'

DS Bailey rang the cleaning company and he was told that the cleaning was stopped for a week due to a holiday. There was a woman who rang in yesterday to cancel the job for a week.

'Oh thank you, I don't suppose they left a name did they?'
'Yes I asked for one, and a lady said she was the sister and that was all. But then she put the phone down. It sounded a bit odd but hey who am I to say, we're very busy.'
'Well thank you for your time and you have been so helpful.'
'Sir, said Bailey, she cancelled the cleaner for a week. She got in by disguising herself as the cleaner. Look sir, she's one clever lady and I would love to meet her. She's as crafty as a wagon load of monkeys as my old mum would say.

'I just want to find her Trevor, I have a feeling she knows our every move and now she will be after Harry. We have to give this guy round the clock protection and that's going to be very expensive, but we have no choice. Because, look if she can come and go as easy as this then we are in trouble, or rather Harry is, but like you Trevor I would love to meet her. That's if we ever do.'

'I reckon you're right on this sir. I have a strong feeling this woman is going to leave this next killing for a while as she knows we are on to her so I think she will slip away and then turn up again in a month or two. I feel this strongly. Look sir we know it's Sarah Lambert but how do we prove it though, she's apparently still in America on FBI leave, extended leave and that's a great alibi. We have checked out the airlines and she hasn't been in the country, well only for the Tom Lambert family funeral and then flew back to America again.'

Sarah decided to keep her flat on for another three months but now she had to get back to America. She knew the police were on to her and she didn't want to kill Harry yet. Because she wanted him to suffer the pain of losing his family, the same as she had done. Harry Dolan had brought this on himself and now he knew the pain of losing his family. She wanted him to feel fear before she dispatched him to hell. Monica Sheldon was another name she had used before while in the FBI. She had the passport and the bank details so she booked a flight back to America, her friend Elizabeth Mallory had been taking care of her flat in New Jersey and had been driving around upstate New York and using Sarah's credit cards for food, petrol, hotel bills, and entertainment.

Sarah had really been in England. Elizabeth was a dear friend who asked no questions but did as she was asked without question.

Elizabeth had an email sent from Sarah's local library saying she was on her way home and would be landing in New York at 4.27pm and could she meet her. She would check in this time as Monica Sheldon a restaurant owner. This passport had not been used for a couple of years and she was clean with no convictions or bad debts. And so any trace on her showed a normal 100% American woman. She turned up looking frumpy with a walking stick and she was also wearing a short dark curly wig and heavy rimmed glasses. She had put a block in her shoe so it was difficult to walk, hence the limping and walking stick.

Sarah met Liz in the arrivals lounge and the first thing they did was have a laugh and a coffee. Hey, 'so what's with the disguise,' Liz Laughed.

Sarah explained and together they had a catch up. But she asked her 'did you use my credit cards as planned Liz?'

'Yes I did and a couple of times more so the trace is there if anyone needs to trace them.'

'So how did you get on with the trip Sarah, did you do well?'

'Yes I did Liz and there's just one more trip to go, but not for a while at least. I need a break for now, so Florida sounds good, you up for it Liz.'

'Just try and stop me' they both laughed.

CHAPTER TWENTY

Harry Dolan was not the man he used to be. Every night he was suffering from bad dreams with always the same theme, a woman in black and white with a noose in her hands laughing at him. Yet all he heard now was 'I'm the dead man's sister.' He still couldn't understand what that was. Another thing, he was beginning to have problems with his staff. Now he tried to get his cousins involved in the various businesses he owned and now he had decided he was going to sell up and retire abroad. He already had a place in Spain and now with no family he decided that was the best policy. He had also developed a phobia of scratching his neck and he had lost a lot of weight, which was totally unsurprising in the circumstances.

DCI Arnold had a bright idea and called round to see Harry with DS Bailey, but he had to ring first to make sure he was there and as usual Harry had his brief with him. 'Harry we know you knew the family who were killed in the fire in Alicante, they used to own the Black Swan. Now then Harry apparently according to my contacts you tried to purchase the premises from the then owner Mr Tom Lambert. Unfortunately all his family were burnt to death in a terrible fire and there were no survivors, well only one. He had a sister who lives in America but at the time she wasn't there which was lucky for her. Maybe a bit like you Harry in a way, because she has lost all her family and so have you. Anyway the dead man had a sister.'

Harry said 'what.... the dead man's sister, he had a sister.... I didn't know that.'

'Why would you, if you say you didn't know the man or his family. I think you knew him perfectly well Harry. We also believe you had them killed as an act of revenge and now this sister is coming for you as well. We believe she's leaving you until last, which by the way is anytime now. We want to try and stop her Harry because she will kill you. We may be able to stop her.'

Mr Ben John-Paisley laughed and then said 'stop right there DCI Arnold, you have no proof. You have no evidence that my client is responsible for the deaths of that unfortunate family, none at all. So if you have then kindly produce the evidence to us. Or please leave, because this is amounting to harassment and I have it recorded on my mobile phone for future reference, which I would put before a court if need be Inspector Arnold.'

'All we are trying to do is to catch this woman. This woman is a serial killer and we believe she will be coming for Harry next, but not sure when. She is an expert at disguise and works, or did work, for the FBI. Today I will try again to find out more about her. The problem is, the FBI doesn't exactly give out a lot of information. I don't think they like us Brits much. Christ knows why, but that's the way it is. We could do with some help. But so far this woman has left no clues. To date, only Harry has seen her.'

Ed Warren, who was Sarah's boss at the FBI, had a card sent to him as it was his birthday. It was from Sarah saying 'Happy Birthday Ed, but at this moment having a nice time whilst I'm off. Oh and I have met a nice man. Who knows where it will lead to, so in the meantime don't get too drunk, will be back at work soon, maybe in two to three weeks? Love, Sarah x. Ed Noticed the card was sent from Albany so it looked as though she was heading back to her home. Well he felt pleased she would be back to work she was too good to lose. So maybe meeting a new man would change her life, he hoped so, because if anyone deserved a break it was her. Then his phone rang. Carefully he lifted the receiver. The call came from England it was from a DCI Reggie Arnold from West End Central police station, London, England.

DICI Arnold asked if he could get in touch with Sarah Santana as a matter of urgency.

Ed Warren said 'I'm afraid not, she is still on leave, as a matter of fact I have just had a birthday card from her today, because it's my birthday and the card was sent from Albany. And it also said she would hope to be back to work in a couple of weeks. This is the first contact I have had from her in six weeks,' he lied, 'and as you know she was devastated by the death of her family and we gave her extended leave.

She has been travelling round New York State and further. Look Inspector it's a big state we don't ask her where she's been. I can't reach her because her phone is understandably turned off. She needed some space she has suffered a great loss. Is there anything else DCI Arnold because I'm now late for a meeting.'

DCI Arnold said 'no, oh and happy birthday. If she does show up for work, can you ask her to please get in touch with me, it's important Mr Warren.'

'Yes of course. However it's really up to Sarah, but look I really have to go, goodbye.'

DCI Arnold said to Bailey 'well that went down like a concrete parachute. For fuck sake the guy was as helpful as a broken trouser zip at a meeting with the queen.'

That's very descriptive sir you wouldn't get a Knighthood that's for sure' said Bailey.

But DCI Arnold was now far away in thought. Yet he knew Sarah Santana could have had a friend who could have posted the birthday card and he bet her credit cards had also been in use. Maybe by someone else because that's what he would have done, it was a good alibi. He knew she was travelling in more than one name and in a few different disguises. This was one smart clever lady. Yet after all she had been trained by the FBI. He thought to himself she deserved to get away with it because the Dolans had dished out a lot of pain and death to certain people and he was convinced that Harry Dolan had the Lamberts murdered because he was rejected. It sounded farfetched but Harry Dolan was a twisted evil man and he did not like to lose face. DCI Arnold had to admire this strong woman for her endeavour. However, he did want to catch her and put her away because it was his job and he would do his best to do so.

DS Bailey said, 'Sir I have some good news and some bad news, but the good news first is that Harry and his empire is beginning to crumble. The bad news is we don't know yet who is going to take over. The word on the grapevine is his first cousin Gerald Dolan is making a move on him. It looks as though Harry has cooked his goose and is heading off to a life of retirement in the sun. Well that's being bandied about it looks as though he is on the way out, the new blood is on the way in.'

'What do we know about this Gerald Dolan, Trevor? Let's go and find out and maybe we don't have to keep an eye on Harry so much now. He will probably sell his interests in the businesses and retire as there's not a lot left to keep him here now. His family are gone and all of a sudden he's grown old too, and this woman Sarah Santana has returned to America. But according to the FBI she never left. Let's see what happens in the next few months.'

'Well sir, at least Dolan is growing old, that's more than can be said for Tom Lambert and his family, and also his own family. If he was responsible for the deaths of nine people, then he has to live with that. Can you imagine taking that to bed every night and waking up with the knowledge of what he has done?'

'Yes Trevor, and that's a big cross to bear, a big cross.'

CHAPTER TWENTY ONE

Harry Dolan had made his mind up, he was going to sell up all his interests and as quickly as possible, he had a few million tucked away in various banks and their deposit boxes here and abroad. He didn't want to get ripped off, especially by the so called business consultants or agents who he hated, they all charged around 4 - 6 percent. He loathed the fucking wankers. He'd been heard many times complaining about these scrounging bastards. Now he contacted Gerald who was his first cousin about buying his business interests. As was the norm he was asking far too much and the wannabe buyer had far too little to give as he had other business interests and his spare cash was in short supply. When you start to grow you always have cash problems, and that's just the way it worked. By selling privately he had saved a shed load of money.

Gerald Dolan was another ruthless Dolan and didn't think twice about hurting anyone. He wanted to be at the top of the tree. Standing at six feet ft tall and now aged 38 years old with a heavy frame he was very fit. He weighed about fifteen stone and was also an ex fighter. While travelling along the rocky road he had also hurt a number of people, including a number of women and men. Suddenly out of the blue he had a call from Harry asking if he was interested in buying his businesses. But at the right price of course, he wanted to get the money sorted out now, or he would put the businesses on the open market.

Gerald asked him for the sale price. Well the price for the Loan Star Club and restaurant was £1,500,000, the three betting shops were on sale for £2,300,000 and the large house used as a brothel was for sale at £1,780,000, making a total of £5,530,000.

'That's a lot of money Harry, a lot.'

'Look, forget it. Jesus, the net profits on the takings on paper alone are £650,000. You tell me where the hell can you earn that amount Gerald? You can't, so forget it. I have several organizations who are interested but I would have liked to keep it in the family, you know pass it on to my boys anyway forget I called you Gerald. I honestly thought you had a brain on you.'

'Hey wait a minute Harry, it just comes as a shock the amount you want, that's all. I can't just put my hand in my pocket and pull it out. What am I a fucking magician?'

'I'm not a charity Gerald and all you have to do is carry on the same as me after you give me the money and there is another 20 percent on the top of that in cash every week. So look, if you can't keep up with the big boys go and play in the kids area. After all you could pay this off in seven years or even sooner. Jesus, just forget it.'

'Look Harry let me see what I can arrange and come back to you.'

'Being as you're family Gerald. Listen to me. I am prepared to leave £1,500,000 in the business at 5% because you will pay a minimum of 9 or10 percent, so that's a good deal. Anyway let me know in three days. Go and have a word with the bank. Ask for Mr Rupert Jones at the City of London Bank. Oh and I have already primed him for you Gerald.'

'Ok Harry, and thanks for the first chance. I will ring this Rupert bloke and see if it can be done.'

'Jesus, have you listened to anything I have just said? I have already arranged it for you. For fuck sake I should charge you a broker's fee.'

'Oh yes sorry Harry yes I will do, in fact I will ring him right now my brains all over the place now. This has come as a shock to me.'

Mr Rupert Jones of the City of London Bank was reading the Financial Times when his secretary Linda put through a call from Gerald Dolan. They arranged to meet the same day at 3pm. After two hours of grilling by Jones, Gerald had the money and Harry had his sale. He was out of his businesses and now very depressed because now he had no purpose in life. He had several millions in the bank or various banks. He was aged almost seventy-four years old he had no immediate family. He still had his nightmares and bad dreams and he still had his fear about the dead man's sister. Ye that was beginning to fade a little as each day passed.

Harry had tried to settle into the dream of living in Spain. He had a huge villa in Marbella but he was on his own. Now he was feeling lonely. The problem was he could still feel his son around the villa and the place took on a ghostly feel at night. That was especially true in the early hours of the morning. After a lot of thought he decided to sell the villa but at this moment in time properties in Spain had slumped to an all time low. Still he had to try and was prepared to drop down in price. But he didn't feel comfortable staying in the villa. In spite of that he was now beginning to put some weight back on, he was eating again and ate at the best restaurants in Marbella and the surrounding areas. One idea he had he thought about buying a boat to laze about on but knew nothing about boats.

However, he had a look around the Marina and talked to the owner of a boat yard a man named Simon Dexter. While he was looking the owner introduced him to his mother. She was a widow too who was aged sixty three. She was a stunning looking woman and they hit it off right away. All of a sudden his life was turned around by Maria Dexter. They quickly moved in with each other and the future was beginning to look bright again.

Maria lived in a gated community on the edge of Marbella having its own theatre, doctors, library, and shops. Harry liked it so much he thought seriously about buying an apartment there. In the meantime he was beginning to enjoy his life again. The view from Maria's balcony was superb. You could see the sea and watch the comings and goings of all the residents. It was also a difficult place to get into as you had to have a pass key and strangers never went unnoticed. Feeling safe there he told no one back in England where he was staying. All his money was tucked away and he felt free from any obligations so he started to enjoy his life again especially with Maria Dexter.

Sarah Santana after six weeks back in America decided to take one last visit to London to arrange the death of Harry Dolan. The funeral of Joan who was Harry's wife had come and gone the same as her three sons. Now it was time to finish what she started. With that in mind she said goodbye to her friend Elizabeth Mallory. Still they had the arrangement of keeping in touch by each other's emails and phones, but with Liz doing the sending and receiving just as before.

Elizabeth told her to stay calm and to stay safe and not to worry. Their plan was working out so just carry on as before while she was away. She would drive around as before texting and also using the emails.

Sarah took the flight under the name of Monica Sheldon and flew to London on an open ticket. She soon found out that Harry Dolan had sold his properties and moved to Spain. She already had his address in Marbella.

Harry was trying to sell the villa but there was a shortage of buyers around. There was a sign outside saying VENDI meaning for sale, apply within and the mobile number, Harry's number.

The plane landed at Malaga airport at 2.45pm. Sarah now known as Monica Sheldon stepped off the plane and walked through the customs. She walked to the car rental section and hired a car. Next to the hire car there were several hotels advertised locally. She found a nice little hotel and booked into a self catering apartment. After settling in she decided to look at the Villa again. Not wishing to waste any more time, she wanted to finish this as soon as she could.

The villa looked deserted, so she drove off and waited a mile away in a lay by until it became dark, then she drove back up to the villa. It still seemed deserted, she felt certain it was empty. Harry was not there. But she knew he was in Spain but he was obviously living somewhere else. Deciding to look around inside the villa to make sure he was not there she quietly broke in....he wasn't at the Villa. She could see it hadn't been lived in for a while there was nothing in the fridge and no sign of life. She returned to her car and thought for a while. But he must be somewhere.

Harry was about to go out with Maria when his mobile rang and a woman with a broken French English ascent spoke to him about viewing his villa and how much was it up for sale for. It was difficult to understand what she was saying. So she spoke in French.

Harry said to Maria 'you speak French don't you? Look can you have a word, it's about the sale of my Villa and she's French by the sound of it.' He handed the phone over to Maria.

'Hello how can I help you' asked Maria in French 'is it about the sale of the Villa?'

'Yes I'm sorry about this but could I come and take a look at it? I was driving past the Villa yesterday and it caught my eye. I would very much like to take a look if this is possible with my husband, and as soon as we can. Look we have to go home in three days for a week. We could come back and sort out the finances and we would pay cash for it no problem. If we like it we will leave a good deposit subject to contract.'

'She wants to take a look at the Villa Harry, with her husband, when are you available to show them round?'

'Tell her this afternoon at say 2pm? Will that work for her? Oh and ask her what her name is.'

'Is 2pm good for you, and your name is?' Asked Maria.

'Oh yes sorry its Edith Perrin, and yes 2pm is fine for me. Will you be there as well as communication would be a lot easier,' she laughed.

'Yes I will be there as well, my name is Maria and the owner's name is Harry, will you be on your own Edith.'

'No, my husband will be with me then if we decide to buy the Villa we can get on with it, and it's my money that will be used. The decision is all mine and not his' she laughed. 'I make up my mind very quickly, if I like it then I can leave a good deposit and we can move on this today, or tomorrow as I have to find a lawyer. I'm sure you know of one.'

'Yes we know one. We will see you at 2pm and I have a dark blue Mercedes car, a convertible.'

'Oh by the way, why is he selling the Villa, it looks so lovely.'

'Simple, he is now a widower so it's far too big for him to rattle around in.'

'Okay 2pm it is until later then.'

'Hey this sounds good Harry, do you want me there as well?'

'Yes of course I do, you can speak the lingo, I can't.'

'Oh no Harry, I've just remembered I have a hair appointment at exactly 2 o'clock.'

'Well cancel. It's not a problem is it?'

'If I do that I won't get another appointment for about four weeks and my hair needs a good cut. Sorry Harry I have to keep that appointment, anyway you can show them round. Give me your phone, she will have left her number so I'll ring her, she'll understand.'

'How long will it take to do your hair, we can go later.'

'I can't, I have arranged to meet up with Muriel afterwards to go shopping. She wants me to go with her because her daughter's getting married and she wants my opinion on the outfit she wants to buy. I can't go with you. Look tomorrow I can but not today. I'm sorry honey I forgot to say. Anyway look I will write her a note in French to say I will see her tomorrow if you like, but really you have to strike while the iron is hot, she may find another house she likes, so the quicker you get her signed up the better. You can muddle through and she is interested in the Villa Harry, and not us two.'

'You need to sort out what you're doing Maria, because I'm getting sick of this situation. Christ sake you're always changing your mind or we will have to knock it on the head because I don't know where I am anymore. One minute you say yes then you say it's no. You said we were going out yet now it's your hair that needs doing or you're off shopping, and I'm pissed off with it.'

'Harry I'm really sorry, but even I can make a mistake for Christ sake. Anyway who's bloody perfect? You want perfection then bugger off, because that's not me, I do have friends and have done for years so you can pack your things and go back to your place. I don't much care anymore. So anyway how long have you been in Spain for? Five or six weeks, well I've been here for twenty-three years, so you can get your things and go if you don't mind, today please, because nobody tells me what to do.'

'Yeah well I'm sorry babe. I suppose you're right. Ok I'll meet her on my own. Let's not tell her, she may pull out if you're not there, so it's best if she looks at it, anyway the place is clean and tidy.'

'Are you going to tell her about Jason, Harry? Take in what I said too.'

'Of course I'm not going to tell her at this stage, she's just looking. I don't want to put her off and there's no law to say I have to. I can't see the point in saying. Oh by the way my son was murdered at the Villa and it's not exactly a good selling point is it?'

'Sorry Harry, you're right, anyway honey, the best of luck with the sale. I have to get ready as its 12.45pm now. For god sake get some nice trousers on and a nice shirt. You can't go looking like that in those baggy shorts and you could also do with a haircut as well. For fuck sake comb your hair before you go out. You look as though you slept in a fox hole all night. Oh and that reminds me, take a shower' she laughed. 'But Harry, think on. If you don't like what I say then please move out, and today if you can, it's your choice.'

'Ok, ok!' Harry had a shower and also washed his hair then changed into a pair of blue Faro trousers and a white polo shirt. Putting on his Ray-burn sunglasses he shouted out to Maria 'see you later babe' then he started up Maria's car, a spare VW Golf. It was just a runabout town car which Maria owned and Harry used. Showing his pass he drove off through the security gates and headed for his Villa. The time was now 1.30pm, it was so hot and the sun was blazing down, it was a lovely day and not a cloud in the sky, the sort of day to die for.

Sarah had been waiting and watching for thirty minutes for the pair to arrive. Now she was parked in a line of cars about ten yards down from the Villa in her hired white VW Polo and reading a paper. She saw a black VW Golf driving down the road and turn into the Villa's driveway. It was Harry who got out of the car. Good he was his own. The time now was 1.55pm, she continued to wait for a while expecting a woman to appear in a dark blue Mercedes convertible. By 2.10pm she hadn't appeared and Harry came into the road looking up and down, then his mobile rang, he said 'hello?'

'Oh Sorry I am a little late, I'll be there in about twenty minutes. Sorry for the delay, I was held up in town there was an accident.

'Harry just about understood the message. Ok I will be here, don't worry. I will see you in twenty minutes.'

Sarah rang off and waited. She wanted to make sure the woman wasn't going to be there. She wanted to get him on her own, and all to herself.

Harry was annoyed to be kept waiting. But he was not used to waiting for people, and then at 2.30 the front door bell chimed as Sarah pressed the bell.
She was satisfied he was on his own. She was wearing dark jeans, trainers and a tight yellow T shirt with her hair hidden under a tight

wavy black wig. She had on a pair of dark glasses and a pair of strong surgical gloves. She was also wearing a floppy hat and had a large bag on her shoulder. A man with his dog walked by and gave her an appreciative look.

Harry opened the door and said 'Edith, please come in. Oh where's your husband, is he not with you?'

'He was, but he will be here in about ten minutes. He had an urgent phone call, something to do with his mother.' Her English was a little difficult to understand at first.

'Oh okay I'll start to show you around.'

She said in broken French 'can we start upstairs please. I always do' she smiled. 'I like to start at the top and then work my way down, is that okay for you?'

Harry said off course. And then he led the way. As they go to the top of the stairs he suddenly froze. His thoughts were tall woman, attractive woman, and great legs aged about thirty to forty something. In that split second he knew he'd made a mistake. It was too damn late. He tried to run but she had him round his neck then she banged his head against a bedroom door frame. She quickly kicked him hard behind his left knee where he went down on his knees. She held his nose tight with one hand and held his mouth shut with her other hand until he passed out. It took her less than three minutes to disable him. She wanted him to know why he was about to die. Then again she wanted him to beg for his life and to realise he was being executed for his evil deeds. But there would be no way out for him. Sarah was amazed at how weak he was. He was certainly unfit and not a problem to deal with.

Harry seemed a lot weaker than the last time they met in the graveyard back in England. He came round in a couple of minutes, but he was now tied up against the middle of the banisters at the top of the stairs on the large landing. Now securely tied all he could move was his head. Being trussed up like a turkey waiting for Christmas. Sarah had also used ducting tape to wrap around his lower face so he couldn't speak. His arms were through the banisters and his wrists were tied on top of them with garden ties, like he would be if he were nailed to a cross. His ankles had also been tied but then he realized his neck was gaffer taped to the banisters as well, he knew there was no way out of this situation. Sarah was now sat on a chair in front of him she asked him 'who he thought she was and what was she going to do with him.' But until she removed the ducting tape he could say nothing. Removing the tape she asked him again.

'I don't know. You're the one who murdered my family. Why, and what for? I've never seen you before in my life, not ever.'

'Oh but you have Harry, I saw you when I was a little girl and I know you had my Father killed, and now my brother and his wife and three children. They were my only family and you ordered them to be murdered by Duvall, the French man.'

'Look who are you?'

'Who am I? Well Harry. I'm the dead man's sister.'

'So it's you. I know what you're going to do, you're going to hang me aren't you, the same as my sons.'

'Oh no, no Harry, that's far too easy, oh no, no, no. You're going to burn to death. I want you to see the flames coming for you, to see the flames reaching out to burn you like my family burned. I want to hear your eyeballs pop, and they do you know, but your nose starts to melt first, oh and your ears too.'

'It wasn't me, I had nothing to do with it, honest, it wasn't me!'

She took out her mobile phone and played back the confession that Duvall made. It was all there. He couldn't deny it now.

'Look I will give you money I will give you £500,000. That will give you a good life. Please. This is pointless. Now you have killed my three sons and then my wife, so what's the point in killing me now?'

'What's the point Harry? Why that's simple, its pleasure? That's the point, pure pleasure in ridding the earth of evil people like you, but also revenge. They do say revenge is best served cold, but sadly in your case I have made an exception. So I'm afraid it's being served very hot' she laughed. Placing the tape back round his mouth, she went to her car and came back with two cans of petrol and a box of matches. She left one can downstairs. And then she went upstairs where slowly she undid the cap on the petrol can in front of Harry, and smiled. Then she splashed the petrol all over the floor whilst singing Come-on Baby Light My Fire.

Walking slowly she went into the four bedrooms and bathrooms, the balconies and the landing, then she went down the stairs and poured the petrol into the two living rooms and dining room. She then soaked the kitchen, the conservatory, the living room curtains and the sofas. All had a good soaking and the place stunk so much of petrol it made you gag. Walking back up the stairs she was still singing the same song.

'Harry' she shouted out, 'who sang this song? Can you remember? I've forgotten now. Look if you can remember I won't light a match so who was it. Tell me it could save your life.' She continued to pour the petrol over the stairs as Harry watched with pure terror shining in his evil eyes. He did his best to get away but he couldn't move, then she stood over him. 'Hi Harry' and then she poured the petrol over his legs and his waist but left his head alone she wanted him to see the fire as he burnt and his head would be last to go. She saw more panic in his eyes, his nose was now bleeding badly and the veins on his neck stood out like cable.

His head was covered in sweat. He'd now emptied his bowels and his bladder. She stood over him smiling. But there was nothing in this wonderful world that anyone could or would do to help him now. She pulled the tape off his mouth. 'So who sang the song Light My Fire? If you know it tell me and you live.'

He screamed out 'I know this, it was the Doors. The Doors sang it. He laughed 'see you have to let me go, you have to keep your word now don't you.'

'Oh Harry, sorry you took too long in giving me the answer, and anyway I have taken a leaf out of your book. I don't keep my word. I'm sorry I lied but it's more fun this way.'

He screamed out 'don't do this, please don't do this. The police will find you, they always do. Please don't kill me.' He started to sob 'you gave me your word' and then he cried out loud, he sounded like a wounded beast he was begging. 'You lied to me.....'

'I know I did but what fun' she laughed. 'Harry I'm not here, I'm still in America. I haven't left. I'm travelling around up-state New York having a holiday. It's the perfect holiday alibi, anyway no more of this, if I hurry I can catch the plane in a couple of hours good by Harry.'

As she said this she placed the tape back on his mouth. 'Oh and yes please remember. Now you have a really nice day.'

Harry struggled but to no use. And then he became restless as he slid about in his own filthy fluids. The smell was ghastly, but the smell of the petrol was stronger. As she got to the bottom of the stairs she lit a petrol-soaked cloth and threw it onto the floor in the living room and then she lit the bottom of the stairs. The flames started slow at first but then they greedily gobbled up the petrol as it spread through the Villa and then very slowly at first Harry watched his nemesis the flames. Now they crept cruelly up the stairs tormenting him stopping and starting as they gobbled up the driest parts. The banisters down below had now really started to burn, loudly crackling and hissing and making strange popping sounds as the paint blistered and burned. Harry terrified watched as the flames come ever nearer, but he couldn't move. He carried on crapping himself. All he could see and feel were the red hot fingers of flame slowly heading for him.

Sarah got to the bottom of the stairs and shouted out 'goodbye Harry, hey now don't you get cold.' She opened the front door laughing. Then she quietly closed the door and left the villa.

Now the flames angry fingers crept ever closer to him, they seemed to be teasing him, but he still tried to get free. Not being able to move the flames started to surround him. But at first they were like small dancing devils still teasing him. And then he could hear the wood from the banisters making a louder crackling sound as he watched. Now suddenly some of the flames leapt onto his legs. He tried pathetically to try and blow out the greedy flames. But they slowly crept up to his waist.

Desperately, he tried to move his head away but he could feel the heat as the flames became larger. He was feeling pain now as he watched the flames feed on his legs and his lower torso. He could smell his pubic and chest hair burning and his arms were now on fire. The flames were now so close and getting closer before they all enveloped him in their burning agony. The flames seemed to be inside his ears and in his nose which was slowly melting as she had said it would. Then his head and face started to burn with unimaginable pain as his eyes bubbled in agony as though red hot lava was gushing out of them. Inside his mouth was burning too as he began to die in great pain.

Then the whole Villa suddenly went up in flames, it was a good job it was set in its own plot and well away from the rest of the houses and Villas in the exclusive area.

By the time someone had called the fire service Harry Dolan was a burnt skeleton and the fire took all afternoon to put out. The fire service because of the immense heat could not enter the Villa. They were told there was no one living there at the moment. The VW Golf was still in the driveway and once they did get in they found Harry or what was left of him. He was charcoal and they saw that his wrist had melted plastic sticking to them, the same as his ankles.

There was a very strong smell of petrol about the place and the fire service called in the police who concluded that the owner, a Harry Dolan had been burnt to death. It was probably suicide because of his son had also died in the same Villa. Some said that was also suicide.

Maria had her hair styled and had gone shopping with her friend Muriel. She got home at 7.45pm and was greeted by the police who asked her when the last time she had seen Harry.

She told them 'at Lunch time, he left to go to his Villa to show a lady, well actually a French couple around his Villa. She phoned for an appointment to view the property at 2pm' that was the last time she had seen him, she had only known Harry for about six weeks. They were living together to see how things went between them. But she didn't really know a lot about him, only that he was a wealthy widower from London. She never mentioned the argument she had with him.

They told her they had traced her car, the VW Golf which was in her name.

She told them 'Harry always used it, and there was no point in having three cars, anyway I only have two parking places at this apartment.'

The police asked Scotland Yard if they had any information on a certain Harry Dolan, the enquiry eventually came to DCI Arnold who made immediate plans to fly to Spain with DS Bailey.

When DCI Arnold and DS Bailey arrived at the murder scene they were appalled by the murder and when they enquired about witnesses, there was just one.

He was a middle aged Englishman who lived two Villas down. Now he saw a tall attractive lady entering the Villa. He noticed her as he walked his dog on his usual early afternoon stroll and said 'she had a great arse....'

'What time did you see this lady' asked DCI Arnold 'and what was she wearing?'

'Oh it was about 2.30 she had black jeans or trousers on with a distinctive yellow top. She was wearing a floppy hat and had a large shoulder bag with her. I also saw her driving away in a white VW Polo at about 3.15pm. She just drove normally, as I walked past the Villa I saw nothing untoward at all, and carried on where I dropped my dog back home then went out for a game of golf with some mates. We drank in the bar and then came home to the fire service blocking the road which was a bloody nuisance to say the least and local cops running about like the Keystone cops. It was a complete bloody farce I can tell you what a bunch of stupid clowns.'

'Thank you, err Mr.'

'Oh sorry, it's Mr Berry, Edward Berry, if I can help any more please ask, you know where I live.'

'Mr Berry can you take a look at these pictures and can you see the woman on any of these please? Take your time, there's no rush.'

'No sorry I can't be certain, the height is about the same and I suppose she would have good legs but she did have jeans on. Nevertheless her legs looked good to me. She had on this floppy hat. She was about 5ft 8in or thereabouts I would say, sorry I can't be more helpful than that.'

'Mr Berry you have been most helpful, believe me you have.'

'Bailey what do you reckon, was it the same woman? It was the same Villa as Jason was murdered it just had to be her I can feel it.'

DCI Arnold drove round to see Maria to ask her questions regarding the woman who made an appointment to see the Villa. 'What did she sound like did you see her at all?'

Maria told them she hadn't seen her, but only spoke to her on the phone. The woman was French and she had a fractured way of talking which Harry had a job to understand. When she spoke French she could speak the language perfectly.

'Do you speak French Mrs Dexter,' asked DS Bailey.

'Yes, I lived in Paris for twenty-three years and if you don't quickly learn the language the Parisians soon dismiss you let me tell you. That lot have no time to teach anyone so you have to get on with it or simply go without. Now I can also speak Spanish too, because it's good manners to know the language if you live in their country. Or what's the point?'

DS Bailey asked 'is there anything else you can tell us anything at all?'

'No sorry....mind you, oh no it's nothing really just me being a bit silly.'

'Please Mrs Dexter anything at all helps us at this stage. Tell me what is it, no matter how trivial it seems to be, it could be vital to us.'

'Well I did pick up a trace of another language and I know this sounds daft. I'm sure she had a little bit of an American or mid Atlantic accent. I'm certain now. Yes it was mid Atlantic, definitely.'

'Mrs Dexter, you don't know how much you have helped us, but you have, immensely.'

'Oh well thank you. I'm so glad I haven't wasted any of your time officers, and I feel so sad about Harry but between you and me I don't think we would have gone the distance anyway.'

'Sorry to hear that, what went wrong may we ask?'

'Oh you know, he was just starting to get a little. 'I'm in charge and I want it done this way and where have you been.' You know controlling, and at my age I don't need a boss thank you. So he was on the way out as far as I was concerned. Mind you I told him today to pack his things. I told him in no uncertain words too. Yet to die the way he did was cruel, very cruel and if this woman had anything to do with it, then she must be a nut case.'

'Mrs Dexter, we can't be sure this woman has anything to do with this case, although we are looking for a woman in connection with several homicides back in the UK and we are anxious to speak with her ASAP. If she does contact you again which I doubt very much, well here is my card. And thank you again you have been really helpful, I can't stress this enough.'

'Sir, I have a feeling this lady is not going to be caught, she's always way ahead of us. She is one hell of a woman. And now she has killed all the Dolans off which in a way has helped us out. Now we have a lot more to deal with. By all accounts Gerald Dolan has now taken over the businesses from Harry, so what's he like sir? I haven't had the time as yet to check him out.'

'Trevor when you take one head off another three seems to grow. This Gerald is the same as Harry, although not quite so nasty. Hey, but life goes on and in a way it helps us keep our jobs. Gerald has form, plenty of that for fighting, prostitution, protection rackets, drugs and VAT fiddles. He did a three-year stretch for ABH a few years ago. Since then he's been clean and kept his head down. I have heard he is recruiting for some heavies to help grow the businesses he's just bought from Harry. Anyway I wonder what has happened to all the money Harry accumulated, he must have salted it away somewhere, it must be millions.'

'Sir what do you think has happened to this Sarah Santana, where do you think she's gone now?'

'The one witness who saw her said she had a white VW Polo, what's the betting she got off the plane and booked a car. Let's see if we can get a picture of who hired the same car in the last seven days and who brought it back. Let's get down to the airport and grab some CCTV pictures from the last week and who goes out like today. That's because I think she's got away again. She seems to have all the luck on her side and it's about time we had some luck. Anyway let's see what we can find out' said DCI Arnold.

DCI Reggie Arnold and DS Trevor Bailey walked to the hire car sections in Malaga airport. They made a start, but luckily there were only two hire companies that hired out VW Polo's and Bailey found the first one they came across. They had rented a car to a lady in the name of Monica Sheldon an American lady. They managed to get her driving licence number, phone number and address which was in Orlando, America. The other car hire company rented out two cars but both were men, so this was a lead.

'Trevor this is her, she's the one. Let's face it we're looking for an American woman and she fits the bill perfectly, what do you think?'

'I think sir this was too easy, far too easy. I don't think she would make a mistake like this. Maybe this is to throw us off the scent and give her time to get away, because so far she has not put a foot wrong. No sir this is a deliberate ploy to catch us out.'

'If it is then who the hell is she now? There was a Muslim get up, and then her own name. Clare Edwards was another, and now this name, Jesus this is one clever lady Trevor. Working for the FBI has given her all the skills she ever needed including several aliases, so god knows who she is now and we can't search all the planes leaving for America can we?'

They checked the name Monica Sheldon with the airlines; they found she was booked on the flight from Barcelona to New York Kennedy airport at 3.15pm 'she's booked on that flight Sir.'

'I almost don't want to go now because she won't be there Trevor. Because I just know she's somewhere else that's guaranteed, but we do have to go, just in case. In fact if she is there then I for one will be so disappointed to catch her because I have great respect for her.'

CHAPTER TWENTY TWO

Making her way back to her hotel, Sarah quickly picked up her packed case. Now she paid for the room and drove away to Barcelona. That's where she would get a flight back to America. Now she booked into a hotel under the name of Monica Sheldon. In her room she used a computer to book a seat to New York the next day. The flight was due to take off at 3.15pm. She had already told her friend Elizabeth to use her phones and to use her email making out she was still in America until she came home.

However Sarah was really catching a flight to London from Malaga in the name of yet another woman in the morning at 5.35am which was her ace card. She didn't even tell Liz about this name, only this time she was now Juliana Benitez, a Spanish lady. She also sent a text by the other mobile to say she would be home in two days, but for now she would just chill out, but she wasn't going out, only to the airport tomorrow.

Sarah felt nothing for what she had done. She knew her family would never come back and killing all the Dolans would not bring them back either. She just felt numb as though she had done nothing, because in the cold light of day it solved nothing. However, she would have to live with what she had done. Revenge is not sweet at all, it just brings the badness out of us then you feel guilty because you almost become the person you wanted in revenge.

Harry Dolan had in some way to pay for what he had done because the law would have lost and he would be free to roam at will again. So in her eyes that was to put it simply....not right! Now she had to decide what to do with her life. But she knew she couldn't go back to the FBI because of what she had done, that would have made her a hypocrite and she was never one of those. So she would have to resign her position, take her pension and leave.

She would take a long holiday. Anyway she always wanted to see New Zealand and Australia. Now this was an ambition which would come true and she would also take her best friend Liz with her.

At 5.35am Sarah boarded the flight to Heathrow airport. She had a wait of four hours before she boarded her next flight to Boston airport. Only this time she was flying in first class, she thought she deserved a treat and she was tired of it all. She was tired of the stress and just plain tired. She had decided to throw anyone off the scent once more and fly to Boston and then she was going to take a Greyhound bus back to New York. If anyone was waiting or watching for her at New York Kennedy airport they were going to be a little disappointed. She hoped that Liz had been putting the miles on her car.

The air hostess asked everyone to buckle up their seat belts then Sarah pressed the send button on her mobile phone. She had the conversation taped of Duvall confessing his guilt. The message went to DCI Arnold's mobile. She had taken his card from Harry's apartment. Within ten minutes they were airborne and the message pinged on DCI Arnold's phone, there was the message of Harry confessing.

DCI Arnold was not shocked about the text messages, because he knew Duvall had killed Tom Lambert's family and he also knew that Harry Dolan ordered and paid for the hit. He also knew that Sarah Santana had killed Harry and his family the motive was simple, it was revenge. Ten people dead in a Tit for Tat scenario was just utter madness and so the world keeps on turning.

They had searched all the airlines for a Monica Sheldon and found nothing else which would indicate where she was. The two policemen were just walking back to their cars and DS Bailey looked up at a vapour trail left by a plane high in the sky he laughed 'she's probably up there now.'

DCI Arnold knew she was somehow on her way back to the States and there was nothing he could do about it. She had left a deliberate false trail which she knew would lead to nothing. He had to respect her ingenuity and her skills. But he knew she had done wrong and now she would get away with it. Harry Dolan had brought this on himself. Because he was the one who instigated the whole thing, but he forgot one important factor, the one thing.The Dead Man's Sister.

Four days later Sarah returned to her home and her friend Liz was waiting for her. They hugged, cried and they laughed. Sarah asked Liz where she had been or rather where both of them had been.

They had a map out and all the miles were recorded on a pad, along with the Motels she has supposedly stayed in, with all the petrol receipts and meals. Then she saw the text messages and her computer history emails. But the police in England would have one hell of a job to prove she had left America, because she had a ghost leaving a trail and the ghost was her best friend Elizabeth Mallory.

'Sarah, can I ask you what happened to you?'

'Yes you can ask Liz, however, that's all in the past now. I have to get my life back and first thing in the morning I'm going to hand in my resignation. Perhaps I can start again and put all this misery behind me. Liz I can't tell you what happened as it would only affect you. Please don't ask me again. I love you and you're my rock and my best friend. You always have to remember that, and I will always be grateful for your help.'

DCI Arnold spoke to his superiors and told them what he thought had taken place, but there was no way Sarah Santana was going to be brought in. Yet there was no proof she was in the locations at the time so the case was dropped and left unsolved. Secretly the police were glad that Harry Dolan had gone. Once more DCS Stewart called in DCI Reggie Arnold and DS Trevor Bailey. Again he opened his whiskey draw and poured out three large slugs. He smiled and said let's drink to the dead man's sister. Here, here they said and drank the slugs in one, as was the custom.

The next day at 11.30am Sarah Santana walked into Ed Warren's office at the FBI and handed in her resignation which was not unexpected. There were a lot of tears and laughter and there were a lot of questions unanswered about why the British Police wanted to chat with her. Ed said 'not to worry,' he winked and said 'they won't be asking again.'

Sarah asked not to mention her leaving she just wanted to slip away in silence. Sarah wished Ed good luck and they hugged.

Ed kissed her on her cheek and said 'Sarah, if ever you need me or I can do anything for you, all you have to do is ask. Oh and you said in your text you had met a nice man Sarah, well I hope it works out for you.'

'Thanks Ed but time will tell, and now I have plenty of that waiting for me.' Then she slipped out the back way and down the stairwell to the bottom. She opened the door which led into the street filling the stairwell with light. And now it was a new day, a sunny day. She stopped and breathed in the air, she felt free and she felt light, but most of all she felt vindicated. Now her time was her own, it felt good to be free. But she knew the guilt would stay with her forever, but not doing what she did would have been even worse and guilt wears off in time, the shame of not doing anything doesn't.

Liz rang her to say 'have you packed your things Sarah? Mind you we don't need a lot; Hawaii at this time of the year is hot. I've hired a car and booked the seats so it's time to go. The plane leaves at 7pm this evening and I can't wait, we'll have a great time Sarah, a great time.'

Sarah laughed 'good, because I'm ready for this Liz. I have just resigned and it's time to start living again, this will give me a new start and I have an idea for a new business. I want you to come in with me Liz.'

'Hey you don't hang about do you, so what's this business all about Sarah. Security and private detective work. I want you to run the office Liz, do you fancy that?'

'Hey you try and stop me. Look we make a damn good team!'

'I know, we can now go global if need be. So remember I'm also English so there can also be work overseas, especially in England and with the skills I have and also the connections, and with you in the office we can have a nice interesting non-boring business, and you know what Liz?'

'What, tell me Sarah?'

'Well, with you in the office and moving about the way you did, what's to stop us using this again to get an alibi. I can get a hundred different aliases if required.'

'Sarah what would we call ourselves?'

Sarah thought about it then she said 'how about SGI that stands for, Santana Global Investigations.'

THE END